To Dance With Fireflies

by

Kathie Harrington

This is a work of fiction. The characters, incidents, and dialogues in this book are either the product of the author's imagination or are used fictitiously. Any resemblance to actual persons, living or dead, is completely coincidental. The places in this small Iowa town are real places supported by facts. The business establishments and locales are real and can be visited. No part of this book may be reproduced or transmitted in any manner without written permission from Willow Moon Publishing, LLC, except in the case of brief quotations embodied in critical articles or reviews. All rights reserved.

Willow Moon Publishing, LLC
www.willowmoonpublishing.com
Contact Information: info@willowmoonpublishing.com

To Dance With Fireflies

To Dance with Fireflies
**is dedicated to the men in my life who instill
in me the desire to dance every day.**

Although my father is gone,
he knew the indelible mark
he left on my life.

my father
my husband
my son
my brother
my son-in-law
my nephews
my friends

The author of *To Dance with Fireflies* gratefully acknowledges
Command Sergeant Major, Kraig A. Kasischke
Vietnam Veteran, 199th Infantry

During the writing of *To Dance with Fireflies,* COMD SGT MAJ, Kasischke openly shared his experiences of the Vietnam War. In doing so, he struggled with death, violence, depression, anxiety, and reawakening the reality of emotions he thought had gone to sleep.

COMD SGT MAJ, Kasischke wept, wrote, recorded, and relived in order to bring the Vietnam experience to life in the pages of this novel.

It is his hope as well as this author's that, by sharing one man's personal journey, it will give other veterans solace and freedom to know they are not alone.

To the brave men and women of the 199th Infantry and to all Vietnam Veterans, in this author's eyes and heart, you will always *dance with fireflies.*

Kathie Kepler Harrington

"Love has nothing to do with what you are expecting to get—only with what you are expecting to give—which is everything."

Katherine Hepburn

When I began the joyous task of writing *To Dance with Fireflies,* I thought I was writing Audrey's story: a view of womanhood with all its colors and flavors: a garden of hope that springs forth from each of us in a distant land we proclaim as fantasy. I felt the need to take a very special slice of my past and bring it into today. We retain our childhood, adolescent, and young adult experiences, and we all find those relationships grow more endearing as we mature.

As the words and phrases of *Fireflies* unfolded on paper, I realized that this was more than Audrey's story. It was a tale of Iowa, her people and her places—those who had left her boundaries, and those who had never wondered what lay beyond them. I set forth on a journey in exploration of a man's emotions. His pain, his desire, and his needs were spread before me, calling my feminine spirit to tell his saga.

What a delight I experienced in telling the story of Stephen Grant and his Audie. The love and passion which reside in them are not far from my own, nor from any of ours. We dream, but if not for dreams, life would be dull and filled only with empty echoes of what might have been.

It was a dream, an adolescent dream when I was a young teenage girl that drew me to the name, Stephen Grant. I remember sitting up in bed one night and that name came leaping forth from my head just as sure as sugar plums had danced there when I was even younger. I have never met a man by the name of Stephen Grant, and yet, he's been a part of my life.

Stephen Grant—there is only one Stephen in my life. Although I dreamed his name so many years ago, it was simply that—a name. I am truly blessed for his name is not Stephen at all; it is Tim, my husband of forty-five years. We all dream of fireflies, Stephen's, Audrey's, and all of the many things that might have been. When I dance with fireflies, My Tim holds me in his arms. He always will.

****

I begin this story with a woman, Audrey Benway, secure, loved, steadfast, and committed, only to find her relinquishing ideals that have taken a lifetime to accumulate. A man, Stephen Grant, burned by marriage, torn by war, callused by life, but given a chance to awaken through love's timeless touch. It is this author's desire that, while reading the story of Stephen and his Audie, you will release the gravity of your doubt and set yourself free—free to sing a new song and *To Dance with Fireflies*.

Chapter 1

Audrey's flight from Las Vegas to Des Moines arrived on time, which was surprising with all of the rain that swamped the Hawkeye State in the summer of 1993. Her car waited at the Rent-A-Car. She'd selected a red Thunderbird over the white model; atypical of her personality, but Audrey Benway wanted to arrive in her hometown of Iowa Falls, Iowa with flare. After all, it was July 2nd, and fireworks were on everybody's mind as she headed for a mini-reunion with girls she had known since the first grade.

"Out this door, to the right, slot ten. If you have any questions during the week, here is our number. Call if you need anything." Bruce, the rental car man, dropped the red Thunderbird keys in Audrey's hand.

"Thanks, Bruce. I'll take good care of it. After all, I'm used to Las Vegas drivers. I think they were trained at the *Bumper Car Academy*." She laughed, but Bruce barely cracked a smile. A quick call on the pay telephone to let her family know she'd arrived on time and Audrey was on her way.

She adjusted the seat, mirrors, and made sure that she turned the radio to the oldies station before leaving the lot. She did not need a road map to find her way out of Des Moines and onto Interstate 35. I-35 was a direct shot from Kansas City to Minneapolis. It probably went further in both directions, but it did not matter to her. She would head north on I-35, get off at the Williams exit, and drive into Iowa Falls about twenty miles away. Before it became an interstate, when she was a teenager in the 60s, the drive to Des Moines always seemed so long. After the interstate, life changed, it had made time more accessible—an abbreviation of the past.

The interstate was not very crowded today, or could she just be used to the city now? The metropolis of Ames was still there as she passed it by, right where the pioneers had placed it. It had not moved, nor had the Land Grant College, originally established on March 22, 1858, known around the world as Iowa State University. The land for Iowa State and its Cyclones was from an original farm of 648 acres and purchased for a cost of $5,379. Everything was as it should be. All in place. All in order. That reassured her. She liked order, predictability, and harmony in her life. She needed all of these, and her husband of twenty-six years, Jeff, brought those qualities to their relationship. *My rock, as stable as Iowa State itself.*

Being here stirred up Iowa thoughts and memories of a time that had not been calm, orderly or predictable in Audrey's life; a time of anxiety, discontent, and upheaval, filled with only questions for tomorrow, which now spun from the far corners of her mind as sure as the rain clouds twirled on this July evening. Late adolescence does that to most of us, but for Audrey, it brought turmoil in the form of a pregnancy, and it had always been difficult to wash the name of Stephen Grant from her mind even though she had not seen him in all these twenty-six years. She knew only the margins of his life as revealed at class reunions through rumors, because Stephen never attended, but it didn't matter anymore, did it?

The Iowa earth itself dusted her eyes as she scanned the fields she now passed. She observed the rich, black earth as it permeated her sense of smell. The fragrance of Iowa topsoil was too much to pass by, and there appeared to be a dry oasis alongside the road. She pulled over the scarlet T-bird just as the sun was saying its first farewell for the day and stepped from the car's interior. As she knelt to examine a small specimen of the world, her hands lifted a rich portion from which she had come. The earth felt like liquid silk running through her fingers. It could be crushed Oreo cookies without the middle as she drew a handful up to her nose. "Ah, the smell of Iowa," declared Audrey. "The senses remember well." She was home.

The sun danced for a while longer before settling down for the night and enjoying its slumber. It would be there in the morning, but for now, the moon and the animalistic nature of the night would carry on. An order prescribed by God and accepted by man; an assurance, a secure, warm, cozy place to be. "A gorgeous sunset tonight means a beautiful day tomorrow." Audrey could hear her grandmother saying the words, as they watched the sun set from Webster City, Iowa, when she was a little girl. Grandma had been right most of the time, so she could count on tomorrow. *Grandmas are usually right.*

All of a sudden, there they were dancing before her. Audrey had almost forgotten about the magic of fireflies. How could she? How could anyone forget the waltzes, the two-steps, the Charleston's, the line dances, the beauty and mystery that surrounded every Midwestern summer's evening? The fields were ablaze with delight, and her eyes were glowing as bright as the lanterns that shined from the millions of fireflies dancing in the Iowa fields. They never seemed to end. Miles and miles, dances and dances, their show went on with a streak here and a bolt there. Into the bushes and out again—no rest at night—fireflies had business to watch over. The sunshine of the day would be their repose. Audrey caught them as a child. She followed them into the bushes as an adolescent. She ignored them as a young adult and even moved away from both of their homes.

How would she relate to the fireflies of Iowa today? The winds that blew through her life between yesterday and her life today were strands of memory cohesively held by her perceptions of a world that was, and the island she had fashioned. She imagined the winds calm, the past as settled, and the fields standing silent in their vigil. However, for Audrey Benway, the winds were kicking up, and fireflies were dancing all around her.

Chapter 2

Audrey enjoyed the dance of fireflies because she did not get to see it very often. Her life as a wife, mother, and physical therapist was busy in Las Vegas, and the opportunity to visit her hometown of Iowa Falls, the Scenic City, was sparse. Fireflies do not live in the desert, and although she had a fake jar of them on her desk at home, they did not fulfill the same principle as the live dancers who now bowed before her presence as she slowed to exit I-35 and enter Highway 20.

A hometown image popped into her mind that came from echoes of long ago. It was a picture of the Swinging Bridge with its gentle downward slope from Rocksylvania Avenue. This scenic bridge crossed the Iowa River and connected to its base at the Baptist Assembly Grounds. Its twisted cables, locked to the concrete arched pillars that first sunk into the riverbed back in 1897. The present wooden structure was first built in 1909, again in 1925, 1956, and 1989. The bridge still creaked with every foot that stepped on its slatted boards while hands clung to the railings. Audrey's thoughts centered on two people standing about one-third of the way down from the top of the bridge. They were not talking, laughing, singing, or kissing right then. They pointed to the bushes and trees that grew on either side of the Swinging Bridge. They spotted the thousands of fireflies as they danced in their furious flight. It was in the early fall after a high school dance. It was Audrey and Stephen Grant. The thought of him filled her mind. They looked. They smiled. They kissed, and they fell in love. How could a thirty second, adolescent kiss on a bridge over the Iowa River linger for a lifetime?

Audrey continued to drive toward Iowa Falls, over William's hill with its steep side drops and little railings that seemed to go on into oblivion. Only about twenty more miles—Audrey's heart picked up the pace. It was dark early this night for July in Iowa, as the clouds covered the evening sky. At least there was no rain and very little traffic. This allowed more time to gather shadows of the home Audrey left behind some twenty-six years ago and to explore as phantasms reached into today.

She loved her hometown, from her personal history, to the detailed facts her daddy taught her over the years. They both instilled their love of Iowa Falls in Audrey's son, Scott. Scott was born with Down syndrome, a lifelong disability, and like the birds of the air, the winds whisked him through the sky of life. They lifted him up when he was down and set him gently on a limb for balance when storms blew his way. Both Audrey and Scott were grounded in Iowa Falls. Scott enjoyed spending two weeks every summer with her parents. Grandma and Grandpa Harris showered Scott with patience and love. When they passed away, it was a difficult concept for Scott to understand, but he had Audrey by his side and as he said, "The wind under my wheels."

Audrey remembered how she would always be *hungry* for Scott when he was visiting in Iowa Falls, even though they'd talk every day about Grandma and Grandpa Camp. She never had any trouble understanding Scott's speech. It was just that—Scott's Speech. The nice thing about his absence was it gave Audrey and Jeff time to spend with their daughter, Heidi, just the three of them as it had started out in married life. *Raising a child and young adult with any disability isn't easy. The breaks were good for all of us when Scott was little.*

"Mom and Daddy, I love and miss you." Two fireflies darted across the headlights at that moment in time.

Scott knew all of the historical buildings in Iowa Falls by name, the dates constructed, and usually some important fact about them. For Christmas and birthdays, nothing pleased Scott more than to receive old post cards for his collection and T-shirts from the Red Rooster Grill, or the famous Popcorn Stand. When Scott was in Iowa Falls, he frequented the Princess Café for a strawberry milkshake every time he could talk his Grandpa Harris into strolling downtown. Scott adored his assortment of River Bend Rally T-shirts and always held his chest high when he wore one of them in Iowa or Nevada.

Audrey couldn't help but think of all the times she and Scott sat on the old family porch in Iowa Falls as she read facts and stories from Ira Nichols books on Iowa Falls history. Over and over, he'd want to hear about the Iowa Falls Popcorn Stand manufactured in Texas during the 30s. Louis Knudesen plopped his four-foot by six-foot business south of Estes Park at that time and called it "Louis' Korn Krib." Word has it Mr. Knudesen's favorite memory was making caramel corn during World War II and shipping it overseas to the G.I.s. He kept all of the thank you notes he received and shared them with local popcorn addicts. *My, how the popcorn flowed all of these years and likely still did—plain, buttered, and caramelized—mmm—sounds good right now, I wish Scott was here with me.*

"I rather doubt it's ten cents for a small bag anymore." She lifted her eyes to the air.

Like all parents of a child with a disability, Audrey and Jeff had made themselves knowledgeable, provided excellent care, and most important, gave Scott as much independence as he could handle growing up. At nineteen years of age, he worked in a community center. Her heart was filled with pride for his accomplishments. A room embellished with ribbons and trophies from the Special Olympics provided immediate conversation for those who entered Scott's world. All of the family, Audrey, Jeff, and Heidi, were active not only in Scott's Special Olympic events but in the city and statewide efforts. It had been one family's journey through tears of laughter—tears of pain, but always tears of joy and pride rose to the top of their emotions.

As Audrey continued to drive toward Alden, six miles from Iowa Falls, she could not help but think of Stephen Grant—yikes…Stephen—how did his name pop up, again? She was actually, genuinely, sincerely, thinking of Floppy. Audrey wiped her forehead in bewilderment. If Scott loved hearing and talking about historical buildings in Iowa Falls, he even more enjoyed having Audrey tell stories of her favorite television programs from when she was a little girl. Stephen—*oh, my goodness*—Floppy was a balsa wood-headed puppet dog loved by all of Iowa on *The Floppy Show*. Duane Ellett broadcast from WHO on Channel 13 from Des Moines. Duane used to tell his TV kids that Floppy was born in 1957 and that Duane's mother-in-law, Cora Nystrom, knit his red sweater with love in every loop. They were on TV for thirty years! Audrey smiled as she remembered taking Scott to the Iowa State Historical Building in Des Moines to see Floppy. They could not leave until they had watched several of the shows. Scott loved every minute and Audrey loved sharing her childhood with him. For weeks afterward, Scott asked everybody he saw the famous Floppy joke: "Why did the man put the car in the oven? Because he wanted a hot rod!" She shook her head in delight, in pure delight. She could just visualize Scott attired in his I ♥

Floppy T-shirt.

Right up there with *The Floppy Show* was *The Magic Window*. This was big and came into her home from WOI in Ames beginning in 1951. Betty Lou Varnum hosted it, and when Betty Lou said it was time to march, Audrey marched. She showed Scott and Heidi how Betty Lou would call out names from her *Magic Window,* and as a child, she'd say a little prayer she'd call her name each day. The name Audrey was not high on Betty Lou's list but her mother assured her that life would go on. Scott and Heidi loved to play their version of *The Magic Window* and Audrey was able to teach both of her young children a lot of imitation, compliance, sequencing, following directions, and all of the skills that are so necessary in helping children with Down syndrome. Many years later, a good friend of her's pointed out that Scott had been as good a teacher to her as she had been for him. So true…so true.

And who could forget *Howdy Doody* and *Sky King*? Audrey rolled along with television memories from her childhood while the speedy tires rotated on Highway 20 toward Iowa Falls. Howdy Doody had forty-eight freckles, one for each state of the union, back in 1947 at his first appearance. Buffalo Bob Smith was the original voice of Howdy, who was a marionette operated with eleven strings. Stephen now resides—*am I thinking Stephen again?* Audrey tapped herself on the side of her head.

"I mean Howdy Doody now resides at the Detroit Institute of Arts." Scott especially liked hearing about Clarabell the Clown who could not talk but used a horn to communicate. Audrey bought both Scott and Heidi their own horns so that they could go around the house honking like Clarabell. That did not last too long because it drove her crazy. She remembered reading an article stating that, "Bob Keeshan once played Clarabell until they fired him." Keeshan went on to become Captain Kangaroo—and of course, that hadn't hurt his career.

"Why do you suppose the name Stephen keeps popping up? I have no idea where he even lives." *Why is it that when you go back to your hometown roots, they carry you to a land of yesterday? Some of those yesterdays you want to forget as if they were crumbs from a dried up cookie that need to be brushed away. Other memories from those same yesterdays resurface every time with emotions that twist themselves more tightly than a spring tornado scalping a path of destruction. A path that gave choices so long ago. A path of what might have been.*

Audrey questioned the phantom in the passenger seat next to her, watching the highway, admiring fireflies, thinking about her family, reminiscing about old buildings and television shows from her childhood, anticipating the weekend, and wondering what Stephen Grant, Floppy, and Howdy Doody had in common. She broke her own silence and decided to concentrate on the latter thought.

"Stephen—Floppy—Howdy Doody, well, two of them were dummies. I'm just not sure which two." Audrey laughed, and if a Thunderbird could respond in kind, this one did.

Chapter 3

The little town of Alden came and went with only five miles to go. Audrey could feel herself smiling, her heart beating a bit faster, and her anticipation speeding up. Plans were to spend the night at Carol's, her best friend since second grade. Sandy was going to join them for a slumber party. Audrey had reservations at The Scenic City Motel the following two nights and then home to Vegas on July 5th. It was a short visit, but plenty of time to see old friends, make her rounds to the sites, and enjoy the festivities of the Fourth. Audrey always stopped in to see her minister whenever she was in town as well, so she hoped he would be there over the holiday.

Always lots to do and never enough time when Audrey was in Iowa Falls, but she would rather go home wanting more than feeling she'd stayed too long. Her family needed her back in Vegas and her job as a physical therapist. After all, there would always be a next time…

Iowa Falls, we're here to boost you while our banners fly.
Always true in all we do, we'll hold our banners high.
Rah! Rah! Rah!
We will always stand behind you, backing up our team.
Fight!
Iowa Falls, we're yours forever, sink Algona, sink Algona High.

The sound of the *Iowa Falls Fight Song* came bellowing from the T-bird on the far side of Alden. Another chorus of the *Iowa Falls Fight Song* was in order, but Audrey wanted to save her voice for talking with the "girls" once she got to Carol's house.

The population of Iowa Falls was somewhere around 5,000, give or take a few cats, dogs, and chickens. Fred Grandy, "Gopher," from *The Love Boat* had represented this district in the United States Congress since 1987. Everybody knew everyone else, his or her shoe size and how much his or her husband had spent on last year's Christmas gift. Audrey always thought of the song, "Mira." She sang it in high school chorus and remembered the last line well tonight: "Everybody knew my name."

One more hill, one more corner of Iowa and Audrey would be there. Iowa Falls, her hometown, a "Field of Dreams" lit by the glow of fireflies dancing in the night. The city lights were far from those of Las Vegas and so was the pace of a day well spent.

Iowa Falls never changes. Good things mellow, they do not change form. They leave you wanting more, and for Audrey, Iowa Falls was more than a destiny, it was a desire. A desire to touch the roots of her youth and hold them firmly; to grasp a part of the past and pull it forward into the present, whether it wanted to come or not.

There stood the Iowa Falls National Guard Armory and new baseball diamonds on the right side of the road. Young boys and girls were acting on their Nolan Ryan dreams that July evening. The Dairy Queen, Spin's house, Judy's yard, Cindy and Dan's, all stood proud in the middle of Iowa. Audrey's old house, on the left, still looked pleasing and fresh. The spruced up green shutters on the two-story frame and a second garage added to the single stall changed the appearance. She wondered if the children of Florence Drive could still play "Annie, Annie Over" and get the ball up and across the doublewide structure. Did anyone play "Kick the Can" down the middle of the street anymore or "Hide and Seek" on a hot July evening after the sun had gone to bed? Were the voices of days gone by hiding underneath coats of paint? Could the walls of her old family home speak of laughter and pain; could they tell the secrets that Audrey had told them long before she left on her life's journey?

The Washington Avenue Bridge that spans the Iowa River on Highway 20 replaced a steel structure known as Foster Bridge in 1934. *Adults enjoy its beauty more than when they were children.* Audrey slowed her car to a crawl. This two-span concrete arch structure was built by the Weldon Brothers Construction Company of Iowa Falls at a cost of $51,710 back in its day and opened on July 24, 1934.

Across Washington Avenue Bridge and toward the steepest hill in town, Audrey gave the Thunderbird an extra jolt of gas. She remembered that hill was a curse as she learned how to drive a clutch in the little burgundy Corvair she shared with her older sister. Stoplights came and went as she let in and out on the clutch trying to creep to the summit. The hill did not seem nearly as high today as the T-bird took it with ease. Dad had insisted that his girls first learn to drive a clutch—they did, but not today.

   With the top of the hill mastered, Audrey was on her way down the two-block jaunt of Main Street. The two and three story facades were mainly intact with only one hole where a blaze had left the opening for the Ellsworth and Jones Building when a fire struck in 1976. The Princess Café sat on the right, and close beyond that, the First National Bank at the Southwest corner of Washington Avenue and Stevens Street. However, what caught Audrey's eye was the Metropolitan Theatre. Eugene S. Ellsworth commissioned the design and construction of the Met at the turn of the 19th century. In 1899, this miniature metropolitan opera house began absorbing the refrains of such greats as John Philip Sousa, making the opening evening the "biggest social event in the history of Iowa Falls." The main floor of this opera house with its maroon velvet curtains once seated 441 and the balcony seated 390. The stage itself was 66 feet wide and 30 feet deep with large wings. Since made into a movie theatre, its ornate structure and silver screen has reflected Shirley Temple to Meg Ryan. Its stage tapped upon by vaudevillians and *1776* reenacted 200 years later by local thespians. Several of Audrey's high school friends who worked in the Met always talked about the old stage and movie posters archived on the third floor. *My, what a treasure trove that would be today*. Audrey shifted her eyes up to the top floor with the four circular windows, two on either side of the center.

   As she headed north toward Carol's, Audrey passed the new McDonalds. The launch of Ronald's place a year earlier had been the biggest event to hit Iowa Falls, probably since the opening of the Met. There sat the Red Rooster Grill on the corner of Oak Street and Rocksylvania Avenue opened by Mary and "Kep" Kepler in January 1953, destroyed by a grease fire on Thanksgiving Day 1961, only to reopen in early 1962. Iowa pork tenderloins were always the order of the day when she ate at either the Rooster or the Princess.

   There was a new Fairway Grocery Store where Central School once stood. Bricks from the school sold for a dollar a piece. Audrey's mother had given her one as a gift with a ribbon in the school colors tied around it. A dollar invested in one's history is not too much to ask. Therefore, it sits in a closet collecting whatever bricks might collect, but Audrey knew exactly where it was. She figured that many more were scattered throughout the United States in various homes of Iowa Falls Cadets doing much the same thing.

It was time to head on over to Carol and Cole's home for the slumber party. Time was ticking and it was already dark out Silom Road and across Whitesell Bridge. Audrey did not notice too much mud on the road, but she drove with caution as Carol had advised.

The letters on the mailbox sitting toward the end of the drive read *The Kings.* Audrey had arrived at the Cape Cod home. The lane, lit by electric lanterns to look aged were accentuated by the millions of fireflies that swirled in the tall oaks, maples, pines, and buckeye trees surrounding the King's home like Essex Miniatures guarding their command post.

The front doors of the King's home flew wide open on their hinges and two very familiar voices shouted, "Audrey, you're home!"

Chapter 4

Six arms flung around each other and stuck like gobs of Silly Putty held by spheres of friendship. It was always like this when Carol, Sandy, and Audrey reunited; safe in the palms of each other's hands they bonded to a touch. The three friends rolled their feelings in one ball and shaped them to create new forms. Then, they pressed the new forms against life and picked up images of the past and present. These images again rolled into a ball and bounced into the unknown future. Yes, Silly Putty has its place just as sure as old friendships endure.

Luggage unloaded and attired in their jammies, the *girls* first concentrated on a blender- full of peach piña coladas and plates piled high with vegetables and dips. Sandy especially loved the cheesecake and chicken wings, and the apple slices topped with hot melted caramel brought a smile to Audrey's face. Carol had made a batch of Iowa Maid-Rites that simmered in the crock-pot just in case they wanted something more substantial.

"These drinks are great, Carol," said both Audrey and Sandy in choral reflection as Sandy directed with her hands and arms. "Let's keep those pitchers flowin'," added Sandy.

"And, the food," added Audrey. "I'm sure grateful God invented elastic in our lifetime!" The girls were on a roll, and so were the food and drinks.

"Cole got called out to deliver a baby just before you arrived, Audrey," said Carol while taking a few steps to get into the family room. "In fact, it's a set of twins. He said he'd be home late but wanted to welcome you back."

"Cole's a gem, Carol. 'Ol' King Cole.' Remember how we used to tease him about that?" questioned Audrey. Cole was from an even smaller town around Iowa Falls, and because his name was Cole King, it was an obvious twist in the name game. However, he was filled with confidence, and he never let it bother him. He went on to become an OBGYN and, obviously, did very well.

Carol's kitchen, which merged into her family room, was decorated in shades of blues, yellows, and beige with accents of forest green. A bay window highlighted the kitchen and overlooked a backyard filled with trees native to Iowa, wild flowers, and a multitude of bird feeders and houses. Carol and Cole loved the Iowa wildlife and enjoyed watching the native squirrels and birds as they passed through the various seasons of life. The tall oak trees provided the acorns for the squirrels to store for each coming winter, and Carol and Cole made sure that plenty of suet, spun with birdseed, was always ample for the birds when snow blanketed the ground.

Carol named her bay window the "bay window observatory" as the seat, with its stuffed floral patterned cushions filled with matching pillows, provided inexpensive *cuddle therapy*. A light-blue, knitted afghan, decoratively placed, with fringed edges dropped gently over the side of the floral window seat and looked like a spring shower had just passed overhead. The drops of moisture lingered on the flowers and eventually found their way to the waiting ground as they rolled off the fringed edges.

Carol, the avid reader of the group, often read the words of Emily Bronte, Ann Tyler, or Robert James Waller while snuggled in her bay window observatory. It was one of her favorite places. Carol chronicled her whole life in her Reading Journals. She started recording every book she'd read, from the time she was sixteen-years-old. Within these journals, she documented the title, author, copyright date, and a paragraph about the books themselves. Carol had shown the journals to Audrey several years ago and Audrey noted the significant part of the journals were not the facts of the books, rather the details of what Carol recorded about her life at the time she was reading any particular book. The dates she started and finished were, of course, always there and where she lived at the time of the read. Carol even documented her favorite soft drink, or perhaps, a significant food that she liked. But, there was more, so much more to her journal entries.

Audrey addressed Carol as she admired the warmth of her home, and the thoughts of Carol's Reading Journals seeped to the core of her memory. "Carol, I'd love to see your Reading Journals again. You're the only person I know who's done something as unique as those. Can we take a look at them later? I'm sure that you still write in them on a regular basis."

"Of course. I'd love to share my journals with my two best friends. You know, those journals are the story of my life. I don't feel as though I've ever really accomplished a whole lot, but those journals hold all of the details I want to leave as a footprint on earth that I was here. I'll get them out later. I complete about one journal every year or two, so figure it out, there's a lot of them If I'd ever been on *This is Your Life* with Ralph Edwards," said Carol, in a mimicking, deep voice, "he could have just brought each of my journals out and they would have represented my life more than people."

"I never had time to write in journals," added Sandy with a smile. "In fact, I don't know how you always find so much time to read, Carol, but I admire you for it. Right now, I'm eyeing a refill on all that great food you've prepared and those piña coladas. Well, what can I say, other than, I'm thirsty?" They all laughed and dove right in once again.

Sandy had married a farmer and lived close to Iowa Falls all of her life, where she and her husband had raised three children, cows, chickens, a couple of goats, and always had at least two horses to ride. They were now raising a grandchild, and, of course, had crops to agonize over in trying to balance their farm books during this flood of 1993. Most years are a financial stretch for independent farmers, and they know how important it is to keep smiling at their banker.

Audrey watched her two friends eating, drinking, laughing, and sculpting thoughts together until they became three younger forms sitting in the middle of another room, another home, from another time. Images and thoughts of Carol, Sandy, and Audrey as they were at eight or ten years of age floated back into Audrey's mind as they talked of Barbie Dolls, gymnastics, and boys. Then how they were at fifteen and seventeen waltzed through the various compartments of Audrey's memories—friends, as they chomped on homemade pizza and were flabbergasted as they watched their first Fizzies Cherry Drink Tablets dissolve in a glass of water. The discussion centered on cheerleading, and movie stars, like Troy Donahue and Sandra Dee, periods, and boys. What did teenage girls talk about in the 1960s besides proms and kisses? These three friends talked about life and what they wanted their lives to be. They shared secrets with one another that would last a lifetime, and they pledged to keep those secrets.

As teens of the 60s, the girls had heard about a war in Vietnam.

In total, 853 Iowans were killed or declared dead as a result of the Vietnam War. Older siblings of some of Audrey's and the girl's friends had enlisted and gone to Vietnam, but the war didn't seem to have an impact on the innocence of life in this small Iowa town until one of their own came home in a flag-draped coffin. The war in Vietnam was something viewed on nightly television. It wasn't real— or was it?

As Audrey looked at both of her childhood friends, she knew they were special. Together, they had roots planted in the most fertile soil in all of America: Iowa. Audrey had moved away from her Iowa roots, but roots spread far, deep, and in all directions. Roots of life gather nourishment from sun and rain. Those same roots, however, are fed by love, faith, trust, and security. Audrey knew she had them all— they all sprouted in Iowa Falls with tentacles that could reach across distance and time.

Audrey's mind floated back into today, seeing that the girls had weathered the storms of childhood, adolescence, children, marriage, and for one of them, grandchildren. They had experienced the passing of parents and siblings, not with ease, but with thoughts of joy at lives well spent, and the fond gift of memories that families bestow upon one another with rituals and routines. The rhythm of life continued, enriched by those who proceeded, waiting for completion, as many would follow.

"Now, Audrey, we think you should know something." Sandy was speaking, but Carol was shaking her head with a slight negative response.

"Something. Something. Something." Audrey thought it was some kind of a game and her eyes popped out with anticipation.

"I don't know, Sandy, we didn't really agree on that," said Carol with concern in her voice.

"I thought we did," Sandy responded.

"Well, girls, just what is this something I should know?"

Sandy and Carol looked at each other for what seemed a long thirty seconds. Of course, Sandy broke the silence. "Stephen moved back to Iowa Falls some time ago."

Audrey did not say a word. She did take a bite of her cheesecake, however, and then a large gulp of her peach piña colada as both Carol and Sandy looked on. "I'll take another one of these," she said to Carol as she handed the empty glass to her. Carol complied.

"I guess that's nice for him—to be back here. Do either of you see him?" Audrey had her fresh colada in hand.

"No, oh no." The response was instantaneous and simultaneous.

"You've never told him about Heidi—have you, Audrey?"

"Of course, I haven't, Sandy. If he's found out about Heidi over the last twenty-six years, it's not because I've ever told him. I haven't seen him or talked to him. He fathered our baby, but that doesn't mean he was Heidi's father. Jeff has always been Heidi's father. Jeff knows that. Heidi knows that. I know that. You two know that, and God knows that. I simply don't know what Stephen does or doesn't know. Does that cover it?" Audrey was emphatic, and her blood pressure was showing.

"But, why is it…?" Audrey continued after taking another and yet another gulp of the now even better tasting peach piña colada. "Why is it that Stephen's face and name won't leave me alone? He haunts me. He chases me. He follows me. He hunts me down wherever I am. Why? Even on my drive from Des Moines to Iowa Falls, his name kept creeping into my mind. He won't leave me alone, and now I find out he lives *here?*" Audrey' arms flung wide as she asked the rhetorical question.

"It's unfinished for you, Audrey," Carol, the wise, the homespun, down-to-earth one of the three spoke the truth. "Even after twenty-six years, it's unfinished for you. You don't know what he knows or doesn't know or knew at the time or didn't know way back when."

Audrey began to cry, just a little, just baby tears as they sprinkled into her piña colada. "It was such a very hard time for me back then, we all remember that. You two were the glue that held me together. If it hadn't been for the two of you and my parents, and then Jeff, I don't know what I would have done. Stephen…" her voice trailed off.

"I want you to read something, Audrey." Carol got up from the couch and opened the levered door of the cabinet by the television. "You wanted to see my Reading Journals. Well, I know you've seen some before, but I never let you read what I'd written in the fall of 1966. I think you should read it now, or maybe, I should read it aloud. Shall I?"

Audrey couldn't speak, but she shook her head in affirmation of Carol's question.

"August 20, 1966," Carol began with the date. "I had just completed *The Scarlet Letter* by Nathaniel Hawthorne. The quote, I picked from Chapter II The Market-Place, 'Ah, but let her cover the mark as she will, the pang of it will be always in her heart.'"

"I'd started reading *The Scarlet Letter* long before I knew you were pregnant, Audrey."

Neither of the women made direct eye contact at that moment, and Sandy fidgeted with her hair.

"What I really want you to hear is my personal note about what was happening at that time in my world—in our world, Audrey."

Audrey gulped, sat her empty glass of piña colada on the coffee table, and snuggled up with a throw pillow that she squeezed tightly between her arms. She cradled the pillow with the same fervor with which she used to hug her favorite Humpty Dumpty. In times of need, this Humpty Dumpty and Audrey provided each other with strength to stay on top of life's wall.

Carol preceded reading from her journal. "I found out today that Audrey is pregnant. She's not the first girl in Iowa Falls to get pregnant, and I know she won't be the last, but she's my best friend, and I love her. I'm mad. I'm mad at Audrey for loving Stephen so much. I'm mad at Stephen for not being more careful. I'm mad at the people of Iowa Falls, because they won't understand. I know how they treated Jenny and Sue. At least, Audrey has graduated; otherwise, she wouldn't be allowed to go to school. If she stays around here, even if they do get married, she'd be shunned just like Hester in *The Scarlet Letter*. Oh, Audrey, what will you do? I'll be by your side—that I know."

Sandy's soft voice filtered through the tide of what life was like for a teenager, who happened to get pregnant in the 1960s, at least, in small town Iowa. "You know, Audrey, things were so different back in the 60s than they are today. I don't even think the first home pregnancy test was out until the late 1970s. You made choices based on what you had available back then, not what there is today. And, after all—you've got Heidi!"

The name Heidi, brought a smile to all of the women, and Audrey's gratitude for her daughter's life was beyond comprehension. Audrey took a deep, deep breath and slowly exhaled with ease. Her grasp of the pillow was less tense as she rolled her lips together, and dipped her chin, but her eyes rose to meet two extraordinary women in her life—the moisture in their eyes was not of sadness, but of joy.

"He's in the phone book, Audrey. Stephen bought the Horton house down by the river, on the little gravel road, behind the tire store, off Washington Ave.," Sandy seemed to know all of the facts and although she wasn't sure if she should tell Audrey—it was time.

Audrey liked harmony in her life, and she always tried to find it. *Routine is such a blessing, and a curse. I depend on it for a steady rhythm, and I rail against it for the drudgery it brings. Life is what happens to you when you are busy making plans.* Plans to see Stephen brewed in her mind as Carol once again filled the glasses with peach piña coladas. Although Audrey rarely drank an alcoholic beverage, piña coladas were in order on this rainy night in Iowa, and they coated her palate all…the…way…down.

Chapter 5

"Audrey's wars" started in her late teens, and Jeff surely waltzed into her life at a time when the first war was raging. He halted all of her battles and healed most of her wounds.

"Looks to me like you're taking pretty good care of your diabetes, Audrey."

"It's hard with all of these great drinks and food like tonight, but this is special, and I've been staying on my diet pretty well. It's Heidi that I'm most worried about." Audrey was solemn. "She had to start on dialysis for her kidneys."

"No!" Carol and Sandy responded in unison.

"She's taking it well. We are all trying to take it—as well as we can. Her endocrinologist says that we need to consider a kidney transplant in the future, and of course, she and her fiancé, Ted, won't be having children of their own. We take this one day at a time. Every day counts."

"If we can help in any way, Audrey, we will."

"Oh, how well I know that."

"How is Scott doing, Audrey?" Carol and Sandy always asked about Scott. He seemed to be as much their son as he was Audrey's. They lavished him with gifts and never forgot his birthday on April first.

Before Audrey could answer the question, Sandy and Carol both handed over their loot of Iowa Falls, Hawkeye, and Cyclone trinkets they knew Scott would enjoy. Oh, how he would!

"Well," said Audrey, "he hated to see me leave, but we marked a calendar so he knows exactly when I'll be coming home. You know, he's into dates and times and minutes and seconds." They all laughed, because they all knew Scott, and they all knew the stress that goes with any family raising a child with a disability. It takes a village.

"Does he still work at the Community Center?"

"Sure and he loves every minute of it. The bus picks him up, and that is a good thing. It gives him more independence and freedom to make choices. I do worry about his vulnerability, but…"

Carol completed Audrey's sentence, "…but it's good that he has that independence."

"It sure is, Carol."

"Did I tell you, our oldest son, Mark, is finally getting married?" Sandy asked with a surprised spark in her voice.

"I didn't know that," added Carol. "When is the big day, and is it here in town?"

"They haven't decided yet just when, and it will most likely be in Minneapolis where Gina is from." Sandy sounded relieved at the prospect of Mark finally finding someone to suit him.

Audrey was silent and looked down at all of the food she knew she shouldn't eat and was not even hungry. She had fixed herself an Iowa Maid-Rite, but it did not hold much appeal right now. She was sad.

"Anything wrong, Audrey?" questioned Carol.

"I'm happy for Mark and Gina and for you, too, Sandy. That's great. All of your kids will be married soon, and you already have one grandchild. Guess there will be more someday as well. I'm really happy for your family."

Audrey suddenly burst into tears. Not baby tears like before, but big, strong, heaving tears that had been building up in her chest for nineteen years. Tears that were stagnate with mold, festered with sadness, hoarded with envy. Tears that had been waiting for a time and a place of safety that said it was okay to release them, to let them go, to give them permission to be themselves; tears that flowed free and words that found safety within the arms of friendship.

They all cried those heaving cries together, because the source was a common one in their love of Scott and their anguish for Audrey and Jeff. Now, to find that their daughter, too, would never have a child seemed to test the boundaries of parenthood. The arms of friends intertwined in holds of assurance and love.

When eyes were dried, bathrooms used, and nerves calmed, Audrey could speak about Scott once again in calmer tones of love's hush. "I love Scott with all my heart, and I wouldn't want him any other way. He's the only Scott I've ever known for nineteen years." Audrey had to stop to take a gulp of air before she began once again. "This journey we've been on is one so many families deal with. When I see children and adults in wheelchairs, I know how lucky we are. And when I see kids out of control, I once again thank God for what we have in Scott. It's just hard and some days are harder than others are. I've heard professionals say to 'get over it.' The parent of any child with a disability learns to accept, but *never* will they or should they *ever get over it.*

"When Scott was born, and we knew the diagnosis right away, of course, I didn't think I could ever have any more tears left in me, but I soon found out that they build back up and come out again and again over the years. Do you know how long it took him to learn how to answer *yes* or *no* to a simple question?" Tears, now forged by Audrey's pain, and not a question meant for an answer by her friends, but a listening question lingered in the heavy air. She continued.

"With the joy of having a baby you dream of going to the stars and finding just the right star for you. Heidi did not start out that way for me, but she has been my galaxy of stars, as you two know. Then we all looked forward to Scott. Instead of finding a star, we had moved into a black hole of sorts—a space we hadn't planned to go by design, but it was still a part of God's universe, and it wasn't in our hands. I guess it never is." Audrey's voice was soft and loving.

"I find Scott to be not just a star anymore and he certainly never was that black hole. He's not just a speck in the sky that I thought I wanted and that I expected God to give me. He's not that at all." Carol handed Audrey another Kleenex, as she knew that her tears of joy mingled with those of pain. "Scott has become my universe. He's more than one star just as God knew he would be."

Tears rolled down the women's cheeks in Carol's beautiful, welcoming home. God listened both on the inside and outside of the house and answered back with a tender clap of thunder, a soothing streak of lightening, and began shedding tears of His own on the bushes, trees, and windows as He reassured them of life and all of the goodness in it.

"We've provided every kind of therapy available for Scott: speech, occupational, music, hippo, and of course, physical therapy. We have often thought that, maybe, life would be gentler on Scott or any special child in a small town like Iowa Falls. The pace of life is slower and—" Sandy cut Audrey off mid-sentence.

"What in the world is *hippotherapy*—learning how to ride a hippo?"

"Well, it sounds like it, but actually, it's riding horses and learning the movements and strides they take. Scott and all the other kids really came to love it. Scott named his horse *Trigger*, because I told him that Roy Rogers used to ride a horse named *Trigger*. Gosh, Sandy, maybe you could learn hippotherapy techniques and teach special kids on your farm."

Sandy cocked her head and put her index finger to her mouth as if a thought just might be galloping through her mind, a thought that Audrey planted for her friend.

"Scott's always so happy," observed Carol.

"He is that. He is happy and content in his world. We have always tried to protect him, and Heidi has always been great with him. She used to read to him by the hour, and he'd ask her these annoying questions over and over and over again." Audrey laughed as she thought about the patience Heidi had cultivated in herself and in Scott.

"Scott calls Heidi every day of the week just to say hi and to see what she's doing. Of course, he usually doesn't listen to her answer, but he asks. He used to be real close to my dad, and Scott would call him every day as well when he was younger. Scott was devastated; you know, when my dad died. Of course, we always visit him up here in the cemetery when we are in Iowa Falls."

"That was a big phone bill to call from Vegas to Iowa Falls every day," commented Sandy.

"I never looked at it. Jeff just paid it and never said a word." Audrey tipped her head back on the couch and a slight smile spread across her face. "Yes, I'm going to count my blessings tonight, and I know they'll add up to five."

"Five?" questioned Sandy with a piña colada in her hand. "Are you counting the number of drinks I've had or what, Audrey?"

"No. I am just counting my blessings in the form of people who are alive today that I can always depend on and hold in my heart: Jeff, Heidi, Scott, Carol, Sandy. That is five. That's enough to last my whole lifetime.

"We have this simple saying before Scott goes to work at the Community Center every day. Jeff actually came up with the idea and it really works. It's *Work Hard and Have Fun*. If Scott follows those two rules, we know he'll have a good day."

"And every good day counts," added Carol.

"It sure does. It *suuuurly does.*" Audrey smiled and raised her empty piña colada high as three glasses cracked in mid-air with an assurance of friendship, love, and solidarity to what they knew was so special between them.

Audrey was very tired from her travel, tears, thoughts, and talking. Her eyes were drifting shut, and she had *promises to keep, and miles to go before she'd sleep—and miles to go before she'd sleep.*

Chapter 6

It was the third of July, hot, humid, and rainy. Sandy, Carol, and Audrey woke from their slumber with stretches and a few more moans and groans than they remembered from past sleepovers. One of them had to grab their eyeglasses to start her day and another grabbed a piña colada glass to start hers. As for Audrey, she collected all of the little trinkets that the girls brought for Scott and put them in a bag. He would have a day's worth of delight from the gifts, and Audrey was forever grateful to her friends, not only for the gifts that she held in her hand, but also, for the ones that she treasured in her heart.

"I have a red, white, and blue breakfast planned before we depart on our day." Carol was hollering from the kitchen. There were red strawberries, blueberries topped with whipped cream, an English muffin with either blueberry or strawberry preserves, and a cup of breakfast tea, all served on the kitchen table looking through the bay window and into the backyard.

"This is so you, Carol. Just right for the holiday." Audrey was sincere and gave Carol a hug.

They all sat down at the kitchen table and ate once again. "I'm going to have to roll back out to Vegas if I continue to eat this much," Audrey laughed, and the laughter was contagious.

"Now, let's plan. We have the parade today, at Estes Park, to see everyone, maybe the Red Rooster, and then we are meeting down at the Princess around one tomorrow as well. More food!" Sandy was right on top of that. "I'm going to take three lawn chairs and set them along River Street by the old Edgewood place so that we'll have them for the parade at five."

Audrey about spit the blueberries out of her mouth laughing. Where else but in a small town in the middle of Iowa could you set your lawn chairs out at 10:00 in the morning and have them waiting for you at 5:00 in the afternoon? She was back in Iowa Falls all right, and she was sure that the candy, Frisbees, and political stickers would rain down from the sky just as abundantly as raindrops. Holiday parades were big events, and neighbors were trusting in Iowa.

"So," continued Sandy, "are you going to see if Stephen is home, maybe tomorrow morning, Audrey?"

"I might. He's probably busy for the holiday." She shrugged her shoulders in a rather nonchalant manner. "What could it hurt?"

The other two women just stared at Audrey as she asked that question, and Audrey, herself, enjoyed a mouthful of strawberries, blueberries, and whipped cream. She licked her spoon in delight and swallowed every last one without spitting any out this time.

"I'm going to go get registered in at The Scenic City Motel, and then, I'll meet you gals down at Estes Park at around noon. Sound okay?"

"Audrey, you are crazy, lady. Why are you staying out there? Carol has all of this, and you are in *that* place?" Sandy really and finally did seem to make some sense.

"I don't know. I just like a little privacy and time to think I guess. I know I could stay here with Carol and Cole, but..." Audrey shrugged her shoulders and grabbed another bite of berries, her suitcase, bag of trinkets for Scott, and headed out the door. "At the park then, by the popcorn stand, I'm buying all three bags. It's surely my turn."

The Scenic City Motel is like stepping back into a time tunnel of the 1970s with a *Laugh-In* style motif. The large flowers of gold, olive green, orange, and a dash of purple prompted Audrey to drop her jaw at least two inches as she entered Room 33. There was a courtesy fly swatter hanging next to the door on a bare nail that she hoped would not have to be used. The room included a television, a telephone, a mirror that hung over a desk, a sink, a bed, one chair, and a small shower. At $25 per night what did one want, expect, or pay for? *Well, I could always go back to Carol's, but first, I'll check out the phone book.*

****

By the time Audrey got her make-up settled in the vintage bathroom at The Scenic City Motel and her clothes and shoes somewhat organized, she was ready to hit the road once again toward the park. She wanted to look around and knew that Carol and Sandy would not be a minute late.

Audrey was lucky as she was able to secure a parking place for her little red, rented Thunderbird right in front of the historic Iowa Falls Post office, which sat directly across from the park on the west side. She noted an open spot for motorcycles on down the block, but did not pay much attention to it as three or four hugged close together.

The Iowa Falls Post Office, built in 1914, was always one of Audrey's favorite buildings in town. Its Neo-Classical design, constructed of dark red brick, rested on a high foundation of North Carolina granite. Four, 22 foot, monumental Doric columns adorned the front of the building. Audrey and her sister used to see if they could put their hands around the 30-inch diameter columns and touch their fingers together as their mother or father dropped their mail inside. When they could touch finger-to-finger, they decided they were too old to play that game anymore. The cement steps, made for running up and down, featured a center door as the main entrance. Above the entrance and white façade was a Della Rubbia style swag that welcomed its mail patrons as if a smile hung overhead. Audrey always smiled back just as she did today.

There is always one pivotal point of any small town, and Estes Park is that point for Iowa Falls. It is in the center of downtown and is the hub of activity for Lawn Chair Nights, teen dances, concerts, and the big draw for the town, River Bend Rally, that takes place every Fourth of July. The park, originally called Central Park, later changed to Estes to honor Jason Estes, a teacher and engineer in1889, had a beautiful wooden band pagoda in the center of the park about where a fountain sits today. In 1931, a Spanish Revival style bandshell replaced the pagoda with $3,622 raised for the construction. Today, the *Bill Riley Bandshell,* in honor of Mr. Riley, a Favorite Son of the Hawkeye State for his Iowa State Fair Talent Search that began in 1959 at the Iowa State Fair, stands proudly on the south side of the park. The Talent Search continues to this day. Bill Riley was a 1938 graduate of Iowa Falls High School. The Elementary School is now a park named for his grandmother, Julia O'Neil. Mr. Riley also served in WWII, as did many of the men and women of Iowa Falls and Hardin County. Audrey's father was in WWII as well and her high school friends knew war from the fields of Vietnam.

"There you are, Audrey," rang out the voice of Sandy from one of the many concession stands that stood on the west side perimeter of the park. Sandy was scoping out the food situation to see this year's offerings. "I know that the Catholics always have a to-die-for ice cream social in the basement of the church that starts about 2:00 or so." Sandy pointed across the street to St. Mark's Catholic Church that sat on the corners of Main Street and Rocksylvania Avenue. "There's always room for pie and ice cream. Right, girls?" Sandy smiled with hunger on her lips.

"We need to *do* the *Beer Garden* tonight too." Sandy was on a roll with food on her mind and a morning peach piña colada lingering on her breath. "Carol was on that committee, you know, Audrey. Carol is on about every committee here in town." Carol and Audrey glanced at each other with affirmation, smiles, and love. "Anyway," continued Sandy, "there was some talk about not having the *Beer Garden* after this year." The corners of Sandy's mouth swayed downward in distaste as if she just gulped a warm beer at that moment.

Carol interjected, "Well, it's not very profitable, and it does cause some problems at least once every season."

The *Beer Garden* was not exactly what Audrey had envisioned when she first heard the name. She thought of it as something rather romantic, with candle lit tables and vineyards running overhead. Something more out of *Rome Adventure* than what it was. Reality hit when she first discovered that the *Garden*, surrounded by chain-link fence, backed up to the alley behind the bank and book-ended between the fire station and one lone building, is no scene from *Rome Adventure*. Beer and wine flowed from an array of raw wooden boards supported by sawhorses. Anyone over twenty-one could buy tickets at the gate for $1 each and redeem them at the tables for their choice of liquid nourishment. It was not Rome, it was Iowa Falls, and that was okay. It was just okay.

"Well, I'll miss the *Beer Garden* along with a few hundred others if you *fuddy-duddies* take it away!" proclaimed Sandy. "It's the social spot of the Fourth."

"I see some coffee over here," said Carol, "Let's get a cup and sit on this picnic table for a few minutes and just people watch."

"Well how boring is that, Carol?" Questioned Sandy as she complied by sitting on the edge of the slivered picnic table. "I could get a sliver up my ass you know, we all could." They all laughed, sipped their coffee, and knew full heartedly Sandy was right.

"Stephen, Stephen, Stephen." Good thing Sandy had a mouthful or the "Stephens" would have come out as a yell rather than a gurgle. Once she could swallow, Sandy flicked her body toward Audrey and continued with the Stephen thought. "Did you see who *that* was?"

"Not really," confessed Audrey.

"Well, I know it was Stephen. He has those bags on the back of his bike and his hair was breezing from his helmet as he flashed by. Did you see him, Carol?"

"I didn't recognize if that was him with a helmet and sunglasses." Carol caught Audrey's curious mood and stood up from the picnic table. "Let's walk over toward the middle of the park."

Audrey also got up and proceeded to walk beside Carol in an *appearance* of not caring who was on the motorcycle although her heartbeat was more rapid. As for Sandy, she was rising slowly, leaning over to watch the cycle glide further out of view, while her coffee cup tipped in the same direction and dribbled down the length of her shorts and leg.

"Sandy, your coffee!"

"Oh, who cares about that. I'm just sure that was Stephen." She tossed her cup in the trash, wiped the coffee off her leg, and strolled along after Carol and Audrey.

"Look out for that hole, Sandy," warned Carol.

"Yes, Mother. I'm right behind you."

Eighty to a hundred people strolled around Estes Park. It appeared much as a scene from George Seurat's 1884 painting, "A Sunday Afternoon on the Island of La Grande Jatte," except that the clothes were more modern and the hair styles less fussed over. A carnival on the east side guaranteed to accept anything that resembled money, and a flavorful array of cotton candy, hot dogs, barbecue, and funnel cakes were arousing to the senses. A ten-year-old girl dazzled the audience with a dance/baton routine to John Philip Sousa's *Stars and Stripes Forever*. More talent waited in the wings for their turn to *fly*.

"I'm buying the popcorn," Audrey spotted the familiar stand on the corner of the park. "Who wants some?"

"Dude, right here," that was Sandy, of course, but Carol's eyes popped with kernels as well.

Just as a lighthouse beacons its travelers, so does the Iowa Falls Popcorn Stand. When he was eleven years old, so the story goes, Bill Riley himself used to sell popcorn at this very stand. His goal was to sell one hundred, five-cent bags in one evening. He often topped that by another twenty-five bags, or so. A dime could still buy a small brown bag of plain popped corn. The three women glowed like the little girls they felt inside themselves as they approached. Then, at that very moment, a *Mrs. Potato Head* with bright red hair approached the trio of friends blocking their ascent to the popcorn stand.

"Carol! You didn't tell me you'd be down here this afternoon; well, not that you had to, but we were talking about the festivities the other day when I worked on your nails. Of course, I know Sandy, aren't you going to introduce us? Anyway, hi, I'm Lorraine Grant. I do Carol's nails and cut her hair. I won't say what else we do to the hair, because that might not be right of me." Loraine paused only long enough to breathe, crack her gum, giggle, and slap Carol on the back.

Audrey's eyes fixated on the redhead who seemed to have a lot to say. She looked familiar, but why? She weighed about two hundred pounds, estimated Audrey, but she carried herself well, and one had to think that *hot air* attributed to some of the weight.

Lorraine grabbed Carol's left hand. "Like her nails, girls? Well, you're supposed to say 'no,' because Carol is *so* conservative. I keep trying to paint holiday designs, stars, and stripes, whatever, on her nails, but she just sticks by her French manicure. Now, look at mine; I'm ready for this July holiday. What do ya' think?" Lorraine extended her fingers, five in Sandy's face and five in Audrey's. The mini flag, firecrackers, star, hotdog, and peace symbol were all decaled on fields of red, white, and blue.

"There's no doubt what holiday you're ready for," commented Audrey.

"Obviously, Halloween!" added Sandy sarcastically. Both Carol and Audrey threw a quick glance in Sandy's direction.

"Why not, I ask? It only comes once a year, and who knows what next year will hold for any of us."

"I'm Audrey Benway from Las Vegas." Audrey noticed the need for a breath from this woman and jumped right in.

"I remember Carol saying that you were going to visit. Now, Las Vegas—that's a different planet all its own. I'm really in my element when I'm out there. Why, the last time I was in Sin City I bought myself a new T-shirt with two giant, glittering dice on it. One comes about right here and the other right here." Lorraine grabbed each of her breasts to indicate the placement of the die. Carol, Audrey, and Sandy smirked and looked around to see who was watching.

"I remember you, Audrey, but you don't act like you remember me from a hill-of-beans." Lorraine was pointing her index finger directly into Audrey's sternum.

"Should I, remember you, that is?" questioned Audrey in a quizzical manner.

Lorraine flung her head back in laughter and added, "Does Natalie sound more familiar? I told Stephen that I wanted to be just like Natalie Wood, so he said, 'Natalie would do fine.' Of course, I didn't carry all of this blubber around with me back then."

Lorraine had by now withdrawn her index finger from Audrey's chest, but proceeded to shake it in her direction. "You were *so gullible.* You made me believe that, maybe, I *should* be an actress." Lorraine was smiling while Audrey was attempting to sort it all out in her mind.

"You're *not* Natalie?" Audrey's face was puzzled.

"Hell, no! I'm Lorraine Grant, Stephen's cousin from Ackley. He never told ya' the truth? Oh, that cousin of mine, he's a dog at times. Like the other day…"

"Wait, Lorraine!" Audrey was emphatic and demanding in her request. "You were his date at that party in late August of 1966. Stephen said…"

"Shit, Audrey, didn't you see then? Don't you see now? Stevie said that he wanted to take me to that party where his girlfriend, you, would be. He wanted to make you mad so that it would be easier for you to leave for college somewhere."

"He wasn't—dating—you?" Clarification still did not come easily for Audrey, and she needed to hear more.

"Noop, I was just his prop. My acting was pretty good, hey?"

"I guess it must have been—both yours and his."

"I'm going to get in line for some popcorn," stated Sandy,

anxious for this conversation to end.

"Glad to see you, Carol, you, too, Audrey and Sandy. Come on in, and I'll fix that nail you've been trying to hide from me." Lorraine pointed to Carol as she turned and walked toward the carnival stands.

"Good grief, Carol, can't you find someone else to do your nails and hair?" questioned Sandy as she turned to get in line for popcorn. "Come on, Audrey."

"You go ahead. Popcorn doesn't sound very good anymore. I'll wait right here." Audrey felt flushed, enlightened, and bewildered all at the same time. She did not often feel anger, but it was creeping in and replacing joy, pore-by-pore.

Sandy and Carol bought their own dime bags of popcorn and found Audrey standing by a large oak tree not far from the popcorn stand. Carol, always sensitive to other's needs, initiated the idea of walking one and one-half block down Rocksylvania to get a Coke at the Red Rooster. It sounded good to Audrey.

"We can't forget the parade at five, and my chairs are holding down our spots on River Street." Sandy and Carol were both taking good care of their friend who had come from a life in the city back to the small town she loved.

The Red Rooster buzzed with business as usual, but there was an open booth in the corner. "Three Cokes," ordered Sandy from the server.

"Make mine diet, please," corrected Audrey.

"Too bad they were out of caramel corn. I thought you wanted some, Audrey. Here, have some of mine." Sandy slanted her bag in Audrey's direction.

Audrey did not see the bag of popcorn right in front of her, and she questioned in a tense voice, "Do you believe what Lorraine said? How could Stephen have done that to me? I thought he respected and cared about me. How could he have lied and used me like that?"

"Forget it, Audrey," advised Sandy. "It was a long time ago."

Carol just listened as Audrey expounded. "How could I forget?" She took a deep breath. "Stephen was jealous when I left for what he thought was college, I knew that, but what could I do. It was not a choice. I didn't ever, even once, think that he'd set me up so that he could get off the hook. I didn't know I had him on a hook!"

Audrey looked to Carol for confirmation of her feelings, but she didn't get it.

"Audrey, Stephen loved you. I know he did. He was not looking to get off the hook as you think; he was looking out for *your* feelings. Maybe, even for your future."

"We had plans." Audrey was not crying, but there was sadness in her voice.

"Okay, but sometimes, lives aren't as parallel as they may seem," advised Carol. "They intersect, but they don't run side-by-side. Sometimes, they don't even travel in the same direction. I read once that 'Discipline, not desire, determines the outcome of our decisions.'"

Audrey took a sip of her Diet Coke, and somehow, managed to swallow it. "I love the direction my life has traveled, but this makes me feel like I was manipulated, and I didn't even know it—not until twenty-six years later."

"It was just a yield sign in the road, Audrey. It made you look at other alternatives. It made you grow and become the person you are today. Maybe, you should be grateful that Lorraine wanted to be like Natalie Wood."

Audrey was silent with her thoughts. Sandy seemed more concerned about the parade and her lawn chairs than with Audrey's current dilemma, while Carol remained the wise, true, and confidential friend she had always been.

Chapter 7

It was the Fourth of July. Audrey had slept well to the prior night's clanging of thunder, show of lightning, wailing of wind, and pouring of rain as it deluged Iowa Falls once again. She was certain that not everyone who lived there welcomed it with such gusto, but since she was used to desert temperatures and dry heat, the storms and God's display of power sang a lullaby to her.

Audrey did not have any trouble finding Stephen Grant's address in the phone book, and she was sure she knew right where he lived. *It was, most likely, the Horton house down by the river on a little gravel road that ran behind the end of Washington Avenue, just as Sandy said.* Audrey had known the Hortons and had babysat for their only child when she was in junior high. The Horton boy, Daryl, was a real terror. He was hard for his parents to handle, aside from being a four-year-old. Audrey could always understand how Mr. and Mrs. Horton would need a night out by themselves, away from "Dennis the Menace."

Other than Daryl's behaviors, Audrey always thought that the Hortons were the ideal family. Young, well-educated, attractive, nice house, nice clothes; they seemed to have it all, and Daryl would surely grow up one day. A couple of years after Audrey graduated from high school; she heard that they were getting a divorce. It seemed that Mr. Horton had been embezzling money from his construction company for years, and prison was his next home. Audrey always let that be a lesson to her; what is on the outside does not always portray what really happens within.

Audrey had thought about calling Stephen before she just dropped by his house; had dialed the familiar Iowa Falls 648 prefix, but hung up. She did not know what she'd say. It seemed too awkward; perhaps, he would be home, and perhaps, he wouldn't. At any rate, here she was on her way to Stephen's house. It was that simple, that innocent, and that nerve-racking. Just the thought of seeing Stephen made Audrey's heart beat with a few more pulses than usual as she got in her car at the Scenic City Motel.

Audrey balanced her head on the steering wheel before starting the ignition. She felt *heavy*. Her arms anchored down at both sides as her right hand rested on the seat, and her left hand dangled by the door. Suddenly, the secret she was not sure was hers alone overshadowed the anticipation of seeing Stephen. She had not seen him in so long and she was unsure she could or should face him after all these years with what they shared. Audrey did not owe Stephen an apology, but she'd always felt like he had a right to know that he had a daughter—a lovely, bright, loving daughter walking around in the world because of him. Audrey had not seen Stephen for twenty-six years, and in all that time, their daughter had been a part of her life, not his.

Did it matter to Stephen? Audrey could not answer that. Maybe, it would have mattered if he had known. Maybe, he *did* know and just chose not to do anything about it. The rhetorical questions buried for so many years were swimming around in Audrey's mind. She had never found answers. What's more, what would she have done with the answers if she had found them?

Audrey had to make a choice at a very difficult time in her life. She was young, afraid, vulnerable, and pregnant. She knew that she loved Stephen in 1966, but she also knew that their love was not enough. It would have never carried them through a lifetime, and just when living seemed impossible, Jeff came riding up like a white knight to save the day.

Audrey, only one time, let her mind think that Jeff was a substitute for what she might have missed with Stephen. There are roller coasters in every marriage and theirs was no exception, but laughter and joy filled most days. The tough times were resolved through communication and mutual respect for each other's feelings. Audrey and Jeff always resolved a problem before it really became one. Even with raising Scott, knowing, and accepting his lifelong disability, they worked together and had made Heidi Scott's legal guardian. Life seemed in order that way for the Benway household. Heidi belonged to Jeff just as much as Scott was his biological son.

If I see Stephen today, will I be denying my faithfulness to Jeff? I love Jeff. I respect our marriage. I don't want those things in my life to change. I wish Stephen wasn't living in Iowa Falls. I wish... I wish... The steering wheel tipped and Audrey lost her balance.

Audrey once again started the ignition, backed out of the Scenic City Motel, and headed down Highway 65 that would soon turn into Oak Street. She passed the red, metal building on the left known as the Moose Club. Their Sunday morning breakfast specials were a draw to the locals with chatter of farming matters, illnesses, and families. As in many small Iowa towns, when a catastrophic illness or disaster struck a family, there were fundraisers held at the Moose Club or the Elks Club to assist with finances. Audrey's family had always been a part of these.

A railroad trestle used to run over the highway, just as it curved into town, but that had been gone for several years now. Railroads were more important and prominent in Iowa back in the 50s and 60s than they were today. Replacement tracks linked the cities to the small towns and provided necessities and transportation over the years.

Audrey's only real experience with a train happened every April 15th, five minutes before midnight. Her father refused to pay his taxes until then. He and Audrey would make a run to the Iowa Falls Union Depot on the east side of town just as the "Midnight Express" was pulling in so that the postmark always read April 15th. They were never the only ones there with envelope in hand. It was one of those rituals Audrey and her dad shared at this 1902 station erected by the Illinois Central Railroad. Illinois Central erected many depots in small towns from the 1890s to the 1920s. Once Audrey left home, there was never an April 15th at midnight that she didn't think of her father, and knew exactly where he was.

The Brown's Greenhouse was coming up on the right side of the highway. It was not a greenhouse anymore, and Audrey knew that the Browns had moved out-of-state several years ago. It was difficult to see the house itself; because it sat several feet back from the road and has tall, bushy evergreens camouflaging the entire front of it. The greenhouse itself is long and narrow, but somehow, it had looked longer when Audrey was a little girl.

Grandma and Grandpa Harris lived close to the Brown's, and Audrey's fear of large dogs stemmed back to that house. At eight-years-old, Audrey decided to explore the neighborhood by herself. Her curiosities lead her to the grove of apple trees that lined the perimeter of the Brown's backyard on the north side. It is difficult to pick apples from a tree when you are eight years old.

There was a fence around the backyard with old wooden poles

every ten feet or so that supported wire. One of the poles was close to a tree that was loaded with round red balls, and it looked like Christmas had arrived in late July. Audrey could not resist, but her reach was far too short of the one apple she had targeted. The wire was weak, the pole splintery, and the apple dangling high above as Audrey proceeded to attain her goal.

Just as the red sphere came within Audrey's reach, the fence gave way, and she tumbled into the backyard and landed flat on her back in the middle of a small pile of rotted, mashed, rancid apples crawling with ants. The ants were having a picnic, and Audrey was definitely the intruder. Definitely!

The Brown's St. Bernard, Buster, came gallivanting toward Audrey. He looked like a five-hundred-pound white and brown bear charging full speed ahead as Audrey's heart thundered and her feet slid on the "apple sauce" she had created. One step forward...slide back...forward one...back two. Just as Buster was ready to leap on his victim, rather than offer brandy, Mr. Brown seized him by the collar and yanked him on his hind-end. He had trouble holding Buster, but he managed, and Buster Brown minded Mr. Brown's commands much better than Daryl Horton, the four-year-old Audrey used to babysit, had ever thought about complying with his parents. The damage to Audrey's body was minor, but she had been skeptical of large dogs ever since, and she never had any desire to visit the Brown house again.

Audrey continued South on her way to Stephen's. The homes looked old compared to those in Las Vegas. They were. A combination of big and little, brick and wood, kept-up and rundown lined both sides of the rather narrow highway. The highway had not always seemed so narrow. Audrey's T-bird fit just fine, but she continued driving slowly.

What a scandal there had been when the Ramsey's erected that six-foot wooden fence around their backyard, remembered Audrey as she glided by the yellow house that stood on the corner of Pine and Oak Streets. When built, the wooden fence was so tight that not even air moved between the vertical panels. It had been painted brown of all colors. She'd heard her mother complain, "Why would anyone put up an eyesore like that? What did the Ramsey's have to hide from the world they knew in Iowa Falls?" That was the real question, and every female in Iowa Falls wanted to know or think they *did* know the answer.

Were the Ramseys on a rampage and didn't want the neighbors to know or hear what was going on? Were the two Ramsey kids' behavior so bad that they kept them behind a barricade? The *real* answer came back to Audrey as she continued on her way to her destination. She knew it was *real,* because she had sneaked down the stairs one Tuesday night when her mother's bridge club met at their house, and all of the women were abuzz with the *real* answer. Mrs. Ramsey sunbathed in the nude, right in the middle of Iowa Falls!

Then, there was the Furman house. It sat off Oak Street behind the big house made of stucco that Audrey lived in for five years. *Mr. Furman was an old man back in 1954 when I first met him. He was tall and thin, had gray hair and a well-trimmed beard. It would not have mattered, however, if his beard were not well kept, because I grew to love him.*

Audrey was five or six when she was roller-skating with her new silver, metal skates. They attached to hard sole shoes by four little prongs and strapped to the ankle by means of leather and a buckle. The instructions had said to "always carry your skate key while skating." Audrey had diligently put her skate key on a shoestring, tied a knot at the end, and slipped it around her neck. Metal skates, made in the 1950s *always* fell apart. As Audrey sat on the curb of Iowa Street back in 1956, attempting to fix her skate, tears rolled down her chubby cheeks, and she just knew that her attempts were futile. That is when Mr. Furman surfaced in Audrey's life. He didn't have much to say over the years, he never did, and Audrey never asked him much. They sat on his front porch; he fixed her skate with the gentle ease of an artist, and they drank a glass of lemonade.

Audrey often visited Mr. Furman in his home. She would take the six steps up the front porch to the door in three giant strides, knock gently, and ask his wife, "Can Mr. Furman come out and play?" If he were busy at his desk computing tax returns, Audrey would sit and watch, read as he figured, and every now and then, they would smile at each other through the silence. Today, July 1993, Audrey didn't remember how long it had been since Mr. Furman passed away. It had been a long time, but she was sure he enjoyed every peaceful moment, and even more, she was grateful he had been a part of her childhood.

The stucco house with its dark oak staircase, built-in bookshelves, coiled radiators, and cedar closet held many fond tales of the Harris family with antedates of secret confessions made in the dark between young sisters, Audrey and Lilly. The smiles, the arguments, the reality of finding out that Santa Claus was a only a wonderful myth had been revealed during Audrey's five years of life in this huge peach-colored structure. They were magical years, and Audrey remembered them well.

A bag swing once dangled from the sturdy maple tree that still shaded the entire front yard of the old house. Audrey and her father would take a military duffel bag to a farmer, fill it with straw, and attach it to the awaiting, suspended rope. Back-and-forth, high-and-low, up-and down. Twirl, swirl, and whirl as Audrey's father pushed her. "One more under push, Dad." He never refused or was too busy. The hours spent on the bag swing were beyond count, and even Mr. Furman's pencil could not add them up. Audrey was always the one who got the first swing on the newest straw, and the one who jumped the furthest from the porch on this flying cylinder. She would squeal with delight, and only once, did she miss the bag and go headfirst into the sparse patches of grass that caught her like a landing net. Levitation had opened its door, and in dreams, a young Audrey could fly with the fireflies of the evening.

With residential neighborhoods behind her, Audrey approached the business district of Iowa Falls, and memories tumbled in her brain like the balls of a Bingo machine: no order, no sense, no beginning, no end, only a random search of historical tidbits known as Audrey's childhood.

The old Super Value Grocery Store, owned by Grandpa Harris, was no longer standing in the location that was so familiar to a young Audrey. It had given way, years before, to progress. Today, Big Macs were rolling off the assembly line. Memories lingered on the air and waves rippled across the parking lot as if it were yesterday.

Audrey and her sister would walk a block to the Super Value and *help* grandpa after school on winter days. The Iowa snow blew and covered the ground with the sugary, white substance that tasted good as large flakes fell upon Audrey's outstretched tongue.

It was late November, about 1956, and a shipment of toys had arrived for Christmas. Grandpa Harris asked Audrey and Lilly to arrange the toys on the shelves, and with wide smiles on their faces, the girls claimed their job with joy. With most of the toys arranged and only a few left in the bottom of the shopping cart, Lilly pulled out a small gray and white Teddy bear. She proceeded to throw him back in the cart. Audrey's eyes grew large, and her mouth flew wide open with disbelief at her sister's blatant disregard for the little bear.

"Why did you do *that*?" questioned a confused Audrey.

"He's broken," snapped Lilly. "Leave him alone," she added as Audrey attempted to retrieve him from the metal grave.

"Let me see!" insisted Audrey as she snatched him up.

Audrey held the Teddy at arm's length, examined him front and back, and replied in a calming voice, "He looks fine to me." She fluffed the red ribbon that adorned the Teddy bear's neck and centered it under his chin.

"Well, one of his eyes is missing, Dodo. Can't *you* see that?" Lilly was older and always responded in a condescending manner when it came to Audrey.

"So?"

"Nobody wants a one-eyed Teddy bear. Grandpa can send him back."

Audrey swiftly pulled the one-eyed bear to her chest and locked him securely in her arms. "You can't have him back. Someone will want him. Someone will buy him. Someone will care."

"Don't be so dumb," quipped Lilly just as Grandpa came hustling around the corner.

"Girls!"

"Lilly says—"

"Audrey is being a—"

"Enough," halted Grandpa Harris. "Audrey, put the bear on the shelf for now. I think it's time to get home. Isn't *The Mickey Mouse Club* about to start?" Grandpa looked at his watch.

Audrey smiled, and she was sure the one-eyed Teddy bear winked back.

As the long days before Christmas were marked off on the

calendar, Audrey made a journey to the toy aisle of the Super Value Grocery Store every day. She would pull the one-eyed bear from the back of the shelf, discarded by a misunderstanding Christmas shopper, straighten his red bow, and tell him that she loved him.

"Lilly, I know what you can get me for Christmas," Audrey said it every day, and every day, Lilly, snapped in the same way. "Nobody wants a one-eyed bear and I'm not going to spend my money that way."

"I know of somebody who wants him—I do." Audrey's head never bent with an apologetic sigh, but rather, met Lilly by looking her straight in the eyes with all the confidence an eight-year-old could muster. "I love the one-eyed Teddy bear."

Three days before Christmas, Audrey made her usual trip to the store. She rummaged through the toy shelves. Her heart beat faster and the palms of her hands sweat. The bear *was gone!* For the *first* time in her life, Audrey experienced the bitter sweetness that comes with letting those you love go and wanting to hold them forever. Warm tears grew cold on her cheeks as Audrey sauntered through the falling snow on her way home to watch Mickey Mouse.

At last, Christmas arrived with the anticipation that every eight-year-old feels when gifts blanket the family Christmas tree. At this moment in time, as Audrey's car drove by the place that used to be her home, she did not remember anything else about that Christmas so long ago—except one gift—a one-eyed Teddy bear. Lilly had brushed all of her *better sense* aside and bought the bear for Audrey. "Coonie" as she called him, waited every night for Audrey's arms, and every night she knew he winked at her. Chance brought them together—caring brought them love.

Audrey continued on her way to Stephen's. The stoplight on the corner of Oak Street and Washington Avenue was blinking red this sultry July morning, and the cars on all four corners paused and waited their turn before proceeding. Audrey's left turn signal blinked to the pulse of her heart—fast. It was a matter of one small-town block until the next turn. Right.

As Audrey made the right turn, she noticed that the tire store remained on the corner with its display of rubber circles built as a pyramid in the window. Behind the tire store was a small home on the right, non-descript in its exterior. Audrey knew that she would be turning on the only road to the left to get to Stephen's house.

A heap of black wrought iron captivated Audrey's eyes. Strewn directly ahead of her this mangled infrastructure might have been something important from another chapter in history. The iron mountain appeared to be railings and steps ornately designed, now shuffled along the side of the road. Audrey shrugged her shoulders and wondered briefly, where it had come from, and furthermore, where it was going.

The turn left was more like an alley than a street. It was gravel and divided the backyards of a row of houses on the left with a single story structure that sat on the right. An extended yard ran the length of the entire block with the house sandwiched in the middle. It all fit the description and location of the Horton home, and Audrey was sure it was the Grant home today.

The yard was a lush carpet of green, and with all the summer's rain, it would surely remain that way. With manicured perfection, the evergreens, oaks, maples, and century old buckeye tree proudly bowed their branches when nudged by the gentle wind. The river was not visible from the street, as it took a deep plunge with overgrowth, but Audrey knew the river was there. The water did not have too much further to go before reaching the dam and emptying into a larger destination.

The house looked small compared to the size of the lot on which it sat. The flat roof was unusual for Iowa, and Audrey remembered her father telling her that not many contractors in Iowa built roofs that way because of all the heavy snow and rain.

A fresh coat of pale yellow paint with white trim set the house off. Audrey figured that Stephen must have painted just before all of the rains started, because there had not been many dry days in the past few weeks.

Audrey pulled into the driveway but left the car running. She looked to either side of her and admired the orderliness of all she saw. Because of the rain, the blooming flowers were late in emitting their beauty. There were still a few peonies in bloom kneeling low to the ground by the weight of their blossoms, and the pinks and whites accented the yellow and orange of the day lilies that stood tall. The perimeter of the house was further floriated by multicolored hosta and tiny white bells of lily of the valley. A faint scent of lilacs, those purple favorites of Audrey's, perfumed the morning air as her hand landed upon the ignition key and the car was silenced.

Audrey could feel her pulse beating in her lower back, and she hoped that she did not hyperventilate! There were beads of sweat *pearling* along her forehead as tension built in her throat, and she felt that if she were to say anything at that moment it would come out in a very high soprano.

One more look in the rearview mirror to check her face and hair. Plucks on both cheeks for color and a pat under the chin could not hurt. It's the chin and neck at forty-five that capture your attention. An older friend had told Audrey that her grandchildren had asked her why she had a thing like a turkey under her chin. Well, slap them silly! The term *hard body* was losing its meaning day-by-day.

Audrey cautiously opened the door of the scarlet T-bird. Out came her left leg, then her right. She felt as though she had to tell each muscle how and when to move. *Ataxia* was setting in quickly. Would she have to be her own best physical therapy patient?

Audrey felt a bit like Julie Andrews when she hiked up to the Captain's door in *The Sound of Music*, unsure, but for what reasons? Insecure was not in Audrey or Julie's nature, but take a tiger out of the jungle and what do you have: a dull roar in a pet store at a mall. Logic did not abound on this Sunday morning. It had given way to the holiday and perhaps, Audrey would not find that logic anywhere.

The main entrance to the Grant home was on the left side of the garage door. There was no doorbell. Audrey twitched her lips as she pursed them together. "Knock. I could knock. Louder, Audrey, louder," she told herself under her breath. There was no answer.

"One more try." Still no answer. Relief. Audrey closed her eyes and sighed with a slight smile. Well, she had tried. What more could she do? With her body less tense, Audrey turned to make her way to the car.

There was an '86 or '87 black Jeep Cherokee pulled off to the left of the drive, and a fairly new motorcycle pulled up close to the front of the house. *But, that really doesn't mean anything. Stephen could have three vehicles, and he probably does.* Audrey analyzed that the Cherokee and cycle that were there made no significant statement as to the presence of the owner. Again—relief.

Audrey went back to the T-bird, and with her forehead resting on the steering wheel, she caught her breath, let her shoulders and chin slump a bit, and felt her silk panties edge into the wrong places. She sat up to adjust the latter and to start the ignition. As Audrey's eyes rose slowly from the top of the steering wheel, they scanned an object that had not been standing in front of the car before that moment. With her lower jaw dropping open, her eyes at bay, and her panties still in a wad, she recognized a form and face from the past: *Stephen.*

Audrey's lower jaw would not snap back in place by itself, so she took the back of her right hand and persuaded it gently. As she did so, a smile broadened across her face.

"Audrey," came the timbre of a voice she had not heard in a quarter of a century. The car window was open, and as Stephen continued, he spread his arms across the front of the red hood as his hands rested on its rain-spattered top. "I heard you were in town. You weren't leavin', were you?"

Audrey could not speak. Her mouth was there; all of the *fixtures* she needed to talk, but not a sound emerged.

Stephen withdrew his hands and walked over to the driver's side of the car. "It's good to see you," he said as he opened the door.

Audrey got out of the car, but this time she did not check her face or hair, or pat her neck or pinch her cheeks. She had not even had time to straighten out her panties, but somehow it didn't matter. A smile stretched across her face, and the words, "Hi, Stephen," came tumbling out as if they had never been lost at all.

He looks great. His dark brown hair fell slightly below his ears and touched the collar of his polo shirt. Only a bit of a recession was taking place on the front hairline, but certainly more slowly than some other 45-year-old men she knew. No gray hair, no glasses, and not a bit of fat on this six-foot-plus frame that towered in front of her.

Stephen's face was still incredibly handsome. A bushy mustache complimented his full eyebrows, and the chin—the Kirk Douglas cleft in his chin was more dominant than it had been in his youth. There were signs of "weathering" around his eyes and forehead, but nothing about Stephen seemed to reveal his mid-forties. Stephen's high cheekbones accentuated with his wide smile as he looked at Audrey. He had not shaved yet this morning, and a shadow of dark whiskers framed his cheeks and jaw.

Taking both of Audrey's hands, Stephen extended her arms and stretched his body backward. "It's so good to see you, Audrey. You look wonderful."

"And you, too, Stephen."

Two people smiled, hand-in-hand, as they stood in a driveway, down a gravel road, in the middle of Iowa Falls, Iowa. The world stopped churning for a few minutes, and the sky was an elegant shade of blue.

Chapter 8

Audrey thought how much easier it might be to talk to Stephen if he weighed three hundred pounds, had warts all over his face, and wore glasses thick enough to see into tomorrow. Somehow, she managed to squeeze out, "I heard you lived here, down here by the river. I wanted to pop by and say hi."

"Funny, I heard that you were in town, too. I'm glad that you stopped or popped by to say hi."

"Hello, Again, Hello. Who sings that?" questioned Audrey of Stephen.

Stephen snickered and responded as if in school, "Diamond."

"You passed." Audrey smiled and looked toward the ground. *Why did I say that? That was a dumb thing to say after twenty- some years.*

"I thought you'd stop by. I was in hopes that you would." Stephen was still holding onto both of Audrey's hands.

Audrey just smiled and raised one eyebrow slightly. Arrogant! Stephen Grant had always been so arrogant. So sure of himself, or, at least, that's the impression he'd always wanted to leave with Audrey. "Well, I did. Stop by, that is."

"I have some coffee on. Do you drink coffee?" questioned Stephen.

"I'd love some. I was just admiring your flowers and yard. They are lovely. The lilacs are the best." Audrey took a deep breath. "Did you do all of this by yourself?" She glanced around the tweezers trimmed lawn as she asked the question.

Stephen released his grip on Audrey's hands and ushered her to the door as he placed his right fingertips gently against her lower spine. "I keep it up, but everything was already planted when I bought the house. Nice touch, hey? I hope all the rain doesn't turn Iowa into a swamp land; could kill some of the trees."

"I thought a lot of water made them more colorful in the fall," observed Audrey.

"The leaves should be pretty, but the evergreens need good drainage. Otherwise, they get damaged roots and drop all of their needles. And, we've had enough water this year to drown the fish in the river." As Stephen smiled, his mustache spread wider and thinned across his upper lip.

As the two entered the yellow frame house, Audrey could feel herself tensing up again, just as she had when she first went to knock on his door. Stephen pulled the door with a hearty yank. "Sticks most of the time; just takes my touch."

Audrey could see why *his touch* was so powerful. Inside the door, the garage transformed into a personal gym, sporting burgundy tweed carpet that covered the garage floor wall-to-wall. A four-by-six foot mirror hung on one wall and posters of Arnold Schwarzenegger, Bruce Lee, Sylvester Stallone, Chuck Norris, Len Dawson in his Kansas City Chief's uniform, and some unknown in Army fatigues on the rest of the walls. A full size cutout of Elvira also stood guard in one corner.

"Arnold, Bruce, Sylvester, Chuck, Len, and who's that?" She pointed to the one in the Army uniform.

"Ski." That's all Stephen said. She could tell that's all he wanted her to know.

The room had all the necessities for body builders: bench press with weights, skier, free weights, and a strange contraption that appeared to do something for the legs or arms or full body. She was not sure, but she could tell the equipment was top notch.

"You work out a lot, I see," observed Audrey as she glanced around the room. She would not allow her eyes to look at Stephen at that minute for obvious reasons every woman could understand.

"I try to. I can lift about 245 pounds. I don't think that's too bad for a guy my age. I try to keep in shape, but it's hard sometimes."

As Stephen turned his back to lead the way up the one step that lead into the rest of the house, Audrey couldn't imagine Stephen being in better shape than he was at that moment. His worn Levi shorts hugged his lower torso with pleasure in every seam. The zipper was snug and the waist, she estimated, about a 36. The slightly faded polo shirt fit nicely and revealed a ripple effect—of muscle. Audrey, with some effort, finally breathed again!

One small step up and her foot sank in a plush, light-colored carpet. Her feet sank into the depth of an inch or so and left a mark indicating where she had been. A small, silk oriental throw rug greeted

Stephen and his guest with deep colors of burgundy, green, blue, beige, and rose as they were weaved in a pattern of friendly oriental design, fringed along the two narrow edges.

Stephen took a sharp right turn and entered the living room. Audrey's eyes snapped to attention, and her legs did the same as she gazed around the room. This was not a living room; it was a museum. A place where treasures come alive and artifacts of life kept. He went on into the kitchen as she admired the interior designs.

The plush light, almost white, carpet continued throughout the main part of his house; the walls a pale green. The couch and two overstuffed tapestry chairs of burgundy, blues, greens, and black fit the room's mood. Throw pillows accented the corners of the furniture with solid colors, and a large square ottoman sat securely in front of one of the chairs.

A coffee table stood in front of the couch made of walnut and glass. Audrey's eyes caught the titles of the magazines, as they lay tousled on the table, pages dog-eared, obviously read. There was *Architectural Digest, Smithsonian, Audubon, American Fitness*, and in the middle, *Cycle World*. A bronze statue of a wild stallion hugged the upper left corner of the table. Audrey's tongue lodged in the upper left quadrant of her mouth, and she tapped it a couple of times to remind herself to relax and swallow.

An entertainment center on the right side of the room in matching walnut covered most of the wall. The television, although not large, appeared to be state-of-the-art. The CD player, stereo, and speakers took up the rest of the center. Stephen's CD compilation could rival any retail store with its wide selection. She went over to study his collection.

Stephen stepped from the side of the kitchen, over to the entertainment center, and placed his left hand firmly on Audrey's shoulder. "What would you like to hear, Audrey? I know," he answered before she could even open her mouth—although it really wasn't shut. "I had this on earlier, some of my favorites." Stephen flipped a switch on his CD player, then turned and smiled at Audrey just as the strains from "Phantom of the Opera" took the room with ease. Audrey smiled back and managed to close her mouth for a few seconds, at least.

Stephen was in his element. He was sure and snug and had surrounded himself with the finest things in life. He was confident here, Audrey could tell that from a glance, and she was happy that his life was so rewarding.

A ten-foot wide archway lead to the kitchen from the living room, and the rest of the wall was lined with bookshelves and a desk. Harvard classics bound in leather were a focal point for Audrey as were several sets of *Time-Life* series on nature, geography, Civil War, and the Old West, as well as a luxury copy of *Gray's Anatomy*. Placed among the books, used as bookends, were various memorabilia from Stephen's life. A hand grenade, cobalt blue cut-glass vase, a set of bongo drums, a framed picture of the Kansas City Chiefs signed by Len Dawson, and another Frederick Remington statue, "Bronco Buster."

The entire length of the far walls in the living room and kitchen were ceiling to floor windows covered with mini blinds topped with a valance. Mother Nature provided the view, and the Iowa River never looked so beautiful to Audrey.

As Audrey stood looking out the back door, she could not help but sigh, "Stephen, this is simply…*wonderful*. Did you have somebody come in and help with the design?"

"A few flies get in the doors every now and then, but, no, I just have what I need and like."

Audrey opened the back door and stepped out onto an inlaid brick patio. In the corner sat a small gas barbecue and one lounger with a little patio table snuggled beside it, atop, sat one half-empty beer bottle.

A few feet forward and Audrey took one-step up onto a wooden deck that ran the length of the house. It lead to the terraced bank that ran down to the river's edge. A wrought iron railing surrounded the deck and on one opening, a set of several concrete steps carved their way down the middle of the terraced bank. They looked like they led to a grassy landing. She did not take the steps, because Stephen exited the back door with two cups of coffee in black and burgundy mugs.

"Black, sugar, or milk?" questioned an ever-pleasing Stephen.

"This is just great," said Audrey as she reached for the cup.

"What kind of flowers are those?" Audrey's point led to tall orange tulip-looking blossoms.

"Those are wild poppies. There used to be a lot more along here, I've heard. I planted some other wild flowers and put a few rhubarb plants down over there. This will be the first year for that. It's doing pretty well, I think. At least, the stems are getting red. It's supposed to turn red isn't it?"

"We don't have much rhubarb in Las Vegas but from what I remember about rhubarb in my grandma's garden, it does turn a deep red before you pick it. Rhubarb pie. That sounds very Iowa."

"Vegas. People *really* do live there?"

"About a million of 'em. We've been there well over twenty years, now, since Vegas was just starting to grow up. Vegas has a lot of opportunities for all of us."

Stephen leaned with this back against the railing, legs crossed at the ankles, and coffee mug held between both hands. It felt "right" seeing Audrey and having her stand on his deck early on this holiday morning. She looked so good to him: fresh, trim, successful, happy. Her white cotton blouse neatly tucked into navy blue pleated shorts and secured at the waist with a red leather belt. White sandals made the outfit complete and simple. Audrey's light skin looked smooth and soft, not weathered by the harsh suns of Nevada or by the hands of time. She was shorter than Stephen had remembered, maybe about five-foot-four, but her eyes—he'd never forgotten those eyes—as stunning as polished sapphires in a sea of cream.

"You haven't gotten any taller." Stephen wanted to talk about Audrey, not about the flowers, the rhubarb, his house, or the river, or anything but her.

"I guess not." Audrey chuckled. "But, you're still as tall."

"Six-three and possibly still growing."

"Possible, but not probable." Audrey smiled, facing Stephen at a distance of ten inches apart. Oh, how he wanted and was sure she did too, but they didn't. They both took a sip from their coffee mugs and Audrey rolled her lips inward as Stephen licked his.

"What have you been doing, Audrey?

"Since I've been here in Iowa Falls?"

"No. For the last twenty-five years."

Audrey stepped to Stephen's right side and balanced her coffee mug on the top of the wrought iron railing. She looked down the grassy bank before replying, "Living. Living, I guess. I'm a physical therapist. I love my work and I like to think, anyway, that I'm good at it. I work in a hospital and outpatient clinic. It's rewarding most of the time, but you see some things that should *not* have happened to people. I see that you have a motorcycle. You *do* wear a helmet, don't you?"

"Yes, I *do* wear a helmet, but I don't have a motorcycle…I ride a *HARLEY*."

"And a black leather jacket to go with the…*HARLEY*?"

"What else?" Smile matched smile as ashes smoldered in an old flame.

It was Audrey's turn to ask a question, and she was not about to miss her chance. "Are you married, Stephen?"

"Only on paper. I've been married twice, divorced once. My first wife, Toni, and I got married not long after I heard that you had gotten married, but it was a mistake from day one. We stayed married until I got back from—" There was a deliberate pause in Stephen's conversation. Then he continued, "From where I was. It couldn't have worked, and we'd both changed. I moved to California, met, and married Janna in 1976. We've been separated and our divorce is in the works. We just didn't have the same goals anymore. We fought constantly about anything. Nothing we had was *ours*; it was hers or mine, but never ours. Except Emily, that is." Stephen was somber, and then, a smile broadened across his face.

"Emily is my daughter. She's wonderful, sixteen and beautiful, tall with long dark hair, just like Janna. She'd like to be a model. I imagine she could if she decides to concentrate on it. She plays basketball now, ya' know. She's center. Sure wish I could see her games." Stephen's smile dissolved into his emotions. "I miss her."

It was obvious how Stephen felt about his daughter, Emily. She was not only the center on the basketball court, but also, of Stephen's life. She brought happiness out in him and a father's pride. Emily gave Stephen a reason to live. Audrey's eyes watched her coffee swirl in its mug as the question she so long wondered about finally found an answer. From that short conversation, she was certain that he did not know about *their* daughter, Heidi.

51

The names of Lorraine and Natalie crept into Audrey's mind, and she wanted to say something, but the time did not seem right. The conversation had been so positive and to bring that up really was not pertinent. Still, she wondered. She thought of Carol's perception of whether Audrey should have made this visit and knew that it was right. If only Stephen had not been so special in her life. He had given her a daughter and he didn't even know about her existence. He had left something so significant in Audrey's life. She'd have to find a way to tell him. A time. A way. This just was not the time and maybe that time would never come.

"She'll be here for Christmas," tagged Stephen.

Audrey's mouth was hanging halfway open, her eyes now set straight ahead. All she heard from Stephen was something about Christmas. "Christmas?" responded Audrey.

"Yes, this next Christmas, the one that comes in December. Emily is going to be here with me." Stephen smiled in Audrey's direction, but Audrey continued looking straight ahead across the river and down toward the dam.

"I should leave now, Stephen." *I found out everything I came to find. What would Jeff think if he knew I was here? Where will this lead? Why are my feelings for this man still so strong? Why do I feel so vulnerable and open when I know that what I have waiting for me at home is what I need and how much they need me.* Audrey's logical and grounded self was pleading for her to run. Run fast. Don't stop. Don't look back. While she grappled with that side of her brain, the other side was busy playing emotional games from her adolescence. These roots were pulled from beneath the ground as if they had been planted there years ago in the tulip beds. Dormant in the winter, they would bloom each spring until somebody pulled them up. *Don't pull at me, Stephen. Please, don't pull.*

"Come on, Audie, let's go inside and get a refill," said Stephen as he raised his coffee mug.

"Audie. I haven't heard that in a long time."

"Audie. Audie. Audie. I like the sound of it, again. I always did like the way it tumbled out of my mouth." Stephen held the door as Audrey entered.

"You make a good cup of coffee. Are refills free?" asked

Audrey.

"They are for special guests, and I haven't seen one this special in twenty-some years."

"Then fill me up." Audrey and Stephen both chuckled ever so slightly.

The living room and outside so engrossed Audrey that she hadn't taken time to survey the kitchen. The plush carpet from the living room extended through the archway, past the outside door, and under the table with its four chairs. The tiled floor in the rest of the kitchen was *spit and polish* clean.

"I think you're expecting company, so I won't stay long." Audrey gestured toward the table that was set for what looked like an elaborate dinner to her relief. The walnut pedestal with its matching top was set for four. Plates of burgundy were resting upon navy blue placemats. Napkin rings of pewter horses secured their linen counterparts of navy, burgundy, and forest green. Two each, forks, knifes, and spoons hugged the sides of each place setting, and four goblets of rose crystal stood ready to hold a beverage. A vase with three artificial birds of paradise graced the center of the table as if it were their sanctuary.

"Oh, no. I just like to keep it set. It makes me feel…polished." Stephen rubbed his knuckles on his shoulder and smiled with a knowing grin.

"Well, it's a nice touch, just like the flowers in the front yard." She moved over to examine the items Stephen had placed in a small hutch alongside the far wall of the kitchen. There were more goblets and a decanter. An oriental teapot with six cups encircling it sat on the bottom shelf along with a small ceramic picture frame holding the likeness of two women who looked very much alike. Audrey presumed it was Janna and Emily.

There was a center island with an inlaid tile countertop. The tile matched the rest of the counter area in Stephen's kitchen, and various appliances like a pasta machine and bread-maker were obvious signs of one who enjoyed cooking.

Stephen slid Audrey's coffee mug across the shiny tile of the center island. She reached for it with her right hand. Stephen placed his left hand on top of hers as he leaned across, in a pulling motion.

53

"I need to give you a hug, a very big hug." Stephen was serious, and the presence of his hand on hers was secure.

"Do you know what?" Audrey did not wait for a reply, as she often didn't when she was nervous. "It takes at least seven hugs a day in order to feel…" Audrey wanted to say loved, but she thought better of it, "needed." Her sapphire blue eyes were larger than ever as she looked at Stephen across the counter. She felt flashes of a schoolgirl's shyness anticipating her first kiss—yet knowing it was wrong and risky.

Stephen took Audrey's hand from the mug and walked around the end of the island. He folded his arms around Audrey and sighed. It was not an ordinary sigh. It was not a sorry sigh. It was a sigh that had been building for years. A deep kind of relief that erupted from his inner soul and escaped through his mouth. Audrey did more than wonder if she should have stopped to visit Stephen at all, she knew in her mind that she should not have. But at that moment, her heart took the lead and that wondering state lasted for too few seconds.

When the hug was complete and extended to the outer limits of its boundary, as good hugs are, the release slipped into clasped fingers raised to the track lighting in the ceiling.

"You're just as beautiful as you were at eighteen, Audie." He looked down into her eyes.

"I'm glad that I am to you, Stephen, but we're not eighteen anymore. Were we ever really that young? I don't even know how long ago that was."

"It wasn't too long ago to remember."

"I remember it all, Stephen. I remember it very well. We were young and in love and had plans and dreams." Audrey let go of Stephen's grasp, took a step backward, along with a deep breath, picked up her coffee mug from the counter, and took a tiny sip. "Life has changed for both of us. We have responsibilities. People who depend on us." *And for me, one special person who trusts me and believes in me.* An image of Jeff popped into Audrey's mind and yet before her stood Stephen Grant. The man she had fantasized for so many years was real. He was memorable, mysterious, a gentleman, and totally handsome.

Audrey wanted to crawl into Stephen's mind and read all the

notes he had printed on his memory about what he had done with the last twenty-six years of his life. She wanted to know everything about him. She could see the outside world of who he was. She knew what he liked to read. Knew he liked horses, flowers, cooking, rhubarb, and Harleys. She knew he loved music and his daughter. Audrey did not have any trouble remembering—no trouble remembering Stephen Grant, at all.

Stephen just smiled. He wanted to kiss Audrey, and he knew she wanted him, too. He couldn't, because if he did, he didn't know if he could stop. Audrey was so familiar. So warm. So…

"Whenever I used to hear Jim Croce sing, I'd think of you, because I just knew his music was your style," confessed Audrey.

"If I could save time in a bottle. If dreams could make wishes come true…" Stephen paused, and Audrey took over.

"I'd save everyday till eternity ends, and then I could spend them with you." Audrey tightened the grip once again on her coffee mug with both hands. She watched the swirling black liquid in order to avoid letting her feelings speak any louder than they already had. With her chin still lowered, she raised her gaze only to find a silent acknowledgment in Stephen's eyes. Both Stephen and Audrey were finding their way—as if they knew where they were going.

"Whenever I smell greasy hamburgers, I think of you." Stephen sat his empty mug on the counter once again. He laughed aloud at the thought of saying what he just said. "I'm sorry. I shouldn't have said that. It's just that after you used to get off work at Charley's, you'd come by my house, and when we'd neck a little bit in the car, you'd always smell like greasy hamburgers."

Audrey smiled. It felt good that he was comfortable enough to say something like that. "I hope I don't smell that way right now."

They laughed together. "Hardly. You don't look like you flip many hamburgers these days."

"Good!" Their eyes locked in common memories, shared by both. It felt good to be *home*, even if this *home* was from a time long ago.

"It must be about noon." Audrey glanced at the kitchen clock and saw that she was right. "Several of us girls are meeting at the Princess for lunch. I plan to have a Green River and a pork tenderloin.

They still make them, don't they?"

"You bet. I had one there not too long ago."

"Do they still make caramel apples like they used to?"

"I think they do, but only in the fall. That's a fall thing, you know." Stephen walked Audrey out of the kitchen, through the living room, and into the gym.

"What size shoes do you wear?" asked Audrey with a look of concern on her face.

Stephen laughed in spite of the fact that she was serious. "Why?"

"Because I don't know that about you. I don't know if you like kiwi or if you like your steak rare, medium, or well done. I don't even know if you go to football games or if you really like the Kansas City Chiefs or just remember Len Dawson. I don't know…"

"Then, know this!" Stephen leaned down from his lofty perch and pulled Audrey into his body with the force of what had been building for some twenty-six years. His kiss was as igniting as metal to a magnet and as sensuous as the smell of the early morning lilacs. When Stephen relaxed his hold and Audrey's feet could again touch the floor, he whispered in her ear, "I wear a size twelve shoe. The Chiefs have always been my team, and I'll have a medium-well steak and kiwi waiting for you at six, right here."

Stephen held the door. Audrey could not quite tell if she was walking on the ground or on clouds, had no idea what day it was, and she could not speak—so, for a change, she didn't.

Chapter 9

Audrey parallel parked the T-bird on Stevens Street and walked a block to The Princess Café. She did not need to hunt for loose change as she had in the past, because renovation took place in downtown Iowa Falls some years earlier and the parking meters removed.

The Princess wasn't busy when Audrey arrived. Ah, the memories that were made at The Princess Café, so fond and deep as she entered the building at 607 Washington Avenue. The tall, vertical Princess Café sign had been a fixture on the main street of Iowa Falls for over sixty years. One of the large storefront windows on either side of the door displayed a pyramid of Princess coffee mugs, T-shirts, and caps. *These are new.* Commercialism had come to the middle of Iowa, a microcosm of Las Vegas style advertising. However, as Audrey entered the front door, the scene confirmed that she was not in Vegas and that time could stand still.

Ernie Karrys and Nick Pergakis came from Greece and established The Princess Café in 1915. Audrey remembered well Chop Suey night at the restaurant with her family and how Harry, Nick's brother, always told the same jokes. Since her dad was a history buff, she knew that on Christmas day, 1934, fire destroyed The Princess. On July 1, 1935, it reopened for business as usual, as it looks today. The Art Deco design with Carrara glass façade and streamlined woodwork is exceptional for a small town in Iowa. The equipment was modern as gas replaced old wood and coal ranges and stoves, and it was the first building in town to be air-conditioned. Harry used to brag that The Princess cost approximately $30,000 to build her up from the ashes during the Great Depression. Harry knew all of the history well and told all of his customers that the Pioneer Neon Sign Company of Minneapolis designed the famous Princess Café Art Deco sign in 1935.

The old-fashioned 25 foot-long soda fountain was in place on the right, just as Audrey remembered with its black marble top shined for the holiday. Eight stools bellied up to the counter, all with black leather seats and brass pedestals. The brass footrest, worn down by the many feet that had found comfort on it, depicted its character with dents and scratches.

The quaint display cabinets that had once been laden with homemade candies and caramel apples now presented boxed goodies, with names such as *Fanny Farmer* and *Sees* that beckoned local patrons to come in. As Audrey stood looking at all the indelible edibles in the glassed cases, she recalled how Sandy was always on a diet—until she entered The Princess. Richard Simmons would probably have been in grade school in those days, and his Dial-A-Meal was not even a figment of anyone's imagination, so Sandy was on her own. She would cheat here and starve there, pinching and plucking her way into adolescent perfection. Regrets? She had none. Sandy was always popular with the boys and her size five or seven put curves in their eyes and molasses in their dreams. Audrey was sure Sandy wished she could wear anything less than a 16 or 18 these days, but obviously, men still found Sandy appealing. She had once confessed to Audrey that she felt, perhaps, her weight gain was a shield, an armor to protect her against any other inner desires. Maybe, caramel apples were more for protection than for pleasure.

The streamlined Café held three rows of booths that were the same as Audrey remembered. Made of two-tone walnut, they demanded their patrons to have a very straight spine. Panels of oriental walnut in lighter shades, imported from Africa, continue to adorn the ends of tables in all of the booths. The pedestal tables, topped with black and neatly trimmed with silver snuggled in to complete each set of booths. The mirrors that accented each booth had remained intact, with a decorative etching on the lower right-hand corner. Over the years, only a layer or two of paint had gone up along with the prices. Audrey did not feel bad about either of these. She was just grateful for the preservation of her youthful memories.

Audrey visualized French fries piled high, smothered in catsup, with a Cherry Coke, or what made The Princess famous, a Green River. That is what Audrey would order today, a Green River. She recalled how Stephen had introduced her to Green Rivers. They not only tasted good, but oh, were they pretty: the color of the emerald isle.

"You're favorite color's green, right?" said Stephen Grant to a naive Audrey Harris over twenty-five years earlier.

"Kelly green—I love that shade of green. Why?"

"Close your eyes, I ordered you something on the way in. I think you will like it. At least, you'll like the color."

Today, July 4, 1993, Audrey's eyes focused on the booth she and Stephen were sitting in when she had her first Green River. It was the third booth from the back on the left side of the Café. Stephen sat facing the double door entrance of The Princess.

"You can open your eyes, now," reminisced Audrey of the conversation as the server set a tall glass of beautiful green liquid in front of her. Stephen smiled.

"It looks too pretty and clear to drink. Are you sure it's not just colored water?"

"I'm not sure of that at all. On the other hand, what river it even came from. But, it's definitely green. Me, I'll stick with Coke."

The server said that lime flavoring and carbonated water were all that went in to making a Green River. Audrey loved them immediately, partially because of the taste and color, but mainly because Stephen ordered it for her.

Today, Audrey just stood there on the marble floor as her mind rolled along with inundating thoughts from a distant time. She recalled that it was upstairs in the banquet room of The Princess where her parents had an anniversary party. That evening had been memorable, not from the party itself, but because Audrey's Uncle Art had walked away from the group and wandered off down by Washington Street Bridge. The effects of Alzheimer's had been on a rampage, and when the police finally found him, he was wearing only his socks and a smile. That was Uncle Art for sure, in the buff. Someone had a striped towel in the car and gave it to him to cover up. He had proceeded to wrap it around his neck as a muffler. *Good thing it was in the middle of August and not cold. Dear Uncle Art!*

The other girls had not arrived, so Audrey selected a booth, third one from the back on the left side. She hoped that Stephen would join the group, but she had her doubts. She had just placed her purse on the seat and settled in when she heard, "Audrey Harris, is that you?"

Because of the high backs on the booths, Audrey could not see whose voice called her name. She turned, placing herself on her knees, her arms draping over the booth's back, and with a cheesy grin, she responded, "Well, if it isn't—" Audrey's voice stopped short of completion and she twisted one of the loose curls on the left side of her head. She did not recognize the weathered face that greeted her. "Well, hi." She was in hopes that he would reveal his identity, or that he would resemble one of the pictures she had looked at in her old annual before leaving home.

"I thought that was you. You look great! Are you here for the weekend?"

After a slight hesitation, Audrey responded, "Yesssss. I'm waiting for a group of gals to meet me here for lunch."

"Audrey, what are you doing on your knees?" questioned a voice coming from behind her.

"Oh, hi, Sandy, I was just talking to—"

"Dan Withers," announced Sandy. "I haven't seen you in a month or so. How is your corn doing with all of the rain?"

Audrey was relieved to know who this was. He did not look like Dan Withers to her. He looked more like an apple-head doll than someone from the class of 1966. It was probably all of the sun, wind, and whatever else farmers expose themselves to. His hair was shoulder length, streaked with gray, and John Lennon glasses exaggerated the wrinkles in his face.

"I don't talk about the weather much anymore," replied Dan. "It just keeps on gettin' worse, and supposed to have more rain tonight, too. I've started my ark in the barn. My wife thinks we should hold a lottery to see what animals get in." Dan chuckled, but it was a chuckle of apprehension rather than joy.

Audrey felt guilty about her thoughts of the apple-head. "Dan, won't you join us for lunch? Please." After all, she had face lotion and her mother's good genes to thank for her nearly wrinkle-free face.

"A gaggle of beautiful women, you bet!"

"At least, you didn't call us a herd, Dan," retorted Sandy. They all smiled that broad *welcome home* smile as they moved to the larger booth in the center aisle. Dan slid in next to Audrey.

"So, Audrey Harris…?"

"Benway. Audrey Benway. I've been that for over twenty-six years."

"Happy years, I trust?"

"Most of them; it's hard to think so many years have slipped by all of us. Isn't it?"

"Damn right, Audrey. I don't know where they've gone. Where do years go when people are through with them; to the year-end graveyard?"

"Good try, Dan, but I think they don't pass go and head directly to the memory. That's where all of mine have landed, anyway."

Dan put his arm around Audrey's shoulder and whispered on his whiskey breath, "Audrey Harris, you always did have all the answers. Have you put them to good use over the years?"

All the answers…all the answers. If only she knew all the questions then at least, she would have a chance at knowing all the answers. "I hardly think so, Dan. I try. We all try, but answers don't always come easily."

"Not at all, Audrey. Less for some of us than for others." Dan seemed sad inside, as though many of his songs in life had gone unsung. Audrey smiled with acceptance, and they both knew that although years had grown into a lifetime, the commonness of their past held a cohesive bond of friendship and caring. Dan squeezed Audrey's shoulder before turning to the others who had arrived at The Princess.

What a group! They rambled in one at a time. Word had gotten around that the class of '66 was ready to roll and time was a wastin'. The server cautiously approached this bunch of Cadets who were equally as loud as they had been as teenagers.

"To start with," announced Spin, who had come from Georgia for a holiday visit with his parents, "you'd better bring us about a dozen Cherry Cokes and the same number of Greeeeen Rivers. Then, put in a slip for ten large orders of fries, with a couple full bottles of catsup. That should get us started." Spin had arrived with his usual flair and boisterous voice. His presence commanded the attention he had always gotten, whether he was pounding on his drums in the band or quarterbacking on the fifty-yard line.

Spencer was Spin's real name, but since *Spin and Marty* days on *The Mickey Mouse Club*, he had never used Spencer again. Audrey had seen him many times over the years, but she knew him better since

61

he'd become a man than when she knew him in high school. Audrey knew that underneath that loud voice hid a man filled with sincerity and warmth, but also a man living in fear. Spin's ex-wife hurt him badly, and he was determined not to ever make himself vulnerable again. He built a shell for himself out of expensive clothes, work, and an array of women. He had confided in Audrey a couple of years earlier that the women had no expectations for the relationship to go any further than the sex. That is all he wanted, or so he said. She always thought that she heard other messages in his words. Spin just needed to let himself be loved for who he was.

Age had not settled into Spin's facial features, but the rest of his body was showing the signs we all face. He was robust, as he would put it, and almost bald. He owned his own sign business in Atlanta and had dabbled in politics over the years. Spin was always a great organizer and loved being around people. Those two qualities seemed compatible for the political arena. On this Fourth of July, Spin was in Iowa Falls wearing a red, white, and blue Polo shirt with stars and stripes and a pair of white walking shorts.

Audrey thought how different Spin was from Stephen. Spin had always been the leader in whatever he chose to do. He had moved to Iowa Falls with his family in his early junior high days. Not that he was a city boy, but he brought with him an enthusiasm for everything. In the terminology of today's education, he would probably be considered attention deficit disordered with hyperactivity thrown in! This quality did not affect Spin's grades, he just had an alternative style of learning: hands on, and he required more attention than many of his peers. He did not have to work in high school, although he played gigs on his drums with some older friends in the small towns around Iowa Falls, so Spin always had time to go out for extra activities in school.

Stephen, on the other hand, was quiet. He was not a leader, and Audrey did not really think that he ever desired to be one. He was not in band, football, or wrestling like many of the other small town high school boys, because Stephen was always busy hustling a job. "You'd be great at basketball, Stephen," observed Audrey. "You're so tall; you'd be a natural." She recalled saying that to him one fall day just as the team was beginning to practice.

Stephen did not comment to Audrey. He simply put his hand on her shoulder, leaned down to give her a gentle kiss on the lips, and said something like, "I'll give you a call after work. I don't get off until 10:30 tonight, hope that's not too late."

"Do you always order in such quantity?" Linda asked Spin as she and others were now arriving and joining in the Cadet festivities.

"Only when Craig's here, this guy looks like Paul Bunyan." Spin roared back, laughing at his own joke.

"And eats like Babe the Blue Ox," added Luke. Craig just patted his stomach in silence, most likely thinking about his football physique, left behind with his letter jacket.

"Now, don't get paranoid on us, Craig. We love ya' just the way you are," added Sandy.

"Oh, I never get paranoid. I call it 'neuronoid' these days," corrected Craig in a confident tone of voice.

"'Neuronoid?' I've never heard of that?" asked Spin.

"Yeah, 'neuronoid.' The fear that someone *will* agree with you!"

Laughter was the most popular choice on the menu: smothered with wit, sprinkled with irony, and topped with hugs. Laughter is always contagious. It is like a yawn; once you see it, you just have to join in.

Audrey sat examining the group of about fifteen friends who had gathered at The Princess. She could not help but recall times shared with each of them: good times, sad times, anxious moments that would dissolve into happiness, and particularly, many days of grief, while she studied Luke's face and manners as the man who sat across from her today. He smiles now, with ease. He laughs now, with graciousness, but he surely wonders about the brother he never had the opportunity to know as a man.

Death finds a small town just as it hauntingly searches in the shadows of a city. It finds its victims in backyards, schools, offices, streets, and jungles far from the security of familiar surroundings. Death had come to Iowa Falls before 1964, but now, in the form of a body shipped from Vietnam. The word of Stanley's death, Luke's older brother, in the rice fields of a land we had all come to know on television, spread quickly into every home of Iowa Falls in late

September of that year. Stanley was nineteen. He was more than Luke's brother; he was his mentor, his idol, and his wrestling trainer. Wherever you saw Stanley, there was Luke, not in his shadows, but by his side. Stanley was an Iowa State Wrestling Champion in 1964, and Luke set his sights on nothing less for himself. At the graduation ceremony, Stanley gave the valedictorian speech in which he said he had enlisted in the Army to make the world a better place for those who would follow. He had turned down several scholarships, because he wanted to do his *duty*. The audience applauded.

Iowa Falls was a naive town back then, in 1964. The baby boomers were only in high school and had not tasted the bitterness of what lie beyond the boundaries of this "sleepy hollow." They were not ready to experience it, but time was not their choice. It took a month and a half for Stanley's body to make it back to Iowa. A month and a half to finally lay to rest on his family's farm. A month and a half to realize that the mighty rivers that lie on either side of Iowa could not keep the world from crossing over—a long time to grieve for the remains of a friend, a brother, a son.

Luke was a state wrestler in 1966, and Audrey was sure that the whole town had gone to the tournament to see him. He held his trophy high above his head, and when interviewed for the local newspaper, they quoted him as saying, "This is for Stanley. I'll always know that the world is a better place because he was here."

Today, Luke raised his glass of Green River high above his head. "To friends: the past, the future, to the time we have now. To Iowa Falls: the places we've been and the journeys to follow. Let's always be with each other."

Everyone raised his or her glass, but nobody said a word. Nobody needed to. Nobody wanted to break the solitude of the moment. They all knew what they shared from this little town in the middle of Iowa.

****

As the glasses once again touched the table, it signaled a spontaneous release of verbal energy from both ends. "Did you know…?" "Do you remember when…?" "Can you ever forget…?" "Wouldn't it be funny if…?" "Have you seen…?" Because Audrey sat in the middle, she was trying to listen to all of it.

"Audrey, remember our kitchen band? I think that was in tenth grade, wasn't it? What was the name of that song we played? I remember that I banged on the glasses with a spoon. Do you remember that?" Linda was full of questions, and Audrey was not sure if she actually wanted them answered or not, but Linda stopped long enough to take a sip from her Cherry Coke.

"Sure, I remember. How could I forget those red and white checked blouses we all had. Yeah, it was in tenth, and we played 'Elmer's Tune.' Clint was our only boy. He was our director with a chef's hat. That was for *Musicalites*." Audrey liked details, and she remembered every one.

"And, didn't you and Clint sing some kind of a song the next year?" June directed her question toward Audrey.

"Right. It was 'A Housewife's Lament.' Clint played it on his ukulele, and he and I both sang. Geeze, I looked awful in that housedress of my grandma's as I wielded a broom. It wasn't that year, though, a couple after."

"Audrey, Audrey, Audrey." Spin was trying to comment on every conversation going on at the table. He was good at multitasking.

"Yes, Spin," grinned Audrey.

"Are you still good at wielding that broom? How about singin' and dancin' with a broom for us today?"

"I'm sure all of the folks at The Princess would love that show! I'll pass for now."

"Hey, aren't you a showgirl in Vegas? I'm sure I heard something about that!" Spin raised his eyebrows and puckered his lips.

"Suuure, Spin," replied Audrey. "But, that's only on my days off at the hospital."

"I'd be *your* patient, Audrey. Where do I make an appointment? Where? Where? Where?"

"Speaking of patients, did you know that Hadley Reynolds has cancer?" Barb was speaking. "I don't think he's doing real well. I saw his mother the other day in Rite Drug."

"What kind of cancer?" inquired Dan.

"Pancreatic. Not a real good prognosis with that," added Barb. "His mother said that he's dealing with it pretty well, and that he's going through chemotherapy. He has a great wife, and she's been there

65

every minute for him. His folks went out last month, too."

"Where does he live?" asked Audrey.

"In Maine."

Audrey continued, "Let's all sign a card for him. He would get a kick out of hearing from fifteen of his old pals; it might just make one day seem better. I'll run across the street and get one."

"I'll go," offered Carol. "I'm sitting on the outside."

"Thanks, Carol, it will be nice for Hadley to know that we're all thinking of him," said Audrey.

Luke winked, Barb smiled, Sandy nodded, and Spin offered the following: "I'll probably write something like, Hadley, just watch those nurses around you; you never know what they might try to insert rectally."

"Tsk, Spin!" said Audrey as she shook her head.

"Don't worry, Audrey. I won't really write that, since I'm not sure how to spell rectally."

"I think its A-S-S. Isn't that how to spell Spin, too?"

Everyone laughed, including Spin who was happy to be back in the limelight.

"Don't mean to change the topic here folks, but I wonder why Stephen Grant isn't here. Does anyone ever see him?" Aaron, who was usually rather shy, contributed to the conversation.

"I've seen him a few times around town on his Harley. He's a hunk, you know." Katie did not hide her observation of Stephen's body as stars flashed from her eyes. "He's not much of a talker, I guess. I heard he had a bad time in Vietnam, and he is just kind of a loner. I don't know if he was a POW or just what happened. Do you ever see him, Doug? You guys were always good friends."

Audrey grew silent trying not to draw any attention to the blushing she felt dash across her face. *So, Katie thought Stephen was a hunk.* All of a sudden, Audrey felt that adolescent jealous feeling of somebody trying to get her boyfriend's attention. "It's My Party and I'll Cry if I Want To" came rushing into Audrey's head. That song of jealousy and protecting *what belongs to you* threw Audrey's feelings back through time

Silly, thought Audrey of this shift in moods. *But, it is funny how being in this town, this restaurant with these people, makes me*

feel like only a few hours or days have passed, not a quarter-century. Once again, she questioned why those roots of adolescence ran so deep and stung so uncompromisingly.

Doug replied, "We had a beer together right after Stephen moved back, a couple of years ago. Yeah, Nam was bad to him; so were a couple of marriages."

"What's he doing in Iowa Falls?"

"He drives a rural gas truck. It's a decent job. He's just not into seeing many people. Seems to like being by himself down there on the river." Audrey listened keenly as Doug continued. "You're right, Katie; he works out and keeps that body firm." Doug, an Iowa Highway Trooper, flexed his right arm and sighed, as no muscle appeared to pop from beneath his black T-shirt.

"Audrey," said Dan as he put his arm back around her shoulder, "didn't you used to date Stephen in high school? Yeah, I'm sure you did."

Audrey lingered on a sip of her Green River as it eased its way up to the end of the straw. "Um-hum," she responded with a mouth full of emerald liquid.

"Did you find his house, Audrey? The other night you were talking about looking him up?" inquired Sandy with a bit of anticipation in her voice.

All eyes of those who had heard the conversation focused on Audrey's reply. "I did find it. It's the old Horton house, remember the Hortons?" All kinds of thoughts were rattling around in Audrey's head. Perhaps she should have given Stephen a call to come down and join the group when it expanded beyond the original plan of four or five girls. She didn't think he would have come, but how was she to know for sure? Audrey didn't want to invade Stephen's world, and it wouldn't be wise if all of these people knew the little bit of Stephen's life she had been able to touch so far.

"The Hortons, who were they?" questioned Linda.

"Who cares," said Sandy, "did you see Stephen or not?"

"He wasn't home when I stopped," fabricated Audrey.

"I'll go check him—I mean, it out with you, Audrey," offered Katie.

"I might stop by again." Audrey looked down at the shine on

the black tabletop. "I'll see."

"I need another Green River," said Craig, as he hoisted his empty glass in the direction of the server.

"Me, too," added Barb and Sandy.

"Ah, just make it twenty!" said Luke. *That was more of a Spin line*. Audrey looked up. Spin was only staring at her, not saying a word.

Chapter 10

Carol returned from Rite Drug with a get-well card in hand for Hadley. "Everyone sign something for Hadley, and I'll mail it off to him tomorrow. He will be happy to hear from us and maybe, it will give him reason to smile. You, too, Spin, now write something nice," said Carol as she glanced in his direction.

"Where do you live, now, Audrey Benning?" asked Aaron.

"That's Benway, as in Ben the rat doing things *his way*," commented Audrey as she responded to Aaron.

"Gross, Audrey. Why'd you say that?" questioned Sandy.

"Well, that came from my, son, Scott, one day when he was *dissecting* our name. Remember that movie, *Ben*? Scott wondered, since our last name has Ben in it, if maybe, he is related. It seemed like a good way for Scott to learn how to spell his last name, so we said that Ben was doing things *his way*."

Carol added, "That was clever, Audrey. I'm sure Scott learned how to spell it easily, then."

"Easier, anyway, Carol." Carol, Sandy, and Audrey smiled as if they had a secret between them, and truly they did, as only they and Spin knew of Scott's handicap. It did not matter to Audrey that anyone else knew, but it had just never come up in a conversation before. "Actually, Aaron, I live in Las Vegas and my Scott has a disability."

"In a hotel on the Strip?" smiled Dan. "Viva, Las Vegas!" He raised his Coke glass high.

"In a regular house, on a regular street, and I have a regular job."

"Oh, come on, Audrey. We all know that things aren't so *regular* in Vegas," laughed Craig.

"Yeah, everybody in Vegas is *irregular*. Hear they have big sales of Correctol out there," said Spin.

As laughter broke out, Sandy added, "Oh, Spin, you're living proof that men have smaller brains than women."

"Naw. You girls just have more hair. Of course, a worm has more hair than I do," countered Spin as he rubbed the bald spot on the top of his head.

"That smaller brain in males is sort of true," injected Audrey.

69

"The brain itself isn't smaller, but research has found that the corpus callosum is larger in women."

"The corpse? Women consider us to be a corpse, now?" laughed Spin and everyone else. "We ain't dead yet; just looks that way some days."

"The corpus callosum is the crossover part of your brain. It's where nerves and impulses from the left side of your brain control the right side of your body and vice-versa. If it's smaller in males, it means that it takes longer to send that kind of a message." Everyone looked at Audrey and knew that she most likely knew what she was talking about.

"Let me see. If the left side of my brain tells my right leg where to go and the right side tells the left leg what to do, who's controlling my middle extension?" inquired Dan as he leaned his face into Audrey's and grabbed his crotch.

Audrey blushed, and when the laughter had diminished, she cleared her throat and said, "I can't speak for *your* extension, Dan, but the hypothalamus is the center of pleasure."

"Audrey! I thought that everyone knew," added Spin, "the bedroom is the center of pleasure."

"You guys are animals," mused Sandy. "Now, promise me you'll never change!"

"Roar," unleashed Craig as he grabbed Sandy's arm and pretended to take a bite.

It was almost 3:00, the memories unraveled and spun into another form, and friends from the class of '66 had made changes in their lives. Many changes could readily be observed on the outside, and those people who had needed to make changes on the inside, had done so. They had molded themselves into their own worlds, worlds where security and familiarity touched. They simultaneously moved from the dawn of their lives into the middle years, and no one could know what the future would bring.

"'Ka Sera, Sera.' Who sang that?" whispered Audrey to Dan.

"Damned if I know. Who?"

"Doris Day."

"Oh, yeah. 'Whatever will be, will be.'"

"That's the one," added Audrey.

"How about if we all meet by the fountain in Estes Park after the fireworks tonight? We can have some brewskies over at my folks, and hey, we'll even put on some 45s and kick-up our heels," Spin had made this as a suggestion, but Audrey knew that, if Spin brought it up, everyone would be there for sure. "How does half-an-hour after the fireworks are over sound?"

"Count on it! I'm ready to jingle my spurs," said a usually quiet Aaron.

"What spurs might those be, Aaron?" questioned Barb.

"The ones I'll be wearin' tonight. I love country dancin'." Aaron shook his booty as he ejected from his seat.

"Are you good at it, Aar?"

Aaron put on his black Stetson, tipped it to the right, and took a slight bow as he said, "Rest up, ladies. I'll be in rare dancin' form tonight." He'd always been cute and age just added to that dimension. His mustache curled ever so slightly at the ends and promised to tickle any part of a body it touched. Aaron was home from Minneapolis.

Audrey had dated him, once, in the tenth grade. They went to the Christmas dance together. She recollected how they were both so shy and did not have a thing to say to each other all evening. Neither of them had danced much, so they sat on the chairs that lined the walls of the old gymnasium. A few teachers had noticed how inept they were at this dating game and had come over to try to stir up a conversation. The attempts had been futile, and Audrey was relieved when the evening was over. Today, Aaron and Audrey had obviously made changes in their lives. That is what middle age does, it brings out the changes that life's path has followed.

"Then, at the fountain in Estes Park after the 'Thunder Rolls.' There'll be a hot time in the old town of Iowa Falls tonight," snorted Spin as he gulped the last of his Cherry Coke.

"We'll paint the town pink," harmonized Linda.

"Does 'Some Enchanted Evening' count?" questioned Katie.

"Strangers in The Night," chimed another voice.

"But remember," said cautious Carol, "The Night Has a Thousand Eyes."

"How about Exodus, like I need to do, right now," added Dan. "Can I give you a lift somewhere, Audrey?"

71

"Thanks, Dan, but I have the car I rented in Des Moines."

"See you tonight, everyone. Dan and most of the group waved as they walked past the rows of booths, watching their images in the etched mirrors along the way. They passed the eight bar stools and the soda fountain that had seen little if any change since its installation, and they were well past middle age. They exited the front door of The Princess and found that the sun and clouds were fighting for dominance in this July sky. It was a toss-up to see who would win. Rain had not given up over the past several weeks, but so far, it was cooperating today, and everyone was grateful that it had passed by just this one time. Maybe, the fireworks could go off on schedule this Fourth.

"Audrey," said Carol as they walked out of The Princess together, "where are you going, now?"

"I thought I'd go to the motel and rest for a while. I am not used to this humidity anymore, so I have to shower and change and I *need* to talk to Jeff. What time does the ski show start?"

Spin was walking out behind Carol and Audrey, and hoping to be a part of the conversation, answered Audrey's question. "It starts at 7:00, but they're always late. By the way, Audrey, I do think that you'd make a great showgirl in Vegas." Spin smiled as he gave both of them a pat on the fanny before going on his merry way. He was Spin all right, and the women loved him.

"Wasn't that fun? Wish the ones of us who live here got together more often than we do. Tonight should be fun, too. I'll see if Cole wants to go over to Spin's later. He rarely likes that sort of thing, and we never know when the hospital might call. It is hard to plan to do too many things together. By the way, did you take my advice, or did you go over to Stephen's earlier today?" Carol questioned Audrey, not out of prying but out of concern. She felt that opening windows from the past might be better off left with their shades drawn after all these years.

The July sun was beginning to peek into the shadows of the building when it did show itself from the side of a passing cloud, so the two friends took a small step back toward the Art Deco front of The Princess. "Remember when we were talking about Stephen a little while ago?" asked Audrey.

"Sure."

"I was at his house this morning, Carol. He was home and…"

"Audrey? What was he—"

"He was home. We had a cup of coffee. He showed me around his house. He kissed me once and told me he would have dinner ready this evening. I don't think I should go. What do you think?"

"Do you really want to know what I think?" Carol did not leave an opening for Audrey to answer. "I think you probably shouldn't go, because I remember how things were between the two of you. You always did have something special with Stephen, and of course, Heidi. However, if you were asking, 'Would I go?' I would only have to say that I would wonder for the rest of my life if I didn't. I have known you forever, Audrey. You like answers. If you go, you *will* have choices to make. Does he know about Heidi?"

"No, I'm sure he doesn't. But, what if—"

"You don't always have to have an ending, Audrey. You have always thought everything should be 'happily ever after.' Life is not that easy or predictable. I can't make this decision for you. Jeff has given you a wonderful life, my friend. Make sure you think things through.

"Carol," Audrey had tears once again as she put her hand on Carol's arm. "I know this is one of the biggest decisions of my life. Stephen has been alone for a long time, and I feel—vulnerable. I don't know how it would change me if anything happens between us, and you're right; I always read the last page of a book first. I want to know life ends 'happily ever after.'"

"Remember how we used to vow sisters forever? Well, Audrey, forever is still ticking. We can be thankful for that."

"Forever, Carol." Audrey tucked her hand around Carol's and squeezed it hard. "Choices are good things to have, aren't they?"

"You bet they are. If you are not in the park after the fireworks tonight—"

Audrey put her index finger up by Carol's lips. "Don't say anymore right now, Carol. I did *not* come back for this reason. I did *not* even know Stephen lived here now. I came back to see you and to be here over the Fourth. I needed a break, a retreat, a little bit of Iowa Falls."

"Go take a rest and change your clothes. Call me before you leave tomorrow, that is, if I don't see you tonight, promise?"

"Of course, sis." Audrey and Carol stepped out of the shadows of the building that housed many secrets—secrets of long ago and secrets of today blended as beautifully as the Art Deco colors of black Carrara glass and pale green design with a Pioneer Neon Sign that read Princess Café hanging overhead. Two women hugged and knew they had vows to keep between others as well as between themselves.

Chapter 11

Audrey stepped into the shower at The Scenic City Motel and let the cool water run over her face and down her neck as she turned from side to side. The water dripped from her breasts and landed on her toes all before each drop made its way to the grate in the shower floor. Audrey was glad she had brought her shower sponge with her. It felt good, and it left her skin soft and shiny.

She patted herself dry and wrapped the stark white towel around her. There was just enough of the towel left to tuck in so that it would stay put. She applied her various creams to different parts of her body wondering just how each cream knew its destination and what part it was supposed to moisturize and smooth. In the dry heat of Las Vegas, moisturizing creams were not a luxury but a necessity. The ever-present winds would blow across the valley leaving faces, lips, and legs dry and pitted with dust and sand.

As Audrey turned to grab her hairbrush, the corner of the towel edged its way free, and she found nothing between herself and the mirror that hung over the desk. She did not smile, frown, or try to act like a Vegas showgirl. She just stared, examining her body. Time had wedged its way into her pores. Gravity's pull, sun's rays, babies, life's stretches all leave their imprints. They're not bad imprints—but rather, signs of having lived. No one escapes them no matter how many creams, pulls, or tucks they pursue. Audrey knew that each wrinkle and sag had come at a price, and the price was a day, a year—time that no one in the world could buy or sell. "A general flavor of mild decay, but nothing local, as one may say."

"Who wrote that, Mr. Fly?" Audrey directed that statement to the winged creature that had followed her into room 33. Audrey had resurrected the line from a poem. "Well, that is 'The Wonderful One-Hoss Shay' by Oliver Wendell Holmes, Sr." She had chosen to recite Dr. Holmes as a high school sophomore at speech contest. She had made it all the way to the state competition with his words of wisdom. "All at once and nothing first, just as bubbles do when they burst." Audrey's father had suggested this poem for her to read at the competition; the same one he had read when he was in high school. Audrey continued to talk to the fly since he was the only one listening,

"My daddy told me that Dr. Holmes was regarded by his peers as one of the best poets of the 19th century. Dad told me that Dr. Holmes' son went on to become a justice of the United States Supreme Court. My dad loved poetry, just like I do."

The fly landed on Audrey, and her patience with his presence was rapidly deteriorating. She was not even sure that he had been listening to her rhetoric. "Fly, you and I are not supposed to be meeting like this." Audrey immediately reached for the courtesy fly swatter that hung in the corner by the door. "Now look, you pesky little guy, we are going to come to terms with this relationship, and believe you me, the terms will be mine." A loud slap echoed across the room. One fly met his match, and he would no longer require testing on movie, song, or poetic trivia by Audrey or anyone else. His days of listening were kaput.

The phone rang at that poignant moment. "Hello," Audrey answered as she stood in front of the desk catching her image in the mirror once again; totally nude with the fly swatter in one hand and the phone in the other.

"Hi, Aud, Honey, I wasn't sure if you'd be there in the room or not."

"Hang tight for just one second, Jeff." Audrey rushed over to her suitcase and grabbed her robe. She slipped her arms in and cinched it tightly around her waist.

"Sorry, I just had to get something."

"How's the weather back there?"

"Wet. It hasn't rained much today, and of course, everyone is hoping that it will hold off until after the ski show and fireworks—"

Jeff interrupted Audrey. "It's dry here and must be about 150 degrees in the shade. Scott said that you told him that, maybe, I would take him to the fireworks display out at the Silver Bowl. Did you?"

"You know how he loves fireworks. We did talk about the possibility of you and him watching them out there. It will give you something fun to do tonight."

"Well, since you've already told him, I guess we'll go. What time do they start?"

"I think between 9:00 and 9:30, but you might want to check the newspaper for sure. It should be in the Leisure section."

"Hey, Scott, grab the paper. Mom said that the time for the fireworks show should be in the Leisure section." Jeff hollered at Scott, and he had not bothered to cover the phone so Audrey held the receiver a few inches from her ear.

"Have a good time at the Silver Bowl. Several of us met down at The Princess earlier this afternoon. I had my Green River. You know, I could not leave without having one of those back here. Oh, and tell Scott that I bought him a new T-shirt from The Princess. He'll be happy to hear about that, and they still serve his favorite strawberry milkshakes like he and Grandpa Harris used to get."

"Yes, he will. How well I know about your Green Rivers, Audrey. What time does your plane get in tomorrow?"

"I've left a copy of my flight schedule there on the fridge. I am pretty sure I get in around 11:30 at night. My flight number and all should be right there. Do you see it?"

"Ya. It's there, Aud, just where you said."

"Scott will probably go to bed earlier, so he most likely won't want to go with you to the airport to pick me up."

"Audrey? Scott and I have missed you a whole lot. You do know that, don't you?"

"You know I know that, and I've missed both of you. I will be home late tomorrow night. Tell Scott I'll bring him something from the Des Moines airport, and that the girls are sending gobs of fun things from Iowa, too." Audrey snickered with the security of knowing how much Scott always looked forward to his trinkets. "And if you talk to Heidi, remind her to pick the dry cleaning up so that she'll have her navy dress that she wanted for next week. I think she mentioned that she is up for a promotion at the bank and wanted to look special in that dress."

"You take care of us all even when you're not here, Audrey. What would we do without you? Tomorrow night at around 11:30. I think that is it with the time difference. Hope you're not delayed because of the rain."

"My understanding is that, because of all of the rains all summer, they've been able to keep the runways cleared with planes landing and taking off pretty much on time.

"Have a good time at the fireworks. I will be thinking about you two. Scott loves them so and I'll miss not watching him enjoy them with his hands covering his ears the way he does every year." Audrey and Jeff laughed together as they knew very well the sensory rituals of their son.

"Sure. I'll take him. Bye now. Love you, Aud." Jeff's voice faded.

"Me, too, Mom. I love you, too, Mom." Scott yelled in the background.

"Give Scott my special hugs for me, Jeff, and tell him I'll find something great for him at the airport."

The phone line buzzed and Audrey hung up the receiver. She sat down on the edge of the king-sized bed. She did not know whether to smile or to frown at the thoughts about Friday morning, as she was getting ready to leave Vegas that were cascading through her head. Jeff was a man of routine. There was no person in the world Audrey respected more than her husband, but when it came to the romance zone, well, Jeff was just a little on the predictable side. For Jeff, sex meant that it could take place on either a holiday or right before one of them went away for a few days. The latter actually happened sparingly, and there were only about six major holidays that Jeff preferred to celebrate by having a close encounter with his wife. Audrey was about to leave for four days, and that sent a signal to Jeff's testosterone level.

"You'll be gone how many days?" inquired Jeff as he and Audrey stood at the twin bathroom basins.

"Four," answered Audrey with a mouthful of toothpaste.

Jeff commented, "Four will be fine," as he stood naked at the sink, as if he did not already know the answer. He picked up his toothbrush and pointed it toward Audrey before spreading the paste in a methodical manner. "That will be Monday, rather late at night when your plane gets in, right?"

Audrey spit the froth in the sink. "Yes, Jeff. I think about 11:30 or so. I put the schedule on the front of the refrigerator."

"We always do something before one of us leaves." Jeff nudged his naked body closer to Audrey who had put on her pink terry wrap after taking her shower.

"Jeff, I'm really not in the mood right now. I have a lot to—

Jeff." He pulled the Velcro on the terry robe loose and flung it over to the bathtub.

"Do you want it on the counter or in the bed?"

Audrey blinked her eyes. "Whatever pleases you." Audrey had learned early in their marriage that Jeff did not expect sex very often, but when he was ready, it did no good to defy the *sign of the time.* This particular morning had offered no surprises. *Sometimes, routine is good.*

"That was good," muttered Jeff as he backed away from the counter, offering a right-handed assistance and allowing Audrey to slide her feet securely on the floor once again. He handed her the terry robe. "Do you know how much I love you?" Jeff went into the bedroom to put on his jockey shorts.

Audrey stepped back into the shower, laying the robe on the basin and answering the questions herself. *Yes, I do know how much he loves me. I know very well.* Women, on a daily basis, crave those *points of love* and add them up. Men, however, don't add love points in the same way. Audrey remembered a sermon one Sunday when her minister explained relationships: "Men can buy a woman a diamond bracelet, and they think they are good in the area of love for a long time. However, for a woman, it counts as one point, just the same as opening a car door for her counts as one point. Women need to know and feel love, daily. The man might crave the act of love on a more frequent basis, but the need to truly express that love in life's little details is not as important as it is to a woman." As the years of Jeff and Audrey's marriage added up, the *points of love*, were not so much forgotten, just neglected.

Audrey stood up by the side of the bed in Room 33 and shook her head back and forth as if transporting herself back into the right time zone. It was 4:30 on July 4th, and she was in the middle of Iowa, not on the bathroom counter in Las Vegas, Nevada. Her wedding ring, however, still circled her finger and her vows, which had never been broken, remained sacred. Nothing had happened between Stephen and her. She knew it would be up to her if it did. *If it did.*

Audrey went over to her suitcase that was resting in the corner of the room to select which set of lingerie she would wear for the evening. She adored all of her fancy lingerie. Jeff could never see the necessity for this indulgence, but she did, and she knew that he liked seeing her in it. She liked matching lingerie, the sensuous feeling of silk against her skin, and the hugging of the lace that crept along the edges of the bras and panties.

Audrey selected a set of white with pale blue flowers along the silk portion of the panties and bra. Flowering lace accented the top of the bra's cups and along the sides of the French-cut panties. She slipped them on her freshly washed body and turned toward the mirror once again. *I can defy gravity*. She settled her hands on her hips and struck a Cindy Crawford stance viewed only by her. She poofed her hair with her hands and twisted them in a dancer's pose that formed an invisible, wide brim of a Marlene Dietrich hat, silhouetting her face as it did for the starlet of the WWII era. Audrey knew the exact names of the muscles on her face to stretch for that glowing, high cheekbone look. She quickly surveyed the room. There was no threat of Jeff watching. No Scott with another "Hey, Mom," question. No phone call from Heidi, or even a dog wanting to cuddle at her feet. She was alone. She could do whatever she wanted and nobody would see but her. This did not happen too often in Audrey's busy life.

Most mothers don't find much time for themselves. It's not so much that they feel regret, but that they miss and need the independence of an inner self that was once their life before it was defined by men and motherhood; to peel back the layers of life and find what was emerging before the journey began.

Audrey flipped her head to the side and turned her body in the opposite direction. She pursed her lips before forcing them into a broad smile that arched up to her ears. She leaned forward watching the realignment of her breasts. The mirror reflected an image Audrey had seldom taken the time to notice.

Audrey parted her lips with her tongue and licked them generously. The glow added to the sparkle of these private moments. She placed her left foot on the corner of the flowered comforter, rested her elbow on her knee as her knuckles sank in her left cheek. It was a time of exploration: a time of observation, a time of examination, and a private time for Audrey.

Audrey held that pose for as long as she could. Was it a different Audrey reflecting back, into her eyes? Or was it just a different part of the same Audrey? She didn't know. She lowered her leg onto the carpet, and her thoughts drifted back to the immediacy of the evening that lay ahead.

She really did not know the man she was going to have dinner with tonight. She knew him as a boy on his way to manhood. A boy with a slight cleft, not a deep one, a shaven face without a mustache, a lanky build not as muscular or filled out, a gentle person who still seemed like he was, a boy who didn't like to study American literature but whose house was now filled with classics...Could Stephen Grant be the same person she had loved so many, many years ago? Was she the same person who had loved Stephen Grant so long ago? So many rhetorical questions in search of answers she could not begin to explore.

Before going back into the bathroom to put on her makeup, Audrey turned up the radio a bit. "Here we are again, folks. I understand they're talking about renaming the Mississippi and Missouri Rivers. It goes to the legislature tomorrow about having seven Great Lakes instead of just five. Let us know your feelings here at the studio! At least, we'd be keeping all of the greats here in the Midwest. On a more serious note," continued the DJ, "we might escape rain this evening. The key word there is *might*. We'll keep our fingers crossed. Do be cautious if you're boating on the Iowa River. It's moving swiftly and is reported to be full of debris from further up north. Be prepared. Now, let's have a Beach Boys spin in honor of all of our newly formed beaches."

"Well the East coast girls are hip; I really dig those styles they wear..."

"Rain, rain, go away, come again another day. Audrey Benway wants to play."

Audrey's words were interspersed by the Beach Boys' "California Girls." She proceeded to apply her makeup in the bathroom mirror: sparing amount of foundation, concealer, powder, blush, and mascara. Audrey always curled her eyelashes just a bit. She remembered how Katie had told her to start doing that way back in the eighth or ninth grade. She claimed that if you trained your eyelashes early in life, they would just curl on their own. Audrey had waited for approximately thirty-five years for that to become a reality. They still needed curling every day. *Guess some things just are not trainable.* She laid the curler on the sink.

As she continued to dress, she wondered what Stephen was doing to get things ready for dinner. He probably had the steaks in the freezer at home as most Iowans do. She was sure he would have to go to the store to get some kiwi. She stepped one leg into a pair of flowered walking shorts. Those did not seem just right for the evening. Yes, she was certain he had to go buy the kiwi. Maybe, she would wear the red ones. Red might be a good choice. No, a skirt, that didn't seem right for a barbecue. She had noticed a wine rack at Stephen's; he would probably have a bottle chilling. The white shorts, those would be the best. Had she put on her blush, she couldn't remember? Well, a little more would be okay. She wondered if they would eat outside or in the dining room where the table was already set. She rather hoped outside. Even though it was humid, it was clearer than it had been, and the Iowa evenings were always beautiful.

Audrey chose a new blouse she had discovered at a small boutique in Vegas. It was blue and white pinstripe, had an extra wide collar embroidered with petite flowers, and sixteen small, white buttons up the front. It would go well with her white shorts. A white belt with gold accent rings and flats would complete the outfit. Three squirts of Caesar's Woman perfume were typical for Audrey, but on this evening, she used four.

Audrey looked around the room. The clock read 6:07. There were clothes strung amongst the dated furniture, bottles of makeup and creams on the tops of any flat surface, and a fly swatter remained on the floor. The DJ continued to combine jokes about the weather in an attempt to lighten the severity of what was taking place in the Midwest. Gene Pitney's "Town Without Pity" started with its memorable strains. This looked more like one of the rooms in *Animal House* than Audrey's. She put the fly swatter back on its hook, grabbed her keys from the top of the television, and her purse from the chair. "Bon Appétit," she proclaimed, and there was no one there to hear her words, perhaps expressed, in the form of a prayer.

Chapter 12

Audrey arrived in Stephen's driveway at 6:20. She knew she was late, and she was not certain at all that she should be there in fact, she was quite certain she shouldn't be there. She had made other choices in life, and for the most part, they had been the right ones. Audrey trusted herself enough that this choice was a wise one as well.

She checked her makeup again before getting out of the car. A deep breath was in order, and she pinched the high muscle bunches on her cheeks. Color and tone were becoming increasingly important these days as the forties kept driving ever onward.

Audrey entered the garage door that led to the main threshold. There sat all of the exercise equipment just as it had earlier in the day. Audrey could see the glint of a small light coming from the kitchen area. She knocked gently, but no answer. A bit harder with the right knuckles, but listening to the level of the music coming from the living room, she was not surprised that Stephen could not hear her. Audrey tried the door, and it was unlocked. She entered while shifting her lower jaw from side to side in an attempt to release apprehension. She pursed her lips together while sucking in on the inside of her cheeks as she shut the door behind her.

"Stephen? Stephen? It's me, Goldilocks." The three bears did not appear to be home, and Audrey rapidly flexed her jaw once again. She cleared her throat.

"I'm out here, Audie." Stephen motioned with his arm from the deck as she rounded the corner of the living room. "Who'd you say was with you?"

"Oh," chuckled Audrey, "just someone from my childhood, I guess; a shadow."

Stephen rolled his eyes and smiled. "Aaaudiee!" The pitch of his voice rose slightly as he elongated the vowels and that proverbial twinge was back.

"I haven't heard anyone say my name like that in a long, long time. That was what you'd always say when you would become exasperated with me."

"Moi, exasperated with *you*!" Stephen clutched his hand to his chest. "Why, *you* could never exasperate me."

"I'm hungry, and you're impossible." Audrey smiled widely as she approached the barbecue pit. "Um," her lips went together in one of those poses she had rehearsed in front of the mirror. "Smells good."

"So do you."

"Not like a greasy hamburger, I hope."

Stephen looked a bit embarrassed. "You smell good, Audie, very good."

Audrey hadn't meant to offend Stephen. After all, he had told her that in complete honesty. "I like the music. What is it?"

"Classical is soothing to me. That is 'Dvorak's, New World Symphony.' It's very dramatic and rather long—not everyone knows it or likes it."

"It's nice." Audrey looked around and again found so many *nice* things about this man, Stephen Grant. "I noticed a picture of John Wayne by your hutch as I came through the kitchen. You must like him."

"Sure do, Pilgrim. The Duke's my hero." Stephen pretended to tip a cowboy hat and vocalize in a true John Wayne dialect.

Audrey laughed. "You're pretty good. It seems as though Wayne was one of the last real hero figures around.

"I met him on the dock of his house lots of years ago. A friend and I were canoeing down the coast in Southern Cal, got tired, and were sunning on this dock."

"Did you know it was John Wayne's?"

"Oh, hell no, we'd just stopped to rest. We were lyin' there with our eyes closed and heard this thumping on the deck coming our way. When we opened our eyes, there was the Duke starin' down at us."

"Was he angry?"

"Not at all. He asked us what we were doin', and when we'd explained, he offered us a glass of lemonade."

"Sounds like a nice guy."

"Great guy. He gave us some advice; said, 'Sometimes when a horse is goin' in one direction, you just gotta get on and ride with him.' Stephen smiled at his recollection of the Duke, and so did Audrey. Perhaps, John Wayne was just as wise as his characters in the western classics he played.

Stephen was wearing shorts, too. They were beige, mid-thigh with a red, white, and blue subtly colored plaid shirt. He had on brown loafers without socks.

"I made some Fuzzy Navels, thinking that's something you'd probably like to drink. Do you like them?"

"I think so."

"How can you think so? It's one of those things you either know or you don't know. Haven't you ever had one?"

"Well, probably."

"Tsk, Audrey."

"I don't drink much. I never paid any real attention to names of drinks. Usually, I stick with diet drinks, except for last night at Carol's."

"Next, you're going to tell me that you've never tasted Tequila or been drunk."

Audrey looked Stephen in the eyes and rolled hers up to the top of her head.

"You've never had Tequila *or* been drunk? Come on, Audrey. Where have you been?"

"Well, not in Margaritaville. I am not against having a drink. In fact, I would love a small Fuzzy Navel right about now." She gave him a quick pat on his stomach. She could feel the strength of his muscles, which hid right beneath the plaid shirt. "Stephen, I don't want you to think that I'm a prude—about drinking anything, that is."

"I don't." Stephen walked over to the table and poured two of the awaiting drinks into crystal goblets from a matching pitcher. "I propose a toast to a very pretty lady," he said as he raised his glass, "and to her first Fuzzy Navel. I hope this one will be memorable." As their goblets cracked together, Audrey was certain that she would remember every moment of this evening, including the Fuzzy Navel.

"H O L L A N D, Audrey," said Stephen.

"H O L L A N D," was Audrey's reply as the past twenty-six years faded with the sun in the western sky. The meaning of that acronym bounced back into both of their minds. Stephen had written it so many years ago in Audrey's annual at the end of their senior year.

How – Our – Love will – Last – And – Never – Die

85

Stephen and Audrey had always been so alike in many ways. Their verbal wit and sparring matched each other's. Stephen seemed more reticent these days, but no less sparkling. They remembered the same things and had been able to throw out those that neither wanted to recall. H.O.L.L.A.N.D. was a symbol of their relationship in 1966, and just maybe, it had been a vision of the future.

It was now dusk on the river in Iowa Falls. Fireflies rest until it is dark enough for them to solicit the attention of a mate; resting they were, contemplating the busy night that lay ahead. For Audrey and Stephen, they had not missed the fireflies, yet. Their senses nested in the aroma rising from the barbecue, the classical tones harmonizing on the CD player, the sparks flying between their gazes, and the anticipating crush of the power of touch. The quintessence of the night was all around them, and it cushioned them like a cocoon.

Chapter 13

"Do you like living here again?" asked Audrey. It seems rather remote, at least, compared to the California lifestyle,"

"It's okay. On days when I want to feel alone, I can, and no one bothers me. Sometimes, I want company, and I find it."

"Where?" questioned Audrey. "Where do you go when you want to give loneliness a break?"

"I never said I was lonely; alone doesn't necessarily mean lonely, Audie." Stephen moistened his lips and dropped his eyes from the fixation they had found in Audrey. He took a deep breath and carried on the conversation about loneliness versus aloneness. "I choose to live this life. There's a difference, Audie."

"I just like being around people. I like talking to them."

"This is the most I've talked to one person in years, and you're right, Iowa Falls is very different than California."

"So, you *are* happy here?"

"Yeah, I'd intended to come back to Iowa Falls for just a while, but I'll probably stay here for the rest of my life."

"I feel like I just intruded on something very private, Stephen, something between you and yourself. I didn't mean to do that."

"Audie, you could never intrude on my life. Intrusion means going where you're not wanted."

Stephen's eyes appeared glazed, as if he was relieved someone cared enough to ask him about his private feelings. Audrey was glad that she had not intruded, glad to be welcomed into a world where solitude was king.

"It's about time for the fireflies to liven up. I always enjoy watching them down here by the river. Remember?" Stephen's rhetorical question knew it needed no answer from Audrey. He walked over to the edge of the redwood deck and spread his arms across the railing, balancing his weight as if his arms were stilts. Audrey followed.

"There were always millions of fireflies," reasoned Audrey.

"There still are. They just keep on dancing."

"'Too many dances, but not enough songs.' Who wrote those lyrics?" tested Audrey, once again, of Stephen.

"'Wanted it perfect, but waited too long,' says Neil Diamond."

"And what's the name of the song, brilliant one?" Audrey smiled broadly with approval at Stephen's knowledge of her musical trivia tests.

"Look, let's watch as the fireflies come out and see them 'On The Way to The Sky,' Audie." Two smiles signaled one beam. Audrey swallowed hard and looked into the darkened night sky. Stephen cleared his throat and followed the view of a firefly as it vanished into a leafy thicket to the strains of 'Dvorak's New World Symphony.'

"I have some other music I want you to hear," said Stephen as he broke the heavy movements of his breathing. He turned and entered the house.

Audrey's brain had a moment to catch up to the beating of her heart, which she so desperately needed. She watched Stephen as he went into the house, his profile weaving between the slats of the mini-blinds through the broad picture window as he walked to the stereo cabinet. Stephen's body seemed severed by the slats that could slice him into layers and examine him under a microscope. If only. There was more to Stephen, so much more, and the thoughts of all of it put together seemed to drive Audrey's curiosity and wonderment wild. She sensed the gestalt of a man she had known only as a boy, and she wondered if she did the same to him.

"This is called Celtic music." Stephen had come back outside on the deck, and Audrey noticed that he had unbuttoned one more button on the way down his blue plaid shirt.

"I don't know the form. But, it's beautiful." The sensual Celtic music blended with the rhythm of the crickets and night creatures that spun to their own intrinsic music they had known for centuries.

"Look," pointed Audrey toward the river's edge, "there's the first firefly of the evening."

"I've been watching a few, now. Maybe, he's just one of the horniest ones tonight." Stephen's eyes followed the invisible line of Audrey's finger into the bushes.

"Uh, well, that's a fine observation. Did he sneak up to your ear and whisper something about his physical state of being? Anyway, how are you so sure it's a *he*?"

"A physical state of being!" He leaned back and his howling

laughter evoked the cleft in his chin to spread widely from side to side until it smoothed across his muscular face. Her eyes popped wide open in amazement rather than amusement.

"You said *he* was   "

"I know what I said. I said that *he* was horny."

"Well, I believe that a condition such as that would constitute a specific physical state of being. In my book it does, anyway."

"And, what book is that?"

Audrey sighed, "Stephen, you're impossible. But then, you always were."

He raised his eyebrows and the corners of his mustache seemed to curl upward. He enjoyed being *impossible*. Stephen always liked being the tease. He liked having the last word. Audrey might never admit it, but as her upper teeth bit her lower lip, the corners of her mouth turned up in a smile, and as she exhaled ever so slightly through her nostrils. She liked it, too. *Maybe that's something that set Stephen apart from Jeff. Jeff was so predictable, routine. That wasn't bad, just different. Not as playful. Not as experimental. Not as Stephen.*

"Let me tell you some things about fireflies," offered Stephen. "You see, I am sure it's a *he* because only the males fly around. They're part of the beetle family, Lampyridae. They have two pairs of wings but fly on only the second pair. The first ones are for balance in flight and protection when they're resting." Stephen's voice was gentle and assured.

He continued, "Fireflies have sheath wings, like many of their other beetle relatives, but one thing that makes them special is their ability to produce light when they're adults: bioluminescence. It's a chemical reaction."

Audrey listened and, at the same time, felt a chemical reaction stirring in her own body. "Only the males fly, and they have two pairs of wings but only use one. Is that right?"

"Yo. The males are the ones we see flying in the air. The females sit on leaves and wait for the males to fertilize them. They signal back and forth and see if they're compatible. That's the way they do it all summer long. That's how I could tell that one was horny. He was flyin' early and divin' into those bushes." Stephen's smile signaled the end to his firefly tutorial. "What's that in your eye,

Audie?" He leaned down and lifted Audrey's head with a finger nudge under her chin.

Audrey brushed her eye with the back of her hand. "I don't feel anything. Did I get it?"

Stephen looked directly into Audrey's eyes. "No, it's still there. I think its bioluminescence is signaling. It's almost blinding me. There it goes again."

Audrey's heart was racing. Every womanly sense in her body was aroused just standing next to Stephen. The touch of his hand, as it had now blended into her left cheek, tingled all over and most certainly, aroused a *specific physical state of being*!

Stephen kissed Audrey on the forehead. She could not swallow or blink, and she knew that if she didn't move *now*, she would be frozen in the emotions of the moment—a place she told herself she would not be.

Audrey ducked underneath Stephen's right arm and stepped off the redwood deck into the neatly trimmed grass. "Look, Stephen, I can dance with fireflies, and I'm a *she*. Do you think they know the difference?" Audrey laughed as she spread her arms to their full extension while twirling with the fireflies. Around she went with a smile and glow that felt so young, so free, and so fresh. She twirled, spun, darted, and dashed while Stephen soaked up the image in his mind like dew on the morning blades of grass.

In a moment's pause, Audrey motioned to Stephen. "Come join me, Stephen Grant." Stephen hadn't needed an invitation. He joined her on the Iowa lawn in front of the moon and the stars and the fireflies, becoming part of this furious frolic.

The fireflies signaled. The moon looked. The stars twinkled. The crickets sang. The river rippled. The music of the Celts played on as the chemical reactions of the night players found a beat of their own. Audrey continued to follow in the fireflies' glide, and Stephen picked up the rhythm as easily as if he had swung to their tune many times.

They became human lanterns of the night as they cavorted in the lush effervescence of the grass. Their arms glided as gracefully as the wings of the maestros. Only the thousands of twinkles that surrounded them matched the glow in their eyes. They were young and free. They had slipped through the tunnel of time and landed in the soft sand of yesterday. It became a day yet untouched by tomorrows: devoid of pain, with a pace slowed to that of the stars, poignant with desire.

Audrey and Stephen twirled alone until their touch, their fingers, entwined. Together, their arms rose to the sky and their bodies swayed in synchronized motion. No pauses. No voices. No doubts. They danced with fireflies.

Stephen leaned forward, brushing his forehead against Audrey's, denying the magnetism of their kiss; forcing the currents of their bodies ever onward—breathlessly onward.

The pace now slowed to a somber wave and calmed as Stephen and Audrey leaned back, forming an arch above their heads with clasped fingers and wanting bodies. Her voice quivered as she broke the silence. "I've never danced with fireflies before, Stephen. I don't really know how the dance goes. I'm only guessing. I've never taken that kind of a risk with my marriage, my life. I'm just afraid I'll want to dance with fireflies forever."

Stephen didn't say a word. He scooped Audrey off her feet and into his arms.

As Stephen twirled around, she hurled her white flats onto the redwood deck. Audrey's head tilted back with both pleasure and pain as they mingled with trepidation in a sphere that would freeze moments like this in time. The breeze swayed along with them as they danced and twirled and summoned more fireflies to join their reverie.

"I've longed for you since the day we said goodbye," confessed Stephen as he slowed his pace for a second time.

"We never had that day, Stephen. We never really ended anything. It just faded." Audrey's face became subdued and creased. "I hate you, Stephen. I don't hate *you,* but I hate…" Audrey still had her arms draped around Stephen's neck as he clutched her tightly. They both were breathless from the dance and dizzy from the twirling.

"I can tell, Audie."

"But, I do. I really do." She sounded as though she was trying to convince herself she meant what she was saying. "Why didn't you ever come and get me? Why did you just let me fade away? Didn't you care about—?" Audrey stopped herself short of saying, "our baby."

He couldn't make any sense of it, so he didn't say anything. He knew he wouldn't have to, and he was right. She went right on talking while cradled in Stephen's arms.

"Twenty whatever years ago, we were in love. We knew we were in love. I met your cousin, Lorraine, yesterday in the park. I guess I'd also met her twenty-five years ago! You remember how she wanted to act, don't you? Just like Natalie Wood?" Audrey's voice trailed off as she looked into the night sky with all of its stars blurred by the teardrops that clouded her vision.

Stephen took command of the situation as he settled Audrey's feet back into the grass. "Audrey, twenty some years ago we were just kids out of school. Yes, we were in love. You went to the University of Iowa, and I was stuck here: no money, no education, and no direction. I was scared, Audie, not *of* you but *by* you."

Audrey felt uncomfortable by Stephen's last remark. Maybe he had known about the baby. God, how she would hate him if he had and she found out now. "Scared of what? How could you have been scared *by* me?" She slipped her feet into her shoes, being careful to keep her back to Stephen.

"I was afraid you'd get pregnant or want to get married too soon, and then, we'd both be stuck in this Podunk town for the rest of our lives. You deserved more than that, and I wanted more than that. Lorraine only helped me out of the situation so I wouldn't hurt you more than I knew I could. You had to go, Audrey. I had to let you go. It was the only way we could see if what we had could have lasted." Stephen's voice was no longer calm. "Look at me, Audrey."

He turned her around with the force of his hands on her shoulders. "I loved you. I knew that then. I know it now. I'd make the same decision if I had to do it all over. Love can't hold people back; it has to let them go."

"But…I was…Stephen." Audrey's speech was fragmented and caught up in the tears of her anguish.

"Audrey, I wasn't the only one who let things fade. It wasn't I who found someone else so soon. Do you know what that did to me when I heard about your new boyfriend and, not long after that, your fiancé? Do you know?" Stephen was stern.

"You never let me know how you felt."

"You were going to the University of Iowa, for God's sake. I was still scooping-the-loop in Iowa Falls and trying to find a job, any job that paid something decent. You always had it all, Audrey. I never knew my dad, and you know how lucky I was just to have money for a date. As I recall, you paid for more than your share of those, too."

"I've never said a thing to you about money," retorted Audrey.

"No, you never did, but it still hurt...inside. I was a *Creeker* from the wrong side of the tracks. You had the money, the clothes, the friends. Why'd you ever look at me anyway?"

"You've always just thought about your own pain, never about anybody else's."

"That's not fair, Audrey, you don't know what kind of hell I had to deal with then or now."

"Nor do you know of mine," recoiled Audrey.

Suddenly, those seemed like the only valid statements exchanged in this course of verbal volleyball. To pursue yet another volley would only point out the invisible net off which it would bounce.

Chapter 14

Stephen had started a fire on the barbecue. "I think they're done," he said, referring to the steaks as well as to the conclusion of the past conversation. He did not like redundancy and did not like opening up his life to others as he had just exposed his inner feelings to Audrey. He felt different about her, however. At least, he thought, he did at the time. Stephen was a man of silence and these feelings didn't seem forced but natural with Audie. He couldn't explain why.

He flipped the T-bones onto awaiting plates. "Grab the kiwi and tomatoes out of the fridge, would you?" requested Stephen of Audrey.

"Sure thing," said Audrey as she opened the screen door and slid into the kitchen. She perceived such an order about things in Stephen's world. Everything seemed to have a place where it belonged. She opened the fridge to get the tomatoes and kiwi. Both sliced neatly on matching plates and presented in cascading rings. She could not miss seeing the Coors lined on the second shelf and the salad dressings placed with the other condiments on the door. Eggs rested in the egg holder and a pound of turkey bacon lay beside them. All was well, healthy, and placed neatly in his refrigerator.

Audrey proceeded to get two serving forks from the top drawer. That, too, revealed a world of organization and continuity. Audrey wondered if all of this was a product of security or insecurity. She didn't know.

Engulfed in thoughts of his own, Stephen leaned against the deck's wrought iron railing. Audrey had come from a world away, he thought, a world of both time and distance. She was familiar. She was comfortable, and he was comfortable with her. She was a rite of passage from his youth, and he had always loved her. How he had loved his Audie. Maybe, he should have told her in that other world before time came between them. It didn't matter, that was past. All that mattered was now. A world had gone before, and a world would come after. They had *now,* and he was a man who enjoyed living for the day, repressing the past and never wondering about the future. A bottle of Fess Parker Chardonnay, chilling by the side of the patio table added to the ambiance. He had already lit the single candle that flickered with the fireflies.

Audrey sat the tomatoes and kiwi on the table and started to take her seat when Stephen rushed to her side and pulled out the chair for her. "I believe this seat is saved for you, milady." Their eyes and smiles connected in a silence between their bodies, minds, and spirits as Stephen sat beside her.

"You haven't told me a thing about your husband, Audie. I think he's the same guy I found reason to hate years ago."

They both smiled as the first forks full of tender Iowa beef entered their mouths.

"Yes, he's the same one. You haven't asked me about him."

"I am, now."

"Jeff is a dentist. He's five-foot-ten and probably weighs more than you do. He's slightly balding, doesn't have a mustache, and always wears neckties and dental jackets when he works. Audrey completed those statements with an air of finality.

"That's what he does and how he looks. Those are great, Audie, but not what I wanted to know."

Audrey raised her eyebrows and shook her head affirmatively while her next bite of steak hesitated in mid-flight. "I know," she said softly, then added, "Jeff's a good man, Stephen. He has always been gentle and kind and given me everything I've needed in life. He has protected me from everyone and everything. I respect him dearly." Audrey wanted to talk now. She'd found someone who would listen, and hoped he wouldn't judge.

"If there's one thing Jeff excels in it's being a great father. He has always been there for our kids; always taken them to wonderful places and has enormous patience. When Heidi, our daughter, was just about ten, Jeff and she went on a three-day camping trip by themselves. He wanted to teach her how to be a survivor in the wilderness. I thought she was a little young for survival skills, but not Jeff." Audrey chuckled. "When he showed me some of the pictures they'd taken, I was furious. I felt that he'd put her in jeopardy." A slight sigh released Audrey's tension. "Heidi was exhilarated over the experience. They made a poster of the pictures and talked about it for years. She was safe, and today, she is a survivor. What can I say about a dad wanting to teach his kids when you see success?"

Audrey knew that she was betraying what she just said. *How could I love and respect Jeff and yet be here with Stephen? It didn't make sense in her systematized, predictable world that seemed so far from this back yard, the fuzzy navels, and the fireflies.*

"Stephen briefly interrupted, how old is Heidi today?"

"She's just about twenty-seven. I'm so proud of her. We're good friends. Not all mothers and daughters can claim that relationship." It was all Audrey could do not to add, *you would be proud of her, too,* but she didn't—not then and maybe, not ever. *I've held this lie to Stephen all these years, now will I hold a lie to my husband as well? A lie I can never reverse? A guilt I can never confess? A trust that will be broken in my heart?*

Audrey wondered if Stephen would have taught Heidi about survival in the same ways Jeff had, if his hand of parental discipline would have been the same, more firm or gentler. If Heidi would have been the same loving person she is today. Some things are better off unknown. Some questions are better off unasked and some prayers, better off, unanswered.

Her immediate prayer was to make a choice she knew was looming. It would be a choice that would follow her for the rest of her life. It would impact her marriage—somehow. It would steal energy from daily thoughts. It would add footprints where none had been before. Audrey knew that desire and want were not always bound by need. *Selfish. My feelings right now are for only myself and no one else.* She was caught—trapped in a human field of unaccountable desire.

As Audrey speared a slice of green kiwi, she opted to change the subject and her thoughts from her daughter to her son, Scott. "You know I have a son, Scott, who is nineteen."

"I do think I knew that. Is he a good friend, too?"

Audrey swallowed with a broad smile and answered, "The best." Stephen didn't ask any more, so Audrey didn't tell and the shift had afforded her mind some reprieve.

Audrey slowly chewed another bite of Iowa corn-fed beef as she studied Stephen's profile by the light of the candle that shimmered from one side of the wick to the other. It was getting darker on the deck, and the shadows of Stephen's hairline, eyebrows, and mustache silhouetted a man she found very attractive. Audrey's thoughts shifted quickly back to Jeff who was nice looking but not dramatic. He was gentle. He was kind. He was giving. He was always there. He always lived up to his word. *He never let me down, not for one minute, not even twenty-seven years ago when I needed him most.* The guilt was as sharp as the forks prongs. Why could she see Jeff standing in front of her even now, not raising his voice to a quiet dinner with an old friend? Would the pleasure she was having now and the want for more with Stephen be her punishment? Would an image of Jeff be standing in front of her no matter how many fireflies danced on this night in Iowa Falls?

"Audrey. Audrey. Audie? Stephen's voice finally sliced through Audrey's silent questions. "Are you okay?"

Audrey came back to the world that was happening before her. "I am now, Stephen. Right now, I'm very much okay," and she smiled into eyes that reciprocated the sensation her heart was experiencing.

"And you, Stephen, are you okay?"

"About tonight? About seeing you?" questioned Stephen.

"About life, I guess."

Stephen was in the world of modern marriage, mishap, and mental mayhem. He'd experienced the defeat of a broken relationship and self-doubt and had come out on the other side. He went back to the recognizable surroundings of his past by moving back to Iowa Falls and blended them into a world he could claim with comfort—as long as he kept that comfort within his arm's reach and did not allow others to intrude.

"Life isn't always easy, Audrey. Maybe it has been for you. I've seen things I wish I wouldn't have and been places I regret." Stephen was somber—then, as if lit by the light of a firefly, he changed his mood, he smiled, and added, "I don't regret tonight—with *you.*"

"Nor, I, with you," added Audrey in a soft tone as she turned her eyes and witnessed a yard full of fireflies dancing in the darkness.

For Audrey, life was much different, and certainly not the ease of existence Stephen conjured up in his mind it had been for her. That mishap and mental mayhem reminded her of the days before she met Jeff, had Heidi, Scott, and a career of her own. The decisions she made back then turned out to be wise ones. To raise a child with a lifelong disability is a challenge for any parent and Audrey knew how lucky she was to have a family and friends who formed a circle around Scott and supported her through this unique journey. Jeff was the foundation. Heidi, the cornerstone. Grandparents, friends, and community all contributed to Scott's growth. It seemed to be Scott and Audrey's close relationship that hugged her heart with tenderness.

Audrey once again asked herself why she was here, at this moment, on this day, with this man. Perhaps it was to answer questions or, maybe, to ask them. Perhaps it was because *something* is lacking in her relationship with her husband and that *something* found a home in Stephen. Maybe, the stresses of life had piled up and this was a familiar someone who simply showed desire for her—just to be herself at this moment in time. Audrey reminded herself of a quotation she read on the plane flight to Des Moines that went something like, "We don't remember the days, we remember the moments." Yes, it was always the special moments with Stephen that Audrey knew were unrivaled in her bank of memories. Just as adult questions are not answered easily; adolescent memories are not easy ones to erase. For Audrey and Stephen, it seemed that neither of them ever wanted to eliminate the memories of each other from the past.

****

"How's your steak?" inquired Stephen.

"Just like I like it."

"Not too charred, I hope."

"No, Stephen. How could it be?"

Stephen seemed to concentrate on the meal at hand as the two, who had frolicked just minutes earlier, were now silent. Audrey knew that the verbal hush was welcome just as it often was when she worked with her clients in physical therapy. It allowed time for deeper thoughts as the noises of the night were settling in. Maybe they both needed to think things over. Stephen was surely confused, not with feelings of guilt, just the uncertainty of what the future could bring and not knowing what he wanted or how much. For Audrey it was much more. So much more.

"Will you spend the night, Audie? I hope you'll say 'yes.'"

There it was. The question. Audrey didn't think it would be

quite so blunt when it came but it was. It was right out there in the backyard, in front of the stars and the fireflies. It wasn't a hint or a nudge but a simple question. *Stephen's voice didn't even shake and he asked me between bites of his steak.* Audrey laid her fork on her plate.

"I propose a toast to later," Stephen was always so assured of himself.

"Why is it, Stephen, that the true identity of a relationship between a mature man and woman seems to be defined in the bedroom. There's a lot of life that takes place outside of the bedroom, but that seems to be the place we all culminate to find out whom we are or if we're good people or how we should feel about ourselves. Why do we use that as the center of our existence?" Audrey wasn't sure if she was avoiding an answer to Stephen's question or just why she'd said all of this. Maybe, it was the night. Maybe, it was the steak. Maybe, it was the kiwi. Maybe, it was the wine. Maybe, it was Stephen, himself, or, maybe, it was the fireflies.

"Love is so much more than the bedroom, Audie. You know that."

"Yes, I do know that. One of the things I've learned in my marriage is what the bedroom could be, and what I'd like it to be more often with Jeff."

Stephen felt overwhelmed with warmth and now more love than ever for Audrey. He wanted to hold her in his arms and never let her go. He knew, too, what it was like to have the bedroom used as a thermostat of rewards and punishments for living outside of it. The *game* of behavior management played in his home, with the winner hoping to manipulate his every move, using sex as the motivator. Stephen had chosen not to be a *game player* in the bedroom, but he and Janna had moved the pawns in different directions for many years.

"Love isn't just sex, is it, Stephen?" Audrey had asked this in the form of a question and made it a statement at the same time. "Sex is something different than love, I think."

Stephen smiled. "Audie. You think a lot."

"There was this fantasy I had many years ago about the two of us. I'm confused now if it dealt with sex or love or both. Golly, Stephen, do you want to hear it?"

Smiles were back and the question avoided for the moment.

"Well, golly, Audrey," said Stephen, "I imagine I do, and whether I do or not, I imagine I will."

"It involves us, of course, and 'doing it' on the dining room table. We were young in that adventure and I've never done it on the dining room table."

"Never on a dining room table?"

"No. Have you?" Audrey didn't need to hear that answer, or because she could see the affirming smile as her eyes glanced upon Stephen's face. She quickly looked away. "Anyway, you'd just laugh at me, because I say it's too cold on my back. There you stand with your hands on your hips, ready to go and laugh."

Stephen laughed as he put his hand around Audrey's and stood up. "The mosquitoes are getting bad with all of the rain we've had. Let's go in the house." Stephen had changed the subject so gracefully. Audrey was a bit surprised that she'd told Stephen that, but it seemed okay. It seemed safe, she guessed.

Audrey and Stephen carried the dishes inside to the kitchen, and stacked them in the sink. Stephen went back out, retrieved the bottle of wine, and set it in the living room by the couch along with the two tall crystal glasses.

"Look," said Audrey, "A firefly came in with us. That is unusual. I'll bet *he* is frightened."

"I don't think we have any female fireflies in here. Maybe *he* is after you, Audie."

"Come on Baby Light My Fire," Audrey clicked her fingers and bopped around as she sang the line. "Let's catch Mr. Firefly and put him back outside with his male buddies."

"There he goes. He's coming your way, Audie. Catch him." Stephen pointed in the air, trying to direct Audrey to the confined insect.

"Fudge, I missed him," proclaimed Audrey. "There! He's by the window." Stephen and Audrey both moved toward the wall of windows that overlooked the deck and down the bank to the Iowa River. Audrey's hand clasped the stray firefly first, and Stephen's hand landed upon hers as the mini-blinds rattled in their designer tracks.

They both released the clasp of their hands, and the once encumbered firefly flew free, toward the white ceiling. If he illuminated his incandescent light, no human in the world saw it. Stephen's and Audrey's eyes held no vision of anything but each other, and they knew that Mr. Firefly would have to find his own way out into the evening rush of what was happening in his own world.

With her hand in his, Stephen brushed the side of Audrey's face with an upward stroke. His left hand met the right side of her face, and as she dropped her hand from his clasp, Stephen's fingers continued to merge as they parted the sides of her hair.

Audrey embraced Stephen's torso with tenderness as they made their way to yet another room of Stephen Grant's home, and the millions of fireflies continued to dance their dance of love in Iowa Falls.

Chapter 15

Stephen's reticence was on high alert. With all of his passion, he pulled Audrey's body against his. Audrey's hands readily embraced the back of Stephen's head like passion released from a volcano. The tips of her fingernails caressed his hairline with rhythmic strokes, and Stephen quivered with delight.

Stephen's hands were gentle but firm, just as Audrey had remembered from the past and in her fantasies. He always liked to French kiss, and he was good at it. He knew when to insert and when to withdraw; when to catch the corners of Audrey's moist lips; when and how to rotate in slow, sensuous circles, with just the right amount of pressure, always coming back to the center for another thrust. Stephen knew it well, and Audrey's acquiescence was unmistakable.

"The bed is ready," whispered Stephen, "and so am I. I love you, Audrey. I've never stopped loving you." Stephen's breath was heavy, and his eyes were piercingly sincere.

"I'm scared, Stephen. I want you, but I'm so scared."

"I knew you would be, Audie. I don't know what to say to make you any less scared other than to say, I love you. Every ounce of me loves you."

"I've never been unfaithful to Jeff." Audrey's eyes clouded with tears as fear and ecstasy danced together in her mind and body, tugging against each other with every turn. Audrey struggled to merge the sides of her soul as one, but she knew that she made her choice when she came for dinner, rather than in the heat of this moment. She had wrestled all afternoon and probably, long before that with her feelings for Stephen. Audrey had always fantasized about this moment. What she'd do. What she'd think and what her weakness would be. She struggled deep in both her heart and in her mind, yet, she knew the answer, but never sought the opportunity until it presented itself. "I…"

"I love you," whispered Stephen softly in Audrey's ear once again. "We love each other. It's *all* we have." Stephen's eyebrows rose, and the furrow between them on his forehead grew ever more prominent.

"I love you, milady. I love you." Stephen's emphatic words left no doubt in Audrey's mind. His question was answered in her simple, tender manner.

Audrey tilted her head to the left as she exhaled with a deep, breathless sigh. Her heart was thundering as loudly and boldly as an Iowa thunderstorm, and her fingers were flawless. The air between them was heavy with the impatience of their longing. After twenty-six years of withholding passion's fire, they were ready to explode, and the time was now. Their lips locked in raw physical hunger.

Desire was met, as neither of them had ever known before, lost in each other and content with what they had found at last. They could not speak nor did they need to.

Audrey's hands moved up and down Stephen's back with light, caressing touches. She could feel the intense sweat as it beaded on his skin and her face, smothered in the aroma of his passion. The back of Stephen's neck dripped with perspiration while her tongue caught droplets as they fell upon her lips. He tasted salty…sweet…Stephen.

Chapter 16

It was 10:00 when Audrey brushed her hair from her eyes. She rolled on her side and studied Stephen's back. He hadn't moved a muscle since he landed there in total exhaustion, completely spent.

Stephen was right; he had learned a lot over the years. Audrey was sure there was plenty he could teach her. As she lay on her left side, she tenderly placed her right hand on his back and massaged it with ease. Stephen sighed with gratitude and pleasure. The sweat had diminished, and Audrey caught the glimpse of a small bottle of body oil spray sitting on the table behind the pillows. She wondered if this was a regular fixture or something new.

"Mind if I use some of this?" she asked in an allegorical manner as she reached over Stephen's back and nabbed the bottle of body oil.

"Oh, yeah, I got that along with the condoms," replied Stephen with a giggle in his voice. "I know that a physical therapist is so much more than a masseuse, but I thought that maybe you'd find some use for it."

"Well, I think I can." Stephen had everything under control. He appeared to be a man of vision, at least, when it came to Audrey. She sat up slightly and balanced herself while pulling the lid off the oil. She warmed a small amount by rubbing it in the palms of her hands before spreading it smoothly and evenly over Stephen's back, which felt like a sparkling, clean piece of fine china as if being coated with melted butter, but soaking in the essence and the aroma of the oil.

"I know the names of all these wonderful muscles, tendons, and ligaments. I had to learn them. I'm glad I did. Let me see," Audrey traced the outline of several muscles with her index finger as she named them, swaying smoothly with deep pressure and a touch of body oil.

"The deltoideus is right here on the back of both shoulders." Audrey's index finger moved slowly with deep pressure as it traced both of the deltoideus muscles. Next, she took the palm of her hand and continued to the midline of Stephen's muscular laden back.

"This is the levator scapulae," she whispered sexily in his ear as she stretched the muscle running downward from the base of his neck. "The rhomboideus minor and major attach about here," continued Audrey as she massaged down both sides of Stephen's spine. "Your major and minor are covered by the trapezius."

"And, here we have the latissimus dorsi." Audrey had positioned herself so that both hands spread around Stephen's middle back and sides. She squeezed, pushed, and pumped his muscles into the fullness of her hands, letting them go to relax, begging for another squeeze.

As Audrey's hands slid gracefully from the base of Stephen's neck to his gluteus maximus, the biggest, tightest muscle of the body, she could feel the strength and firmness of Stephen. His muscles didn't feel 45-years-old. Audrey's fingernails gave a lighter touch as they stroked the hair that deftly covered Stephen's backside. It gave him shivers, and into his pillow, Stephen uttered a small squeaky sound. She felt assured of a second kind of pleasure he was experiencing at her touch. She, too, was pleased, once again.

"Mmm," cooed Audrey as she spread her right hand across Stephen's triceps and squeezed with a commanding firmness. "You pump a lot of iron."

"Yeah," commented a content Stephen. "Don't stop—ah, right there." Stephen was relaxed and Audrey's hands felt so good.

The physical therapy session complete, Stephen rolled over on his back and put his arms under his head with his elbows sticking out. Audrey, by his side, her breasts pressed softly into his hair-crushed chest. Stephen sighed again and raised his eyebrows as Audrey twisted her little finger in the deep cleft of his chin.

"My daughter, Heidi, has a cleft in her chin, too. Did I already tell you that?"

"No. But, you know what they say about cleft-chinned people?"

"I guess I don't. What do they say?" asked Audrey.

"That they're very zealous."

"And, are you a zealot?"

"I'm diligent, enthusiastic, and devoted about what counts to me. Couldn't you tell that from all of the zeal I just displayed with you?" Stephen smiled broadly, as Audrey's blush revealed her affirmation of the *zealous manner* with which Stephen had made love.

Zeal, thought Audrey. *Heidi has zeal.* Audrey doubted if zeal was an inherited trait, but she knew that cleft chins were. She had touched on the matter. She had planted the first seed of telling Stephen about Heidi. Should she continue? Was this the right time, while they were lying next to each other—naked—in Stephen's bed? Audrey opened her mouth with caution.

"Stephen?" She'd caught him in the middle of a yawn.

"Um."

"A long time ago—"

"Ho! What was that?" asked Stephen as he completed his yawn cycle.

"I was just saying that…a bunch of old cronies are getting together tonight at Spin's parents' house. They're probably wondering where I am."

"Did you tell them you were going to be with me?"

"Only Carol. I really thought that maybe we'd just eat, and then, we'd go down and join them. Do you want to?"

"That's meant as a joke, right? Not on your life." Stephen pulled Audrey's face down to his and licked her lips and mouth. "We did eat, that's true. Mmm—dessert was best."

"Sure was." Audrey's face lit up, and she knew this was not the right time for *cleaning the closet* of the past and brushing the cobwebs out just because they were there.

It was now Stephen's turn to explore Audrey's muscular masses. He ran his index finger around her breasts in the form of a figure eight. "I wonder what nerves are lucky enough to run through these."

"I think they're called *turn-me-ons*." Audrey swallowed the clump that had immediately lodged in her throat. Together, their hormones were like those of teenagers and desire was again sweeping through their eyes. "Want, want, want. We could never keep our hands off each other."

"Good things never change." Stephen pulled the whole evening together in one simple sentence.

Audrey rolled out of Stephen's arms, planted her feet on the floor, and located his blue plaid shirt. She put the large shirt on her body and was not amazed to find that it covered all of the necessary

106

parts. She wrapped it around herself. Only one button dangled on the top of the shirt, since Stephen's force ripped away all of the others.

"I'm going to go tinkle, and then, get a drink. Do you want anything?"

"Audrey, who in the world says *tinkle*?" Stephen let out a deep breath and a belly laugh exploded from within.

"This must be a test. Let me see. Audrey Harris Benway calls it tinkle. That's who." Audrey turned and stuck her tongue out at Stephen when she reached the doorway. He had pulled up the sheet, propped his pillow up against the headboard, and was leaning on it, grinning all the while, and shaking his head from side-to-ever-loving-side.

Audrey returned to the bedroom with a couple glasses of Fess Parker wine. She hadn't had time to notice the decor of the bedroom until now; after all, she'd been a busy lady. *It's very male, done in tones of forest green and burgundy to match the rest of the house.* All of the rooms flowed together like one continuous succession—strung by common colors, patterns, and personality of the man who assembled it.

The bed sat kitty-corner with a triangular table and large reading light tucked behind it to serve as a headboard. From that corner, and all along the two adjacent walls, were knee-high to ceiling windows. The windows gave way to the large side yard view and down the bank to the Iowa River; its fast flowing fury right before it found its way to the dam. The backside of the dam had been a popular place to visit with its falling water and trails. In the 1960s and probably even today, teenagers liked the seclusion that the river and trees provided. The dark, burgundy mini-blinds and valance of the windows assured the sun of its presence only upon Stephen's request. His bedroom was his sanctuary of sounds and sights, where he could let them in or turn them away upon his command.

Two oak dressers and a closet the length of the wall completed the room. One of the dressers appeared to be reserved for various male sundries and *treasured* items like soiled socks, old movie tickets, and notes scribbled on whatever had been available. The other dresser was clean, orderly, and content in holding numerous pictures of whom Audrey assumed was Emily.

"Emily is just as beautiful as you described, Stephen. She should be a model with her height and a face and figure like that." Audrey stood facing the pictures and wanting Stephen to include more about his daughter.

Stephen nodded his head and smiled with acceptance of Audrey's approval, but chose not to add to the discussion of Emily. *He's very private,*. Of course, Audrey's thoughts of her daughter were private as well.

Audrey spotted something else in the corner of the room. Perhaps, this wouldn't be taboo. "Is that the same guitar sitting there that you had twenty-six years ago? Is it the one you used to play "Wipe Out" for me?"

"The one and only. I dust it every now and then," snickered Stephen. "It's good at collecting that. Watch out for cobwebs in that corner," said Stephen as Audrey walked over to resurrect the guitar from its dusty grave. "It still has all its strings. Twenty-seven years isn't too long, not if you're made of wood and catgut, I guess." Stephen smiled a familiar smile.

"Can I use this?" asked Audrey of a towel that was crinkled on the edge of the rumpled dresser.

"Sure. Watch out though, the dust might be the only thing holding that relic together."

Audrey sat down on the end of the bed, curled one leg under her, delighted to dust the old guitar as it nested against the plaid shirt whose hem had fallen between Audrey's legs. The top of the shirt lay a bit open with both breasts exposed in a tempting pose for Stephen's pleasure.

Stephen welcomed the quiet as Audrey's hands serenely traveled down the shaft of the guitar. Stephen observed in his vocal silence, while his mind received visual messages with the intensity of a roaring jet. The shaft of the old guitar was long and just large enough around to fit in the palm of Audrey's hand. The frets cleaned, one at a time, as Audrey tucked her finger under the strings and pulled it back out again—gentle, rolling motions, avoiding any unnecessary tension on the aged musical tendons. Always gentle. Always.

"The wood is so pretty," commented Audrey as she stroked the upper body of the instrument. Audrey's right hand edged around the waist of Stephen's guitar and onto its hips. She stroked the wood with tenderness. "It only has one nick. That is pretty good for being so old. No wrinkles around it anywhere and, just think, the same size around the middle as twenty-six years ago."

Audrey treats the guitar like a baby in her arms. A part of her life he had missed.

Audrey's voice became softer, and she appeared to be addressing whomever or whatever might be listening. "How nice it must have been all of these years, being your guitar, watching you from the corners of your life, never judging. Just watching. Observing. Even collecting dust." Audrey grew pensive as she bit her lower lip and once again, a hush fell over the room.

"You aren't crying, are you?" inquired Stephen. Audrey lowered her eyes and kept her hands steady as they held the guitar between them, balancing on her legs.

Stephen pushed the sheet back and crawled down to the end of the bed. He cautiously turned Audrey's face toward his. "You aren't crying are you?" he asked again. A tear rolled down Audrey's cheek, leaving a streak on its descent.

Stephen took the guitar from Audrey's hands and stood it up beside the bed. Without a song, without a chord, he clasped her face within the palms of his hands. "I know, Audie. I know." Stephen caught a salty tear on his thumb. He drew Audrey up toward the pillows, draping her gently over him as he lay on his back. Stephen's hands invaded the plaid shirt, and he felt the symmetry of Audrey's form.

Two bodies harmonized as one on the now wrinkled, dark green and burgundy paisley sheets, their love strummed by the stings of their hearts and played to the symphony of life. All the while, the old guitar watched and listened to the sounds of pleasure and desire, want and need, but never—never judging.

Chapter 17

The early hours of July 5th came suddenly in Stephen's house. Although it seemed as though time turned itself backward in the bedroom, the hands of the clock signaled a different direction. It had no compassion for its owner and his guest.

With desires spent and emotions at low tide, Audrey and Stephen could sleep in the peacefulness of each other's arms. He molded himself around her body like a new layer of skin, a shell, a sheath that would have to provide assurance and affirmation of their love for a long time to come.

Stephen had slept well, amazingly well. There were no nightmares. No jungle scenes had flashed before him, no killing, guns, or fear that permeated his mind. The hours of sleep may have been few, but the rest was welcomed.

The sun peeked gently through a crack in the mini-blinds and reminded him that, along with the river, time had moved just as it should. Stephen uncoiled as Audrey remained in a peaceful slumber. He pulled the sheet up over her left arm and back, and she embraced the warmth.

He stood by the side of his bed and studied her, this woman to whom he had proclaimed his love, and wondered what had compelled her to step into his life once again. What force had brought them together in the first place, and why had he always felt like something in his life had been missing. What brought her here on the 4th of July 1993?

The night, one of the most wonderful nights in Stephen's life had just ended. *The sex was wonderful but it was much deeper than that.* It was more with Audrey than it had been with any other woman in his life, and it felt good. They could talk, laugh, and even cry with each other, and this kind of sharing was familiar only with his Audie. Stephen knew that he was private and found it difficult to compromise his feelings into conversation but he had opened the doors of portions of his clandestine life to Audrey many years ago, and when she walked back in, he was comfortable—comfortable about some things anyway. Stephen could trust Audrey—he knew that.

Stephen turned and went into the bathroom. He stepped into

the shower as if this morning were as routine as any other. As the last drops of water found their way to the bathtub's drain, Stephen climbed over the side of the tub and grabbed his royal blue terry loin wraparound. He continued with his morning ritual by retrieving his razor from the medicine cabinet.

The deep cleft in Stephen's chin had once presented an obstacle to his shaving, but he had long since developed a successful method for removing the stubbles from within the concave configuration. First, the neck, then the cheeks, around the mustache, all smoothed to the texture of a vine ripe tomato. Stephen advanced to his chin where he placed his left index and second fingers to stretch a smooth path for the head of his razor. He shifted hands, commanding the same of his right fingers. With one long and two short strokes, the depilated cleft was smooth. A splash of aftershave, deodorant, and a thorough brushing of the teeth completed the beat of the morning. Although, this Monday morning wasn't quite routine, he felt alive and energized with an enthusiasm he hadn't realized until now had gone to sleep.

Stephen went into the hall closet, and then into the kitchen through the living room. He stopped at his CD player and started to put Bach on the turntable. Stephen then thought differently and rummaged through his oldies selections. He found one that he felt Audrey would enjoy waking up to. The strains of The New Christy Minstrels drifted through the air and into the bedroom.

> *Today while the blossoms still cling to the vine*
> *I'll taste your strawberries and drink your sweet wine.*
> *A million tomorrows shall all pass away*
> *Err I forget all the joys that are mine today.*

A million tomorrows…Audrey opened her eyes slowly. She examined the dark paisley sheet by running the hem through her hands, and then pulled it up under her chin. As she lie on her back in Stephen's bed, all of her senses knew very well where they were and why. She did not want to get up and run away. She did not want to go home and pretend that her night with Stephen hadn't happened. Audrey wanted to spend time with Stephen, but *time* was the very thing they had so little of to share.

Audrey looked around Stephen's room. Knowing what had taken place now written upon her life, no longer could it remain just part of her fantasy. She knew that it was real, and she struggled to accept the joy and dilute the pain that was inevitable. Audrey had never been unfaithful to Jeff. Now, she was in another man's bed, lying naked, wrapped in his sheets. Her wedding vows had been broken, and her marriage violated. It was not the time to think of all the guilt and consequences, but Audrey couldn't help it. She wasn't used to living impulsively, but yesterday and today were hers and Stephen's. There would be a time to deal with emotions that would, for now, need to remain tucked aside.

Audrey could hear Stephen rattling around in the kitchen. She sat upright in bed, and as the sheet dropped to her waist, she swung her leg over the edge. She opened Stephen's closet door. There were two bathrobes hanging on hooks along the side. She passed up the silk one for the shorter white terry and put it around her slender body. Made for a six-foot-plus man, Audrey was five feet four inches tall when her hair was puffed up, so a sea of terry hung to her ankles and the sleeves practically touched her knees. Audrey gave each of the sleeves a couple of rolls and wrapped the belt around her waist a few times.

"I'm going to take a quick shower, Stephen," said Audrey as she made her way down the hall.

The water was warm and tingling. Audrey was careful not to get her hair too damp, because her hair blower and curler were at The Scenic City Motel in room 33. Such is life, she thought. She hoped that she wasn't in for a "bad hair day." She was used to those BHDs because the winds of Las Vegas often swept through the valley leaving hairstyles as its victim. But, not today. Oh, please, not today.

Audrey turned off the water and grabbed a green bath towel from the rod. She dried herself off, and once again, put on the white robe. She tied the belt in a double loop and watched its ends settle well below her knees.

Audrey always brushed her teeth and flossed as Jeff had told her. "No toothbrush," said Audrey aloud as she could hear "Leavin' On A Jet Plane" playing in the background. She opened the medicine cabinet and a red toothbrush lay on a shelf alongside a tube of Colgate.

She figured it wouldn't hurt to use Stephen's toothbrush. She guessed that, after the night she had just spent with him, it shouldn't bother either of them in the least if his bristles united with her teeth!

Audrey, again, thought about what the day would hold. Her plane left for Las Vegas at 10:00 p.m., so she'd have to give herself plenty of time to get to Des Moines, especially with all of the rain looming in the forecast. She promised Carol she'd call, and after not showing up at Spin's last night, she knew that Carol would definitely want to hear from her. She also knew Carol's thoughts about Stephen and her feelings of where this could go and shouldn't. Oh, the complications it added to her life with just making a phone call to a friend. Maybe she'd wait until she was in the security and sanctity of her home in Las Vegas. Maybe only then, with distance and time, could she talk to Carol.

Then, there was Stephen. Audrey wanted to spend any time left with him, knowing that it would be a long time before she would see him again. Maybe, she would never see him again. Maybe, this was all there was ever meant to be. Audrey contemplated those thoughts; they were difficult ones to deal with, especially while she was standing in Stephen's bathroom, wrapped in his robe, and brushing her teeth with his red toothbrush.

Audrey wondered if she should and could tell Stephen about Heidi. She kept asking the same questions repeatedly in her mind. She'd settle on an answer only to find that it was illusive. If there were an answer, it would just have to find its own window of opportunity. Somewhere, sometime would be right or maybe not.

Audrey fluffed her hair in front of the mirror. It wouldn't be such a BHD after all. After all—that really didn't matter.

Chapter 18

As Audrey entered the kitchen, she noticed something was different. It didn't occur to her at first just what it was, only, something seemed to be missing. Her senses caught the potent aroma of bacon coming from the microwave. It smelled good: bacon, eggs, toast. Audrey licked her lips and thought how good it would be to eat breakfast at the dining room table. It was so graciously set with masculine elegance. That was it! The dining room table, there was nothing on it!

"I have a blanket for milady," said a masculine voice from the threshold of the living room, "so her back won't get cold."

Stephen stood in the doorway with only a blanket draped over one arm, held directly in front of him. He was wearing a smile. Stephen had not felt so alive in a long time, and his soul and senses throbbed with desire for Audrey. Their eyes penetrated one another and went far beyond where words could go. The language of their love heard, without speaking.

Stephen spread the light blue blanket on the table. He turned toward Audrey and extended his right hand in her direction. She took it. Stephen's hand felt good, warm, caring, and gentle.

Stephen slowly untied the belt of his terry robe that hung down to Audrey's ankles. He could smell the freshness of the shower that lingered on her skin. His hands followed the outline of her body allowing the robe to crumble to the floor as he eased her body onto the awaiting blanket. Eyes were sparkling more loudly, but in easy, tender tones of love's hush.

The tenderness and endurance of their passion defied time. It was a love that dares to dance slowly in prolonged motions of want and need, a love of desire, expanding every moment. Those moments let it breathe of the love between them, engraving their minds with memories that would last a lifetime.

Time. The enemy was time. It could not be saved in a bottle or matted in a frame. It could not be carved in a mountain or cast in bronze. Their time together could only be spent now and remembered—in dreams.

Stephen straddled his hands on either side of Audrey's head.

His chin raised and his eyelids closed. His chest sparkled with fresh perspiration as his heart set the pace of its throbbing. Audrey's arms twisted around Stephen's as they wound their way up, hands and fingers molded firmly into his biceps. He flexed his arms at the elbows as if he were doing push-ups, lowered his torso, and kissed Audrey on her forehead.

"You *are* the love of my life," he whispered.

Then, so unexpectedly and simultaneously, and almost as if it had been scripted in a movie, both Audrey and Stephen saw in each other's eyes, tears as they pooled and slid to the corners of their agony. What should have been their rapture became their anguish: the anguish of time, the sorrows of yesterdays, and the pain of tomorrows. Stephen laid his head between Audrey's breasts and together, they cried. His hands cradled her head firmly as she applied deep, tender pressure to the back of his head. The transfer of love was once again silent and stilled.

****

As the fantasy of the table, with both its pleasure and pain, came to a climax, Stephen offered Audrey his hand to assist her to an upright position. She secured the robe around herself. It was a funny feeling, like being able to put Humpty Dumpty back together again. Many had tried but failed. Audrey and Stephen exemplified this hero of Mother Goose. They had been around when Humpty fell, and now, this many years later, they found he had waited for them to come along, to fit the pieces back into the whole, giving them a second chance to cradle his fall.

"I'll bet the bacon's crisp by now, Stephen."

"So was that!"

Audrey blushed. "My back didn't even get cold, but I'm getting hungry."

"I've been starving, Audie," said Stephen, "for you."

"Yeah, I can tell." Smile met smile as the bacon's sizzle smelled mighty good.

"Can I fix the egg? How do you like yours, Master of the Table?"

"The Master will have his scrambled. I'll take four, please. I'm famished."

"Four eggs at one time. Well, I hope that's enough. That's more cholesterol and fat than I eat in a week."

"I know. I know. But, I'm a big boy, and I did get turkey bacon instead of the real Iowa pork."

Audrey rolled her eyes in an obvious state of approval as Stephen's bare chest loomed from the other side of the kitchen island. "Four eggs for you, and one for me." Even their eggs mingled together in one frying pan as Audrey scrambled them, and Stephen took the well-done bacon from the microwave.

"I have a pontoon. How would you like a cruise down the river on a Monday morning after breakfast?" suggested Stephen. "Hopefully, we can get down there before the rain does." Audrey knew that a pontoon ride would be fun. There were several of these floating party barges on the Iowa River at Iowa Falls. Her parents had owned one many years earlier, and they used it on a weekly basis. Two large, metal flotation tubes supported a deck. The motors were powerful, as they would float their passengers up and down the river. Many of the pontoons could carry up to twenty or twenty-five people and displayed the finest barbecues, leather covered benches, and holds to secure the necessities of nautical travel and fun. Classy canopies topped off the roofs and they always had their own names.

Stephen continued. "The forecast is for more rain later today, but I think we'll be okay. It's early and the river should be quiet." Stephen looked at the clock on the kitchen wall and saw it was a little after nine. Time pursued their very existence. It was in itself the enemy. To stop time was impossible and to buy it, not an option. Time marched to a constant beat inside the hearts and minds of both Audrey and Stephen. Neither of them wanted to talk about it, so they didn't—not for now.

The clouds threatened this July 5th, but as all Midwesterners know, if you wait for a clearing when the clouds don't show a threatening sign, you may be waiting a long, long time. The summer of '93 was an exception; there was no thought of a clearing sky, so life went on in Iowa.

"I haven't been on the Iowa River in a long time. Didn't we use to canoe?"

"Yes. And you taught me how to ice-skate down on the river."

Stephen added, "Keep talking, I'm just going around the corner to get a pair of shorts."

As Stephen rounded the corner to his bedroom, Audrey's eyes were not well disciplined enough to ignore what they saw. Stephen's muscles were tight all the way down to his toes, and his buttock was firm.

"I did teach you how to ice-skate in exchange for pool lessons," continued Audrey as she lifted her chin toward the ceiling, raised both eyebrows, pursed her lips, and exhaled slowly. "I got pretty adept at the corner pockets. Oh, that was fun." Audrey snuggled Stephen's terry robe around herself, giving a hug of warm remembered times. The softness felt good against her buffed skin, and it didn't seem to be a threat that all of her makeup and clean clothes were at the motel. It was comfortable with Stephen, as if the *old shoes* fit fine with all of their wearing and imprints of life.

Stephen came back into the kitchen wearing a pair of khaki shorts.

"The eggs are ready. How is the toast coming?" asked Audrey.

"Looking more like toast every minute," observed Stephen, "do you want yours buttered?"

"No and just one strip of bacon for me, please. I don't *do* bacon very often, anymore."

"Funny, I never *do* bacon either. I just thought that it would taste good this morning, so I got some at the store yesterday. Shit! I put the whole pound in."

"Oh well, it was fun listening to it spit-and-sputter." Audrey's giggle added spice to the air, and Stephen loved it.

The toast popped up like a four-headed jack-in-the-box. Stephen buttered two slices and placed the other two on Audrey's plate. The one egg was scrambled and scooped beside a lone strip of bacon.

"Let's eat outside on the patio," suggested Audrey.

"Let's." Stephen unlocked the door and held the screen for Audrey. "Let me pull out another chair from the storage shed. You go ahead and take the lounge."

Audrey fit comfortably in Stephen's lounge chair. He pulled a well-used canvas director's chair from the shed and sat it facing

117

Audrey. Stephen propped his feet on the side of the lounge so that he could balance his plate on his lap. The morning air smelled good but was heavy with moisture.

"Mmm, this is good." Audrey licked her lips and took another bite of her toast. "The bacon tastes great." She chuckled.

"It's Hormel. Do you get Hormel out there in Vegas?"

"I don't know, since I don't buy bacon. We don't get many things out there though. I miss some of them like Pella Bologna, Anderson-Erickson dips, and Highland Potato Chips. Not that I'd eat many of those even if we had 'em." Audrey leaned her head back on the chair. "I miss Green Rivers and pork tenderloins, and now, I'll miss something else." Audrey was deep in thought.

"You can call me, Audrey. It would be risky for me to call you."

Audrey didn't reply. She ate her one strip of Hormel turkey bacon and savored the flavor.

"Can I borrow a T-shirt? My shorts are okay, but I wish I had another set of lacy lingerie for you and a clean blouse." Audrey needed to alter the conversation.

"Sure. We'll just put the dishes in the sink and get down to the river."

They piled the plates in the sink, and Stephen placed both of his hands on Audrey's shoulders as they marched around the corner to the bedroom. "There's a drawer full of T-shirts. Pick what you'd like."

Audrey opened the top drawer of the closest chest. It was full of socks. She opened the second drawer. It was full of socks. She opened the third drawer. It was full of socks! "Stephen." Audrey was smiling and shaking her head.

"Yo?"

"What on Earth does one man do with all these socks? You can only wear one pair at a time."

"The T-shirts are in the bottom drawer." Stephen's manner of response was unexpected.

"I found the T-shirts, but the socks. Why so many?"

"I like 'em." Stephen was blunt, and Audrey could tell that was all he wanted to hear about the socks.

Audrey pulled a red T-shirt from the dresser. "Think I'll wear this one." She held it up for Stephen's approval.

"That'll do," he said. "And as for what's under it, nothing is fine with me." Stephen's smile was back.

Audrey had never worn "nothing" underneath, but the suggestion sounded ripe. Everything in her life had been upside-down the past twenty-four hours, so why not give it a try? A bit bouncy on the top, but the shirt was extra-large, and it was a dark color. The advertising on the back seemed to tell it all: GLORIFIED BODIES, Your Auto Detailers.

Audrey and Stephen dressed together. As she laid the terry robe on the bed, he removed his shorts. What little sunlight there was shadowed its way through raised blinds of the southern exposure.

"You have a beautiful body," observed Stephen. "Promise me something."

"Anything."

"That you'll take good care of it for me. I'll see it again, someday. I know that."

"And, you'll do the same for me?" questioned Audrey.

"Count on it."

"No fair," chided Audrey as Stephen started to slip on a pair of Jockey underwear. He tossed them upon the ruffled pile of assorted paraphernalia that lay on his dresser, gave her a pat on the fanny, and pulled his khaki shorts back in place. "Okay, now?"

Audrey just smiled as they continued to dress in silence, observing each other's routines and feeling as if they'd been performing these rituals together for years. Stephen slipped his feet into his loafers—without *any* socks.

"Are you ready, River Rat?" questioned Stephen as Audrey tried to manipulate her curls without the benefit of a curling iron. "The river has been high here, but no flooding in the town other than a little over River Road. As you know, that happens every year, anyway. We're lucky, because the banks are so high and the channel so deep right through town. Of course, they've kept the dam open the whole time."

"The farmers are in financial pain, aren't they? Nothing has been gentle in the Midwest, lately."

"Hell, farmers are always in pain; too much of this, too little of that, not enough for their beans or corn or pigs or cows."

"You don't sound very sympathetic?" Audrey shook her head a bit.

"I didn't know I was summoned to hand out sympathy these days." Stephen's voice was cold at that moment.

"We have friends who hurt, Stephen. When one of my friends is hurting, it diminishes me and humbles me for them. I just think we should all try to help each other. Empathy, rather than sympathy, does that sound better? After all, Doug, Dan Withers, Sandy, they all farm and…"

"Audrey, farmers' lives are made up of hardships, and they have depended on the weather since time began," Stephen interrupted Audrey. He studied her and wondered why she would possibly get involved with the problems of these people, and just why she cared so much. After all, she lived in a desert a couple of thousand miles away and certainly out of harm's way.

"*Since time began*, people have cared for other people, *Stephen*. I don't think anybody's ever been punished for caring too much and being concerned about others. There is dependence on and caring for others, Stephen. In Iowa, starting with the farmers on whom everything depends, and in return, those on whom the farmer depends. Like you, delivering gas to their homes and farms to keep them going and thriving, in the summer and in the winter, and even during a flooded summer like this."

"Of course, people have been punished for caring too much, Audrey," retorted Stephen. "They get hurt."

"Hurt?"

"Abused, used, left, those kinds of hurt."

"Maybe you've never *tried* it enough, Stephen. A little caring for others and letting them be dependent on you just might be fulfilling in your own life. You can't live on an island or in a mole hole until the end of time."

"If I wanted to, I damn well could! Audrey, whenever I *have* cared too much for others, I've been knocked back to reality by their blows; their lack of giving anything back or their dropping out of my life for one reason or another. I live for today, and I concentrate on what that day holds."

"A day holds whatever you're willing to invest in it. It doesn't always pay-you-back on that very day, Stephen. The more you *give*, the more you have to *give*. You put it in a bank and its there when you need it."

"You are an eternal optimist, Audrey. I'm glad that life's always treated you so well, small disappointments, but no real big ones." Stephen was sarcastic.

Audrey didn't answer. Her hair couldn't have been more frosted than she felt at that moment! *How dare him.* How dare Stephen judge the disappointments she'd had in her life when he knew nothing about them. She wanted to blurt out: Why weren't you there for me and your daughter? Were you down with that mole then, too? You don't know about my son; you don't know about my pains, my hurts, my wars, *my life.* All of a sudden, it occurred to Audrey, Stephen didn't know about her life, and she didn't know about his.

They finished getting ready in silence. Stephen wasn't used to anybody intruding on his Monday mornings, and at this moment, he didn't like it. *Women. They want to know it all, all the time. They think they know it all, all the time.* He adjusted that thought in his mind. *Maybe I should just say that aloud to Audrey.* Stephen looked in her direction, ready to announce this profound idea, and he saw that Audrey was rummaging through her purse. *Maybe, the wise thing is just to be quiet.* And he was.

"Oh, look at what I still have." Audrey's face was beaming as she pulled a round, brown sphere from her purse. It was about the size of a big toe, a small, big toe. It was dark brown with a yolk of lighter brown on one side. "I've always carried this buckeye in my purse. I see you have a buckeye tree in your front yard. Do you know where I got this one?"

"Should I?"

"Sure. You gave it to me for good luck when I took my SAT test."

"That can't be the same buckeye. It'd be…well, it'd be crushed by now."

"Well, it isn't. Here, take a look." Audrey hurled the buckeye in Stephen's direction, and he snatched it out of the air like Rollie Fingers catching a spiral ball on the pitcher's mound, stroking his handlebar mustache in delight.

"This is really the same one I gave you?"

Audrey giggled. "Yes. I've always dropped it in my purse whenever I change. I've never been without it."

"Audie," grinned Stephen as he returned the toss, "I don't think I'll ever understand *you*."

"But, it's fun tryin', right?"

Stephen just rocked his head up and down in total agreement. Yes, it was fun trying—it was Monday morning, and he was glad she was there.

Audrey put the buckeye gently back in her purse and secured her comb, compact, and lipstick. She combed, patted, smeared in that order, and was ready for the river.

Audrey slid her right fingers through Stephen's left ones, "I'm ready for the river, Huckleberry, said Becky. Lead onward."

Stephen and Audrey proceeded hand-in-hand through the kitchen; fingers gripped and eyes linked as two arms arched from both sides of the center island, clearing the pile of Hormel turkey bacon that sat below.

Chapter 19

Audrey stood on the back wooden deck looking down the thirty-six concrete steps that lead to the grassy landing. Below, the steep bank dropped into the river. It was beautiful, peaceful, with only the sounds of the birds and the river as they rushed impatiently to greet the day.

Audrey took hold of the railing and proceeded down the steps. She could see Stephen's rhubarb, wild poppies, daisies, hosta, orange day lilies, and an assortment of colorful buds and flowers terraced by natural stone set into the side of the earth. Iowa's rich black soil held their roots firmly.

"This is like a botanical garden down here, Stephen." Audrey had reached the grassy landing that extended at least fifty feet to the right and another twenty to the left. She looked up into the denseness of the maple and oak leaves as they shaped figures that shadowed the ground below. A patch of sunshine beamed through the branches and fell upon her face.

Stephen looked at Audrey and found that she was like a little girl again. She had sun shining on her face, eyes growing larger with simple enjoyment of this July day, and swept to another time in her life as she brushed a lock of curls back from her eyes. Stephen watched as a smile slowly formed and spread like pulled taffy across Audrey's face.

"You're happy here, aren't you, Stephen? I mean, you're more than happy here, you're content." Audrey turned her head in Stephen's direction, keeping her body in line as it faced the river.

"Content, I like that word."

"It's safe. Isn't it?"

"Safe?" questioned Stephen.

"From everything and everybody." Audrey looked back out across the river to the bluff that beckoned from the other side.

"It's simple, Audrey. I don't know if *safe* is anywhere in the world. But, life is simpler here than other places."

"Simple is good." Audrey nodded her head in approval.

"Yeah." Stephen raised his eyebrows in agreement. "The pontoon's this way."

Stephen reached out and took Audrey's left hand. He led her to the other side of the concrete steps, along the grassy plain. "Now, you have a treat in store."

"Do I close my eyes?"

"You'd better not. You won't be very *safe* here if you do that." Stephen was sincere.

"I'll bet that's the pontoon down there." Audrey was pointing to what she knew was the pontoon, but it was some twenty feet below where she stood.

"Stephen, that's a pretty steep bank," observed Audrey as she gnashed her front teeth. "What if I slip?"

"Then, you'll get down faster."

"Smarty!" Laughter would have come more readily from her had she not been a bit frightened of the drop.

"You're lucky. I just got these steps in last week. They're from the fire escape on the side of the old Central School building." He was proud of his steps, and she recognized the fact that they matched the pile of mangled metal that sat at the end of the road as she had entered Stephen's house.

"Well, Lucky's my middle name, I guess. How did you get down before the steps?"

"I used a rope."

"Like Tarzan?" Audrey looked up at Stephen's face. A hidden smile in there, she just knew it. "Didn't you forget something here?"

"Like what?"

"Like the railing that goes with the steps? I'm sure that was part of this Neiman Marcus purchase."

"Here," smiled Stephen as he offered his hand and rolled his eyes to the right. "Neiman Marcus!"

Audrey stepped cautiously, and she noticed that Stephen did too.

"I did forget to mention one thing, Audie."

"What's that, Man of the Jungle?"

"Well, I ran out of time last week. It was raining, and I didn't get the last five or six feet of steps put in. That's all."

"Well, what are five or six feet?" Audrey was more concerned about the slippery ones she was stepping on at the time. "Where are they?"

"The steps or the missing yards?"

"Actually, both are a bit important, especially, to me right now."

"The steps are lying on the road and the missing part is at the end." Stephen balanced on one foot. "In fact, we're there. It's just a small jump to the deck, now."

"Just a small jump, just one small jump." Audrey repeated the statement so that she might believe it herself.

Stephen took the jump with ease. "See, I said it was small. Come on, I'll catch you."

"Didn't somebody important say, 'One small step for man…'?"

"He meant for woman, too. I'm sure, Audie."

"Sure he did, but he was on the moon and gravity didn't count." Audrey smiled all the way down, and she landed in Stephen's arms. He rewarded her with a quick kiss on the lips. "That's *my* girl."

Audrey breathed a sigh of relief as she stood securely on the concrete platform Stephen referred to as a deck. Instead of running out into the water, the deck ran parallel to the bank and snuggled in under low hanging branches from trees that tilted, their roots exposed. The roots reminded Audrey of tentacles attached to an octopus or something similar from the deep blue sea. She cautiously stayed away from them.

Ropes at the front and the back secured the pontoon. "All aboard. Just hop on over the rail." Stephen scaled it with ease, and Audrey put one leg, then the other, over the side of the pontoon. "I gassed it up after I docked it the last time, so it should be ready to go. I just like to start the motor before I untie it these days, because the river is so swift and the dam isn't too far behind us."

"Good idea," observed Audrey as she thought of what could happen if the engine would not have started and the ropes were already untied.

Stephen turned the key, and the engine popped in gear immediately. He hopped back on to the deck and untied the back rope. The stern swayed away from the dock in a second. Stephen rushed to the front rope, untied it, and jumped to the bow. He was over the railing once again and sat in the captain's chair as if he were ready to steer the Queen Elizabeth II.

"There's a CD player and some disks in that hold." Stephen pointed to the seat that Audrey was sitting on.

"You keep those under the seats? Aren't you afraid someone will steal them?"

"In Iowa Falls?"

Audrey had forgotten that life is gentler in small towns than in Las Vegas. She remembered that, when she was growing up, her family rarely locked the front door of their house. In fact, it had been quite an adjustment learning to take the keys out of the car every time she went somewhere since she'd encountered city life. Audrey couldn't help but remember when she was in ninth grade and the chief of police lived down the street from her family on Florence Drive. He couldn't find his gun for weeks. When he finally asked his wife where it was, she told him she put it up in the closet while cleaning. Yes, things were always simple in Iowa Falls.

"'The Best of Dan Fogelberg,' how does that sound?" asked Audrey of Stephen as she sat down on the seat once again.

"That's a good one. I have another one there by a pianist, Richard Yusko. A friend of mine introduced me to his music, and I find it's really relaxing when I cruise down the river."

"Let's listen to Dan first and then to Richard. Okay?" Audrey didn't wait for Stephen to reply as she carefully handled the CD. "Does she have a name?"

"Does who have a name?" inquired Stephen.

"The pontoon. It should have a name, you know."

"The Pontoon, that's its name. How do you like it?"

They both laughed, and their smiles would have reflected upon the water more readily had it been a calmer day, but as it was, their faces ruffled and looked much like those seen in funny mirrors at a carnival. "I like to name everything that's important in my life. Let me see…what's a good name for something that floats, provides enjoyment, relaxation, is close to your heart?" Audrey thought for only a couple of moments. "How about *Emmy* after Emily?"

"I like that. *Emmy* the pontoon. Yeah, I like that a lot," said Stephen as he verbally commanded, "Sail on, *Emmy*. Take us to the brink and back again."

Emmy and her passengers made their way up river, against the current as Dan Fogelberg strummed and sang the songs that made him popular.

"His blood runs through my instrument and his song is in my soul." Audrey sang along with Dan. "'Thank you for my freedom when it came my time to go...and, Papa, I don't think I said I love you near enough...' What's the name of this one?" Audrey again quizzed Stephen.

"Try, Leader of the Band."

"You're right. You've passed every quiz I've given you. Are you always right, Stephen?"

"When it comes to you, Audie, I am."

"Well..." Audrey just raised her eyebrows.

There was so much that was familiar to Audrey about this section of the Iowa River and that little conversation. She had paddled, skied, floated, stroked, and skated on the waters that now ran beneath Stephen and her. The limestone bluffs run through the heart of the Scenic City, and Audrey remembered how her father used to say that Iowa Falls was one of only three locations in the world where cliff dwelling pigeons lived.

As *Emmy* made her way under River Street Bridge, the pigeons and sparrows were nestled on the bridge supports. Stephen honked, *Emmy* echoed, and birds flew. The concrete structure with its two graceful arches to span the river was identical to the Washington Avenue Bridge that carried the bulk of traffic. There was a public boat dock on one side of the bridge, but it was quiet this morning.

"It's peaceful down here. Don't you think?" Stephen broke into Dan's singing.

"It sure is. Know what I was thinking about?" asked Audrey.

"Not a chance."

"Stephen! I was thinking about that poem, 'Bridges,' which we had to memorize when we were in Mrs. Leteges' English class. Remember how she would make us memorize a poem each week, and then, we would have to write it perfectly, comma for comma. She'd even pick about five people to get up in front of the class and recite it."

"Who could forget how *she* did it. I don't remember much of anything about the poems though."

"I do. I loved that part of her class. I don't remember if she wrote 'Bridges' or who did but I remember every word." Audrey proceeded to recite it:

You cannot pass through my Iowa Falls without traversing the arched bridges which link the palisades to the opposite shore. A bridge is the symbol of our ties with our world. The river below that feeds the sea, is returned to us as rain upon the soil, a bridge to nourishment, lowly blossoms bridge our union to the Earth from which we were formed; to which we returned. The celebration of freedom is our bridge to the past and the brave colonists who won our way of life. Our vision of steely rails and mighty trains dost bridge us to the world beyond our sight. Bridges unite us: to our past; to our future; and to each other.

"Do you remember it, now?"

Stephen responded by shrugging his shoulders. "How do you remember all of that?" he asked.

"Don't you remember things that you like a lot, just because they're pretty or something like that?"

"Sure. I remember every inch of *you*."

Audrey stood up and put both hands on her hips. "Kiss me you fool, before I attack you on this pontoon."

Stephen hooked Audrey with his fingers around the back of her belt and pulled her against him with one strong arm as he controlled the captain's chair. This time, it was necessary for her to tilt her head down to meet his lips and they kissed in the morning light on the Iowa River—cliff pigeons watched and they were right in the middle of Iowa Falls.

Chapter 20

"Can I steer for a little while?"

"Are you a good captain?" asked Stephen.

"Not a lot of experience, but I'm game to try anything new."

Stephen stepped aside with one arm in front of his waist and one in back, performing a mock bow. Audrey slid into the captain's chair and took over *Emmy's* controls.

"Straight ahead," said Stephen with a bit of caution in his voice.

"But, I like circles," quipped a grinning Audrey.

"Aaaudiee!"

"As you command, Captain Bly." Audrey saluted Stephen as he shook his head with an approving smile.

"The river's pretty forceful this summer," he said.

"So's my maneuvering, as you can see. This makes me feel free and powerful." Audrey dramatized the words with arms flung wide apart.

Once Audrey put both hands back on the wheel, Stephen relaxed as he watched her steer *Emmy* against the current of the Iowa River. He'd always felt freedom and power as he steered the pontoon, and he liked knowing Audrey shared these same feelings.

"Last week, a hog floated past me right before he went over the dam, down by my house."

"Was he alive?"

"*No, Audrey*. I have no idea how far up river he'd come. Later, I looked over the dam, and he was caught in a whirlpool, spinning round and round."

"The flooding has really taken its toll on everyone and everything hasn't it?"

Audrey didn't give Stephen a chance to answer. "I guess that's the 'Little Piggy' who never made it all the way home."

"Never," Stephen lowered his eyes, "never home. Not everyone does make it home."

Stephen was solemn and Audrey sensed something deep and very sad in his voice. It went far beyond the image of a hog swirling in the Iowa River on either side of the dam. She knew there was a

129

shadow lurking in the corners of his soul, and because of what Doug had said at The Princess, Audrey was sure it had to do with Vietnam. She wanted to ask; just blurt it out. However, from her experience as a physical therapist working with veterans, she knew the mental demons were more temperamental and much more reluctant for release.

Audrey had listened to the flashbacks and nightmares of the jungles as she manipulated the muscles, bones, and stumps of Vietnam vets. They hardly ever bared their souls the first few times she saw them. They'd just sit there and grimace as the pain ricocheted throughout their bodies; sometimes, they'd assist with the exercises, sometimes, they wouldn't. It took several visits before most of them trusted her with their private ghosts from the past, and some never did. Vets guard their ghosts with their lives until they're ready to erupt like a volcano; with force, violence, and a total immersion in the mud, sweat, and horror of the pictures running through their minds like echoes of a howling wind.

Audrey had heard stories of scared, brave, heroic men who sobbed with relief as they visualized their year of torment in a land they knew little about. Their stories varied, depending on where they had been stationed, but three things always pronounced the commonality of the war: the smells, the boredom, and the "unreality" of the world they had been thrust into. The pungent odors permeated their senses and were always a part of what they brought home with them. It was as if they had locked these smells in the membranes of their brains and felt it their responsibility to never forget! *Nothing in this world smells like that*, she had been told time and time again.

The boredom, the ever present monotony of wet feet, green jungles, ten clicks to the right, ten clicks back, only to be repeated again and again and again. Up the hill, down the hill, to the river, to the camp; a mindless wonder of voiceless soldiers marching to the cadence of the night, not knowing if the clicking was that of crickets or the cocking of enemy guns aimed at their heads.

And real? What is real? Does it have a face? Rules? Where can you find it? Where can reality hide? The only answer the vets all agreed upon was, whatever real was, it couldn't be found in Vietnam.

Audrey had seen firsthand how war robs—mentally and physically—and it can never fully pay back. Vietnam had been unlike any other war in our history, with its controversy, its distance, its cost to humanity, its fear, and its toll on a generation that asked only for peace. Our government had sent 18, 19, and 20-year-olds off to a jungle and into a lifetime of hell! Audrey hadn't been in that hell, but she'd heard enough about it to be sure that it existed. It was more than the "armchair war" that was coined by the media as it came into our homes each night over the news. The coverage lasted about five minutes and often showed one buddy carrying another to safety or to a chopper. The reality of Vietnam was in the rice paddies and pineapple fields. Audrey had heard it so many times, so many stories with so much anguish that might never be resolved in the mind of a Vietnam Vet.

Audrey knew that if she asked Stephen about Vietnam, he might withdraw. If she didn't, he might not think she knew he'd been in Nam, or worse, that she didn't care. Time was the enemy now—their time together. By the end of this night, Audrey would be in a world far from where she was standing at this moment, and although her fear of knowing would be hard, her fear of not knowing was unthinkable.

Stephen had said, "You could never intrude in my life." Audrey proceeded with caution. She had to get to know him as the man she saw before her. She wanted to know everything.

"Tell me about Nam...please." Audrey kept her eyes straight ahead, not wanting to rock-the-boat too far in one direction or the other.

First, there was silence.

"I was there. What more do you want to know, Audie?" Stephen's voice was emotionless.

"I know you were there, Stephen. I wasn't. We didn't share any of those years. I want to know...to be a part of what I missed, but only if you want to tell me."

Silence again fell on the Iowa River. Even the hum of *Emmy's* engine seemed to accommodate the reticence that hung on the heavy air.

"Just be happy you weren't a part of it. Those days didn't mean anything. That world wasn't real."

"Every day, means something, Stephen. Nam meant a lot to

everyone back then."

"Everyone? Don't kid yourself, Audie." Stephen looked at Audrey through glassy eyes, and she felt that asking her cautious question might *not* have been the right thing to do.

Stephen's body began to tense as ghosts from over twenty years ago called up from some secret hiding place. The ghosts had become a part of Stephen's world, part of his everyday life. His ghosts were part of who he was, until they were buried so deep within him, he feared he wouldn't be able to function without them. To live in a world without his ghosts from Vietnam might be too lonely to face. Misery, after all, is better than loneliness.

Stephen knew that Audrey wanted to share in his secret world, and if there was anyone in the world he wanted to share with, it was his Audie. But, what did she want to know and why? What could she change? Could telling Audrey change his relentless, sleepless nights? Could she alter his thoughts in such a way as to make them seem as though they hadn't happened at all? That was the scariest part: that something in his mind's hideaway would change. Exposing his secrets to another human being in the form of real words might release his ghosts from their prison; give them the courage to change form or, heaven forbid, to float free! Just as surely as Stephen had protected himself in the tall, swampy grasses of Vietnam, he had shielded his soul from a world that asked for much but offered little in return. Could he trust Audrey? How could he not?

Stephen had seated himself to the side of the captain's chair, and in his silence, Audrey watched as he concentrated on a scene far away. She saw a man in Stephen she'd never seen before. She felt the bond that had bridged the distance in their lives, and at that moment, Audrey knew, all over again, why she'd loved him as a young man. She saw the father their daughter had missed, and tears rushed into the corners of her eyes. Audrey's tears had been at their ebbs and tides during this whole time with him in Iowa Falls. It certainly wouldn't change now.

The river was swift, and the cliff pigeons of Iowa Falls guarded their rocky dwelling along the twenty-five foot cliffs as routinely as Stephen looked after his ghosts. Stephen began wringing his hands, and his face contorted with pain. Audrey was sure that Stephen's eyes saw nothing of the Iowa River, or of her. They were fixated on a jungle, in a distant land far from Iowa Falls and the fields of corn and beans that he'd known in his youth. Far from the security of the people he knew, or the place he'd called home.

"I was drafted, 'sucked in,' as a buddy of mine called it, in March of 1968 just before the Tet Offensive. I always thought that was ironic of the Viet Cong to choose Tet to stage the major part of their offense. Tet's the Chinese New Year. I think of a New Year as celebrating—funny—maybe, it's just how they celebrate that's different." Stephen seemed to relax a bit. He rolled his neck, but he didn't smile and couldn't look at Audrey.

Audrey knew that her part in this conversation was as the listener. She could nod and affirm, but not question and never judge. Stephen would not repeat. He would not ask. He would be graphic and revert to language he'd used in Nam. He might not look at her, and if he did, she would be an image of somebody—anybody—nobody. Audrey knew the rules. She'd been a part of that dance, and she knew it well.

Audrey waited patiently, slowing *Emmy's* throttle to a point where it forged the current with persistence, not force. She had to let Stephen find his way out, at his own speed.

"Guess that time was as good as any other, to be drafted, I mean. What the hell? I didn't know what I was going to do with my life. Why not take this adventure? It was free. The Army even paid me for it. All I had to do was follow orders and keep my ass down and my head covered. Sounded easy enough to me.

"I landed in-country at Bien Hoa Air Base. The runway was being shelled at the time, so we weren't there long. I'd never heard such quiet, even with all the shelling, as when we landed. We'd been jokin', talkin' shit, but when they said we'd be landing at Bien Hoa in ten minutes—nobody could even finish their joke. We were so fucking scared, we couldn't think of anything else, let alone a punch line.

"The smell! I didn't know anything could smell like that: gas fumes, dirt, blood, oil, incense, I don't know what else—a mixture so shitty. Between fear, smell, and heat, I could hardly breathe. When I looked around, I wasn't sure I wanted to.

"We were hustled into Army green buses. They had wire mesh

over the windows so that grenades couldn't come flyin' in. An MP in a jeep convoy led us to the 90th Replacement Company near Long Binh. We rolled along winding roads in the darkness for what seemed like an hour. Guess it was only about five miles, but it was an eternity in our heads and our butts as we bounced on the metal seats over the rocks and dirt. I think somebody called them roads."

Stephen cracked a smile for the first time. "You know that sign, like they have on TV shows and in movies with arrows pointing to hometowns?" He paused, looking at Audrey, waiting for an affirmative shake of the head, which she gave. "It's really there, right there where we got off the bus at Long Binh. It said, Des Moines, Iowa, 9,555 miles. I remember *that* number."

Stephen was a long way from home. He talked of time. He told Audrey that he never knew what the hell time it was in Nam, but he always knew what time it was back home.

"On missions, I'd wear two watches; one set for the real world of home and one for the fantasy world of Nam. It wasn't real over there. We were there, but it wasn't the real world. This was the real world. I don't know what it was, but I know it wasn't real life. Nam taught me one thing. It taught me more about what life wasn't than about what it was. I'm still lookin', along with a few thousand other guys."

Audrey broke her silence. "You'll find it, Stephen. I know you will."

Stephen didn't appear to hear Audrey's voice as she responded. He was riding in the curl on a wave of memories, in a land far away, pain now resurfacing and oozing from his pores like a poison leaving its victim's body.

"Watches and socks, I could never have enough of either of those. I always had to know what time it was in the real world, and my feet were never dry during that whole fucking year." Stephen paused, and Audrey now understood why one of his entire dressers was filled with socks. It had nothing to do with Stephen's love of socks, but rather, a fear of not having any, a fear that had tracked muddy, wet footprints across his mind. Each pair of socks folded and so neatly placed in his three dresser drawers. He probably never wore them, but they were there, secure in Stephen's world.

"Why did they let it happen? How could they let it happen?" Stephen's voice was more intense, and Audrey could tell he'd asked these questions time and again. Asleep, awake, drunk, sober, stoned. The answer could never be found.

"I had a job to do in Nam. I woke up, and I did it. My buddies and I crawled in that fucking shit, because we were told to. We shot at whatever moved, because we wanted to live. It was Russian roulette, and you never knew if your name was on the next bullet, mine, or punji pit. You didn't know if the next set of chopper blades would be carrying your body in a bag or the bastard next to you. God—my God—you didn't want to know.

"Nobody died in Nam. You got waxed, smoked, dinged, or danged, but nobody died. That's how we coped with it. We were a young, dumb bunch of grunts. 'On-the-job training' no matter what the assignment. A sheet of instructions, a slap on the back, fifty pounds of gear and we were off to war. Toy soldiers, lined up and ready to kick ass. It didn't make any sense. Nothing made any sense. You always wanted to stick close to a buddy. Shit, the worst thing you can do in combat is stick close to a buddy. Nobody wants to get waxed, and nobody wants to get waxed alone."

Stephen barely caught his breath. It was as though he didn't even need to breathe. He had rehearsed his story so many times in its silence that it wrote itself upon the winds and carried it some 9,555 miles across land, sea, and the invisible time; a time, which only his reality had not forgotten.

"I was assigned to a two week stint guarding the perimeter of the camp. All I was given was a phone if I needed help and some printed instructions. Three of us had eight hours on, eight hours off. At least, it gave us time to get used to the heat, the Vietnam heat of '68, but not the people. I was in their country, and I didn't know a damn thing about what these people were like. All I got to do was watch them from a thirty-foot tower as they rolled down Route 1 on their bikes and scooters. In-between were U.S. military trucks and tanks.

"The only luck I had in the whole year I was there came during those two weeks. I got to know the records clerk. He asked me, 'What's your M.O.S.?' (Military Occupation Specialty) and I said, 'Infantry.' I knew I was goin' out to fight. I was a grunt. Infantry was a bitch.

"This clerk said, 'See those lights down there? That's the Army's 199th Light Infantry known as the Redcatchers. That's where you want to be. They have it easy! All it says here is you have to be light, swift, and accurate. So, he pulled my papers, and the next day the Sergeant said, 'Grant, fall out and load up on this truck for the 199th.' I smiled and soon found out that light, swift, and accurate meant that the 199th was in charge of trouble. Whenever anyone needed back up, they'd call us. Hell, the 199th didn't show-up on the records as doin' much, so the clerk didn't know. But, every time we loaded up, we knew it'd be a hot L.Z. (landing zone). We were just used to round out units. Whoever was in some shit and was gettin' their ass kicked or was low on people and needed a line punched up, it was 'Call the 199th and send THEM in.' Little did my friend, the clerk, know what light, swift, and accurate' meant! Here's this fucking clerk goin' on about 'the 199th never did shit.' He'd read in the paper that The Big Red One, First Cav, did it all. He never read that all this shit was supported by the 199th!"

Stephen had a chance to catch his breath, tilt his head and chuckle. "Yeah, I was a lucky bastard all right to be in the 199th! I let that clerk know, too.

"I met Ski right away, Sgt. Ski. The first time I saw him he came flyin' around a bend in the Ben Tri Dong Tam River in Saigon. That sucker emptied right into the China Sea. Anyway, Sgt. Ski was shootin' about a hundred miles an hour in an airboat. Sittin' high on the seat, no shirt, lots of beads, little purple glasses, and had the crotch cut out of his fatigue shorts. What a sight, even for Nam. He was there to pick us up and take us downriver. Once we got settled, I asked him, 'Sgt. Ski, so how'd you get this job?'

"Know what he said? 'My dad has a plane back home in Kansas with a runway in our backyard, so they thought I knew the most.' Who knows if he knew anything about drivin' an airboat, but he did know how to survive. He was on his third tour then, came back to Kansas, and ended up in politics.

"I am proud of the 199th. It was a small unit, but if I had to be there, in a war, none of us believed in, I was glad to be in the 199th. General Davidson made us feel…" Stephen paused and looked into

Audrey's eyes, "secure. That sounds funny, but secure is the word. This one-star brass was like one of us. He'd always be there in a chopper when the heat started to watch over us. Hell, he'd land and get right down there in the shit with us and ask the commanding officer what the fuck we were doing there. Once, when we were in the middle of all this shelling and he didn't want to lose any men, he turned our company right around and saved our asses. He was one hell of a General and kept the 199th tight."

Audrey's smile caught Stephen's, and their eyes locked as the clouds continued to tumble overhead and Stephen's memories drifted on. She heard another moment of pride in Stephen's voice as he talked about the fact that General Custer and Andrew Jackson had served in the 199th. How his Company, 3rd Battalion, 7th Infantry was the most decorated unit of the United States Army—nicknamed the "Cottonbalers" after serving under General Jackson at the Battle of New Orleans during the War of 1812. After serving in Vietnam, how several of Stephen's buddies had gone to the "Old Guard" when they returned. These soldiers served in Arlington National Cemetery burying up to thirty-five bodies a day during the Vietnam years. Business was steady but never routine.

"I never got hit directly but, shit, I walked into a booby trap one blistering afternoon. Don't know where the fuck we were, but I caught my right arm on a bush and this stick came plunging in." Stephen pointed to the upper part of his right arm where now only a small scar remained. "No one was sure if it was poisonous or not, so they sent me to the Third Field Hospital for blood tests. I was the least of their problems there, and I…" Stephen's face grimaced and he turned his head and eyes upward, accessing the haunting, visual images that lurked in the occipital lobe of his brain once again. "I sat there waiting for the results, shit, if it had been poisonous, I probably would have been dead by then—I don't know if they would have even had time to notice one more body. Two nurses walked by me carrying this vat of some kind. It looked like something you'd cook a huge amount of soup in. There was a boot sticking out. By the time they got closer, I could see that the boot wasn't empty." Stephen bit his lower lip—hard—as tears collected in the corners of his eyes. "The vat was full of *parts*. God only knows who the bastards were who lost 'em.

That was toward the end of my first month in Nam. I knew I didn't want to go back to that hellhole. I didn't have anything I wanted to add to their *soup bowl*.

"I knew a corpsman that smashed all the bones in one of his hands so he'd get a seat on the next plane goin' home. Then, there was Father Joe. Shit, I don't know what his real name was; we just called him Father Joe. He was a priest; wore a little white collar, carried a Bible—and packed a gun. Army said the Bible was okay but the gun wasn't." Stephen pursed his lips together and paused for a minute.

"That's the Army for ya'. Give ya' a book not a bullet as they sit your ass down in the middle of some fucking war. Well, Father Joe was smarter than that. He carried both of 'em and knew when to use each one. He'd kneel at the side of one of our guys and administer last rights right there in the middle of combat. Shells flyin', shrapnel fallin' from the sky like rain, and there he'd be, wafer and rosary in one hand and pistol in the other. He got his Gook count, but only to protect the guy who was already dyin'. He never seemed to be afraid for himself," Stephen raised an eyebrow, "maybe that's where the Bible came in.

"You didn't really want to know anybody's last name. Everybody had a nickname: Papa John, Wheezed Out Wilson, Wired Willy, Spider Man, Lipps. I was Tower. I guess because I was so tall. Last names meant that you would know someone for sure, and then, if they got smoked, it would hurt too much. Hurt would make you vulnerable and a grunt was vulnerable enough in Vietnam. I did know one last name though." Stephen rose from his seat, took two steps toward the front of the pontoon, looked up into a patch of blue in an otherwise clouded sky, and took a deep breath. With his back toward Audrey, he continued.

"His name was Tom, Tom Westover, Westy. We met on our first day in Nam and immediately became friends. Westy was twenty-four, so a little older than I was, and he was even taller than me." Stephen had turned toward Audrey and was leaning on the railing of *Emmy* that surrounded the perimeter of the pontoon, his arms outstretched to either side as he gripped the metal bar in a twisted pose. Stephen was looking past Audrey and into her soul, deep into someone who would listen and welcome his ghosts with understanding.

"Westy was from somewhere in Florida. We had a plan, a survival plan. It was simple; he'd watch my back and I'd watch his. We'd been in an overgrown pineapple grove for over a week. Shelled in—shelled out. It hadn't been harvested in a long time because of the war. We'd planned to go back to the base later that day. We were having breakfast and the mail had just come in; God, how we welcomed the mail. Everybody shared everyone's letters and packages. We couldn't wait to hear. If one of us didn't get anything, it felt like shit, but you knew that the real world was still out there, because you heard from someone else's mom, dad, wife, or lover. We lived for it." Stephen's jaw was becoming set and gaunt. The tension seemed to be extending the length of his body with nails driven into his skin.

"It was about a week before Christmas. Westy's birthday was comin' up, so he'd been lookin' forward to hearin' from his wife and three-year-old daughter. Well, he did!" Stephen swallowed hard and folded his arms across his heaving chest. He took a deep breath before continuing.

"Westy got a tape. He was so happy. You didn't take much in the field so his player was back at base. I knew of a guy, Kauffman, in the next platoon, who had a cassette player, so I went over to get it from him. Hell, we sat this player on a dry rock and called all the guys over to hear it. I cranked it up as loud as it could go. There wasn't a dry eye when Westy's little girl started by saying, 'Happy Birthday, Daddy. Mommy and I love you. We want you to be here.' Shit, even I cried." With a flexing of his right elbow, Stephen pinched the bridge of his nose with his right thumb and index finger. Tears converged in the center of Stephen's face some twenty years later. They were the same tears he had shed in that contemptible field of pineapple, somewhere in a land far away.

"After the tape was over, all the guys slapped Westy on the back or the ass and wished him a happy birthday. As we stood in the irrigation ditch of that pineapple grove, by Saigon, we just smiled at each other with clutched fists held in the air.

"We saddled up and started humping," Stephen's voice suddenly became uncontrollable as tears gushed from his eyes, "and one hour later! One fucking hour later!" Stephen was yelling at the top of his voice as he clinched his fists in the air on both sides of his body; his back once again toward Audrey as if he were calling to God in the openness of the Iowa River which lay directly ahead of him. "Westy was dead!"

Stephen's fists *slammed* against the top bar of the railing, and his head dropped to his chest. The frame of this six-foot man slowly made its way down to the floor of his pontoon and landed in a contorted, heaving pile of flesh and bones. Stephen had buried himself in this private hell for over twenty years, and the reality of a world he had refused to accept, came alive. The pictures that had been black and white now colored with Westy's blood, and Vietnam was so much more than just a place on the map. Time ticked and reality lived.

Audrey's body draped over the top of *Emmy*'s steering wheel as tears streamed to the crevices of her neck. Her lower lip revealed the tooth marks of her anxiety and the reticence of her love. She wanted to hold Stephen in her arms and rock him until he fell asleep. Tell him she loved him and that whatever happened was not his fault. To give assurance that Vietnam was over and draw him from the past; keeping only the cream that remained on the top of his memories; allowing the rest to settle in silence and peace.

Stephen's crumpled body was shattered on the deck and nestled against the railing as his hands released the vertical bars they had clung to so violently. He looked like a marionette whose strings had been released from the taut position of its puppeteer. He had been manipulated. He had been deceived and worse, he had shielded himself from the truth, the realities of war.

****

The river and clouds advanced along with Father Time and Stephen once again sat in the seat next to Audrey as she steered up river. He wiped the tears from his eyes with the backs of his hands the best he could. He'd started something he had to finish. Audrey knew that. It was as if it were a neurological circle with vets; they had to *complete their tour of duty* once it had verbally begun. They had to unite the positive with the negative in an attempt to find the real and throw out what was not.

"Westy was an RTO, radio man. He was good at his job. They were smarter than we were, the Gooks. They were playing in their own backyard. Who's going to win when you're in your own backyard? I know my territory in my backyard, you don't.

"We were crossin' a creek. Westy was tethered to this little prick of a fresh lieutenant by a foot or two of cable attached to his radio. The damn lieutenant was wet up to his ass, anyway, but the Gooks had him pegged. If there were an easy way across that water, a stupid GI would take it. A log went from one side to the other..." Stephen breathed deeply and paused. "When the lieutenant was about a third of the way across, his next step set up a daisy chain and blew the shit out of six men and wounded a dozen more. Westy was one of the six.

"I ran to him and dragged him to the bank. I held him like a baby in my arms while his blood ran back into the water. His legs were gone and the hole in his gut was raw. He was in pieces, but he still had a smile. Letting Westy die in my arms was the best I had to offer. That was the best."

Stephen's jaw shook, and his face flushed with images flashing in front of it. They were slow, agonizing frames of horror, pain, and rage driven by resentment and guilt. Somewhere, during that graphic description, he had reached out and was squeezing Audrey's arm with all his might. His hold was powerful. His pain was real. His ghosts were finally able to begin their journey to freedom.

"Know what I remember about that day? The sky. It was almost yellow, a putrid yellow like dirty dried mustard on a sleazy diner counter.

"Westy never saw his kid again. Never watched her open a Christmas present or blow out the candles on her birthday cake or fall asleep in his arms or watch her face as she played with a puppy; never any of those things.

"I wrote to Westy's wife and told her that 'Westy heard that birthday tape, and that he was a hero.' Shit! There're no heroes in hell! There's no room for them. He died because...I guess because the sky was yellow that day. It was a sickening yellow."

Stephen released his grip on Audrey's arm. She didn't interrupt. What could she say about hell that Stephen didn't already know? She breathed in as he exhaled, and her heart beat to the thunder of his emotions.

"Our country saw to it that all the land in Nam was torn to bits; its rivers red with blood. The smell of 'napalm in the morning' isn't 'great' like some asshole described in one of those Nam movies. It smells of death, shit, and muck.

"Finally, it comes to you. If you're going to survive yourself, you've got to play their game—by their rules. It was the only game in town in the 60s, at least, for grunts like me. The smells of a pipe and cheap pussy were much sweeter than the napalm.

"The drugs and the whores were almost free. The Army handed out methamphetamines like they were Pepto-Bismol. That got you started, and getting high got easier and easier.

"I was married to Linda, my first wife. When I'd left for Nam, she didn't really care, and we fought the whole time during my R & R. I knew it was over between us, so I decided that if I was goin' under in the jungles of Nam, I was at least goin' down with a smile on my face. The whores were everywhere: the camps, the trails, the fields, the villages, even the cemeteries. Anytime of the day or night it was 'Come GI. I virgin for you, GI. See me GI. You buy me one tea!' Shit, no reason not to anymore."

It was hard for Audrey as she listened to the Pandora's Box she had opened, but she knew it was right for Stephen to awaken the demons and to live. To live in a world where the reality of war is death and values are changed. To walk in the sunlight of each new day and look forward to night as its shadows hold you in comfort and peace, and let you rest, for what lies ahead is more than serendipity, it is harmony. To see one's own life as an endowment, and to know that you have shared with others even for a brief time during war is like a rainbow painted by God's hand.

Stephen wanted to continue talking, telling, teaching, trying to understand what his year in Vietnam had been about. Attempting to make sense of it all was like soaking up the ocean with a single sponge.

"It always falls apart. Did you know that, Audie? It always falls apart."

Audrey gave Stephen time to answer his own question, but when he didn't, she asked softly, "What always falls apart, Stephen?"

"My gun!" He shouted as he swiftly raised his eyes. "In my

dreams, it always falls apart! I'm holding it and it just starts falling into pieces. I can't stop it. I don't know how."

Audrey had heard her friends at the hospital talk about this dream many veterans share. In a Freudian context, the gun represents the male phallus and its *falling apart,* impotence and death; either way, lifeless and scary on the battlefield or in a bed.

Stephen stood, shifted his weight, leaning on the steering wheel mount. His manners were lighter than before, but the redness in his eyes was evident as he looked at Audrey. He was relieved that a hush could feel so good and surprised he had revealed his inner most feelings to her.

"There are so many stories, Audie, so many faces that float past me almost every night of my life. Sometimes, just when I think they are getting dimmer, they reappear in 'living color.' They keep it up and just keep marching in my head. I don't know how to get rid of 'em. I don't know if I really want to."

Audrey hesitated before speaking. "Every life has its own war, Stephen. They're just fought on different grounds with different rules." Audrey's voice was soft but explicit with frankness as she reached out to touch Stephen's hand; knowing that her own *wars* had been fought as well. "Westy's or any of the other guy's deaths weren't your fault. It was no one's fault."

"It was everyone's fault, everyone who kept us in Vietnam for no reason and for no good."

"Wars are no good," said Audrey in a calming voice. "But, when people die in them, it's not any one person's fault. I'm glad you knew Westy. I'm glad you touched each other's lives and I'm glad he had a friend like you to give his last smile to. You'll carry it with you forever."

Stephen exhaled heavily to ventilate his body with a new breath of air. Releasing the past of its hold wasn't easy. Scar tissue runs deep and adheres. It stiffens the body and restricts movement. Emotional scars do the same. For Stephen, this was a beginning to rid himself of his ghosts and scars from Vietnam. This was a point from which he could now pivot in a radius wider than before.

"Coming home brought another kind of hell. Where to go, what to do, whom to trust. When we got off the plane at Travis, we were spit on at the airport. One of the guys leaned over to me and said, 'Shit, this is no better than Nam. Only difference is that we could shoot 'em over there.' I'll never forget when I looked into that guy's eyes; they were hollow. No emotion. Nowhere left for him to show his feelings, I guess. Just dark, little round circles pointed right at my head. As we walked into the airport, I watched as he took these 'baby steps,' first one way, and then the other. Then he scampered, like a squirrel and was gone.

"Linda and I got a divorce right away, and getting high had become a habit. No one respected a Vietnam vet. Maybe, the problem was that they'd seen too much of us on TV. We'd come into their houses every night on the news, and we'd intruded upon their comfortable lifestyle as they cut their prime rib au jus and sipped their chardonnay. Americans aren't used to thinking of anyone crawling in the mud of rice paddies and stomping through rubber plantations, let alone gettin' it on with a whore in a hutch right in the middle of a village while shells were blastin' in one ear and agent orange sprayed out of a chopper fifty yards away." Stephen snickered once. "No, Americans aren't used to thoughts like that.

"They aren't used to burnin' shit either. That's what we'd do when we'd dump the shitters. We'd pile it up, pour diesel fuel on it, and burn it. It just added to the other God-awful smells that were part of Nam. Once, when a couple of guys from my platoon were assigned 'shit burnin' duty, they accidentally grabbed the gasoline instead of the diesel. Burnin' shit exploded all over hell and they were covered with it. God, their skin, and clothes were on fire. They dropped and rolled immediately. They couldn't get it off. Far as I know, they both made it and bought themselves a ticket back to the states. It was an expensive way to get home, I'd say.

"And where were you, Audie? Where were you in the Nam years? You weren't in hell, I assure you of that." Stephen's look pierced Audrey with resentment, but she knew, out of pain, not out of spite.

"I was here, Stephen. I wasn't eating prime rib and drinking wine, but I was here. I was going to school, raising a family, sitting in my living room watching the war on TV every night. I might not have been part of the war, but I wasn't a part of those who hated you because of it."

"I've never told anyone about Westy or any of this, Audie. I'm sorry."

"Don't ever feel sorry about what you shared with me, Stephen. Don't apologize for caring too much."

The gentle hum of the motor and the resurgence of the water from beneath its blades as it breathed new life were now the only sounds that came from that corner of the Iowa River on that particular day in July 1993. It felt good—so cleansed and good!

****

"Let's anchor here for a few minutes. I want to see if you remember the bridge." Stephen took over at the wheel and guided *Emmy* to the bank near Assembly Park. He was trying to empty his mind of his Vietnam ghosts, making room to hold other memories from his past.

"I've never forgotten any of it," admitted Audrey.

Audrey couldn't take her eyes off Stephen. She understood more about him; the *successful aloneness* he had achieved in his life and why. The *plainness* he had built on the outside only to expose an ornate structure of labyrinths intersecting one another in an internal maze of temperance and fury.

"It was on our first date, after the Harvest Ball, 1965." Audrey and Stephen stood toward the middle of the pontoon, looking at the Swinging Bridge. "I wore a navy pleated skirt, white nothing blouse with a nubby light blue sweater, and I probably had shoes to match. I still like that matching shoe thing."

"And me?" questioned Stephen who was trying to wipe the lines of anxiety from his face and throat.

"You had on dark slacks, a plaid shirt with a V-neck sweater; I think it was maroon, and your Buddy Holly glasses. You'd driven your grandpa's old blue Ford. We parked right up there." Audrey pointed to the top of the Swinging Bride that came off Rocksylvania Avenue. "We walked down about a third of the way on the bridge. It was cold. We didn't have a lot to say. We didn't need a lot." Audrey's voice tapered to a lull as she affirmed the feelings she thought left behind along with her adolescence, tucked into a file not to be opened again, but here they were, more fervent than before, more understanding,

145

more mature. Stephen had shared so much more than his stories. He had exposed his soul to Audrey, and she fell in love, but this time with a man.

Dan Fogelberg had extended his concert on Stephen's CD player.

Longer than there've been fishes in the ocean,
Higher than any bird ever flew.
Longer than there been stars up in the heavens,
I've been in love with you.

Stephen took Audrey in his arms. She placed hers around his neck and snuggled her face against his chest. "I love you, Audrey." The rage now silenced and only a whispered sigh remained. "How much I love you, you'll never know."

Tears emerged from both dancers as they swayed to the ripple of the water. It carried their emotions down the Iowa River, over the dam, washing them into a larger basin where they could begin to find their roots in the complexity of the past. Dan Fogelberg floated on the air. A slight July breeze ruffled the tall oaks in the park, and the fireflies rested from their flight, waiting for their turn to dance once again.

Chapter 21

Noon was approaching, as it always does, signaling the end of the morning, giving way to the prospect of the afternoon, and anticipating what the night will hold. Audrey had changed the CD from Dan Fogelberg to Richard Yusko on the piano. *Emmy* would need to start heading back toward the dock very soon.

"You were right, Stephen. This piano music is soothing. He's great."

"I like the variety of what Yusko plays. One of his tapes is classical, and this one is more popular. He gives pieces a country sound. Here's "Unchained Melody." I like his ending; it twists from pop to country."

Audrey and Stephen didn't talk during "Unchained Melody." Although there were no lyrics sung, they both knew them well.

When the song was over, Stephen said, "I have a quiz for you, Audie. What were the names of the two movies that this song was played in?"

"I know that *Ghost* was one for sure with, Patrick Swayze, but I don't think that I know of another one." Audrey always liked to test others, and she found it satisfying when they turned the tables on her.

"Well!" gloated Stephen. "Actually, it was a movie from the 60s by the same name as the song. I've never seen it. I guess we could say you failed that one." Stephen smiled in Audrey's direction.

"I guess we could say that," smiled Audrey right back. "But, we don't have to."

Emmy made her way back down the river to where she would find her familiar resting place. They had passed under the Swinging Bridge, Washington Street Bridge, and River Street Bridge. They had drifted along beside River Road and admired the houses whose yards opened to the beauty of the waterfront. There was the Foster home that sat on a point overlooking one of the larger areas of the river. Across the water from the home was Foster Park with all of its trees, large stone shelter house, playground equipment, swings that hung at least twenty-five feet from their suspended frame, mosquitoes and memories. Audrey was sure that there were more of the latter there than anything else. She remembered her eleventh birthday party that was a complete surprise. How her mother and father had pulled it off was beyond her, but she could spot the exact table where the cake and about fifteen girls gathered to celebrate. The table had not gone anywhere in all those years, and the laughter had soaked into the soil to remain a part of what Dr. Foster had created. After the celebration in the park, Audrey and her party entourage had gone to *The Shaggy Dog* that starred everyone's favorite Mouseketeer, Annette Funicello.

"Stephen, why didn't you come to any of our class reunions over the years?" Audrey questioned Stephen as they reached Weaver's Landing. "I've never missed one, and I'm sure that you get the notices every five years."

"I've known about 'em. That's just not my thing. Too many people who I really don't care about seeing, and what would we say?"

"I always have a lot to say."

"I—understand that." Stephen positioned his lower jaw wide open and raised his eyebrows for the *I* part of that utterance.

"Well, it's just fun keeping up with everyone's lives."

"This conversation sounds a bit familiar, Audie. It's not leading to one of those 'everyone should take care of everyone else' lectures is it?"

"Oh, Stephen. People ask about you at our reunions. According to you, they probably don't really care, but they ask, anyway. Over the years, I've asked about you too, but that is because I've really cared."

"You're different. It's okay if *you* care."

"I do." Audrey just shook her head and smiled as Richard Yusko played "The Dance" on his baby grand.

Stephen changed the subject very gracefully. "*Emmy's* a great name for this flotilla, Audie. I'll tell Emily about her namesake the next time we talk. She'll like it. She likes to float down the river with me. I think that she's going to come to Iowa Falls over Christmas vacation. Of course, we won't be floating down the river at that time."

"How wonderful, I miss snow at Christmas."

"I did, too, when I was in California. Emily and I built a nine-foot snow-bunny last year. It was awesome!"

Stephen was talking about Emily as freely as if she were *their* daughter. He had bared his soul about Vietnam and had opened a seam to his feelings.

Stephen continued, "We made ears by bending coat hangers, and we stuck pine cones together and gave the snow-bunny a large pine bow tie. We didn't name him though," snickered Stephen, "I imagine that was going to be your next question. But this year, Audie, I promise we'll do that; just for you."

"Will you build a boy or a girl snow-bunny?"

Stephen smiled and said, "How about both; one about six-foot, three and the other five-four. I'll name them…" Stephen cocked his head to think. "The Ascots of Iowa Falls."

"Why the Ascots?"

"A as in Audrey, S as in Stephen and cot for caught between now and what might have been."

The smiles on both Stephen's and Audrey's faces vanished as the words *what might have been* took on a weight as heavy as a ball and chain. A shackle had been cinched around their emotions and the effort to move it might forever be laden with pain and longing.

Stephen maneuvered *Emmy* perfectly into the dock despite the rapid flow of the current. He secured the bow by the rope as he leaned over the rail and Audrey took care of the CD player and disks. Stephen offered Audrey his hand to assist in getting off the pontoon, but she was already in position with both hands on the railing and one leg straddled over the top. As she planted both feet on the concrete deck, Stephen's body came leaping to her right side. He had his exit down to a gymnast's style, as if flung over a pommel horse.

"You're limber."

"I thought you discovered that last night," teased Stephen.

"I did notice the flexibility of those muscles and limbs. You have a fantastic 'range of motion.' That range thing is very important to physical therapists. Now, I'll see how my range is trying to get up these steps. Just trying to get *to* the steps will be a feat in itself. Maybe, you should have left the rope hanging. What do you think, Tarzan?"

Audrey smiled back at Stephen and noticed that he was dangerously close to the edge of the deck. She pretended to rush at him and push him into the *drink.*

"Not on your life, Lady." Stephen grabbed the railing that surrounded *Emmy* as a smile surfaced on his face.

"Shucks! I missed my chance to push you over the edge."

"I fell over that when I saw you yesterday morning in my driveway, and I don't recall needing a nudge."

Audrey rolled her eyes in one of those circular motions that only women do. It's a roll that all American men recognize, and it makes them feel good knowing they have pleased their lady.

Stephen turned Audrey around facing the steps and grabbed her on both sides of her waist. "Jump on the count of three and put your foot on the first step. I won't let you fall. One, two, three." Audrey jumped. Stephen lifted and, surprisingly, Audrey made it to the bottom of the iron steps as they hung on the cliff's side.

"It's easier going up these steps than it was coming down," observed Audrey.

Stephen followed closely behind. As Audrey bent over, securing her position on each step of the iron walkway, Stephen smiled. His hand reached out to grab Audrey's right cheek emerging from her white shorts, once, but he contained himself since the steps were slightly slippery from the mud that surrounded them. He felt proud of himself; he had controlled that urge in the name of safety.

"Mmm. I love white shorts."

"What about my shorts?" asked Audrey as she reached the grassy summit. She brushed her hand across her fanny, sure that there was something unnecessarily attached.

Stephen shifted his jaw and replied, "Yeah, you got it." He motioned with his hand to go on up the path to the redwood deck and continued smiling as he walked behind her.

"It will take me a while to get my suitcase packed out at the motel. I haven't packed a thing and I'll need to get reorganized. You might know that's a major task for me."

"I'll go with you."

"You'd better. But look!" Audrey's finger was pointing beneath a large pin oak tree in the corner of the yard. "It's a squirrel. I almost forgot how fluffy their tails are. Scott would love to see one of those again. He loved them the last time he was in Iowa Falls."

"I guess you wouldn't have squirrels in Vegas, now would you?"

"Well, not that kind," Audrey turned her head and raised her brows to accentuate the figurativeness of the word *squirrel*. They chuckled simultaneously. "Have you ever been to Las Vegas?"

"Nope."

"Think you might be up for a trip out there sometime," questioned Audrey of Stephen as they worked their way up to the house.

"Audrey. I'm a small town guy now, and with you there, it might be like stepping into a jungle of punji sticks."

"Like I'm poison or something?" Audrey felt a bit insulted and confused.

"No. Maybe, I'll consider it someday." Stephen smiled gently and knew better than to get in a conversation about that right now. He'd learned a lot in the last few hours.

As they entered the kitchen, Audrey and Stephen saw that the breakfast dishes as well as last night's were in the sink and nearly a pound of bacon remained in a heap on the center island.

"Bacon, lettuce, and tomato sandwiches sound good to me; how about you?" Stephen rubbed his stomach as he asked; wanting to indulge in something he had forbidden himself to eat. For Stephen, his diet was a matter of choice, for Audrey, necessity.

"We'll probably both regret it," added Audrey, "but it sounds delicious to me, too. Shall we?"

"I have whole wheat, fat free bread, and mayonnaise. Think that will help us feel less guilty?"

"You don't need to deal with guilt, Stephen, but I do, sooner or later."

"I don't want you to have to leave here with guilt, Audie," said Stephen as he got lettuce, tomatoes, and fat free mayo from the refrigerator. "We love each other. I guess we've never stopped."

Audrey ran water in the sink to wash the dishes. "Whatever we feel, Stephen, doesn't change facts." Audrey dropped her eyes to the bubbles that floated in the sink. "I'm a big girl. I made a choice, and it's now a part of who I am."

"We're all a part of what we do. You did want to, didn't you?"

Audrey quickly turned her face in Stephen's direction. "Oh, yes. Oh, yes."

Stephen put the lettuce on the counter top. As he approached, she lifted her hands, covered with bubbles, from the sink, and pulled

Stephen's head down to hers. Their kiss was long. His tongue parted her lips, and with pleasure, it searched inside. Her hands on his head, his on her fanny and the bubbles, bacon, and bread would just have to wait their turn for that kiss to end.

"How many strips of bacon do you want?" Stephen held up two, one in each hand.

"I'll crumble one around on lots of lettuce and tomatoes," said Audrey as she began painting the bread with mayo.

"My cautious Audie. You have quite a way of putting mayo on a slice of bread."

"I'm known worldwide for my culinary ability." Audrey swiped the mayo jar with her index finger and inserted it into Stephen's mouth.

"Mmmmmm. I love the taste of your fingers. I'll give you an hour to stop that."

"And if I don't?" questioned a playful Audrey.

"I'll whisper for help."

Stephen grabbed Audrey's hand, inserted her index finger into the mayo jar once again, and put it directly into his mouth. "This would even be good with Tabasco Sauce."

"Stephen, it's only been about three hours. I think you need this condition checked out by a professional." Audrey focused her eyes on the bulge in the center of Stephen's shorts. She smiled—broadly.

"I agree. *You* seem to be a professional, and, by the way, the cause of this condition of mine. I *will* let you check it out."

She did.

Once again, the sandwiches had to wait their turn.

Chapter 22

As Audrey and Stephen left his house for the motel, she made sure she followed him out of the kitchen. As she did so, Audrey relinquished the buckeye that had been in her purse by placing it in the middle of the dining room table. That buckeye had brought her good luck all of these years. She would return it to the one who had given it to her. It would be Stephen's fortune now and Audrey knew he would cherish and care for it in the same way she always had. *They're tough, these buckeyes from Iowa Falls.*

Audrey walked through the living room and turned back for another glimpse. She stared at the CD player, the magazines, statues, view of the Iowa River, and the shadows of twenty four hours ago that clung to the walls as if they held a life of their own. Stephen pushed the outside door open with patience and slowness in his stride. Audrey glanced at him and then at the exercise equipment as she took the step down into the converted garage. Her eyes perused Stephen's entire poster collection on his gym wall and fixated when she came to the one in Army fatigues. That was Ski. She knew that now, and how distinctive and impacting he was in Stephen's life.

"I'll think of you when I lift my weights," said Stephen, "but those won't be the only times."

It was all Audrey could do to walk to her car.

"I'll follow you to the motel." Stephen shut the door of the red T-bird as Audrey settled into the bucket seat and rolled down the window. She hesitated before starting the engine. Her eyes fixed straight ahead and the lump in her throat felt like the husk of a dried piece of Iowa corn, trying to go either one direction or the other.

Stephen knelt beside the window, placed his hand on her arm, and bent in to give Audrey a kiss. "We still have a little time. We'll spend every minute we can together. I'll follow you."

All Audrey could do was to make a non-verbal gesture by nodding her head. She placed her right hand on the key and stated the engine. She guessed it turned over, she couldn't hear. Her senses numbed as she backed out of the drive while ominous rain was looming in the dark clouds that hung overhead.

With her eyes, Audrey said her good-byes to the hosta, the day

153

lilies, the lily of the valley, and the lilacs. She etched a picture of every corner of Stephen's house in her mind and savored the scents, especially, the lovemaking. *Making love has an aroma, a pleasant sweetness that kindles the pores to drink of its passion; an arousal of the spirit, daring a woman's desire to be penetrated with the fervent force of a male; a scent, a flavor all its own.*

Audrey backed onto the gravel road and Stephen followed in his Cherokee. The buckeye tree stood proudly at the edge of the yard as it had for about one hundred years. It appeared full of small round seeds covered by their husky shells. The seeds would grow over the rest of the summer and drop to the ground in early fall. Maybe, someone would wander by and pick one up, shell it, and give it to someone they loved as a symbol of good-luck. Audrey hoped that is what would happen, and she stepped on the brakes.

"Something wrong?" inquired Stephen out of his window as Audrey lumbered out of her car.

"Not really. I just wanted to pick up a buckeye for each of my kids from beneath your tree." Audrey hurried over to the tree and easily found some on the ground. She discarded a couple, and then picked up four that seemed full, brown, and ripe. There would be one for Heidi, one for Scott, one for herself, and yes, one for Jeff. She knew they would be safe in her purse.

Stephen smiled, shook his head, and revved his engine. "I'll send you gallons of them if you'd like," yelled Stephen out of the window.

"I'd like. I'd like. I'd like!" Audrey got back in the car and felt in a *safer* mood.

Again, Stephen followed and the two cars pulled up in front of room 33 at The Scenic City Model at the same time.

"What are you doing?" Stephen was whisking Audrey off her feet and she loved it.

"I've never carried you over a threshold before. I thought I'd see how it feels."

"Probably, pretty heavy," Audrey's giggle had returned.

"Naw, but don't fumble too long with that key." Audrey could barely reach the doorknob to insert the key and twist the handle.

"I've got you. I won't drop." Stephen bent his knees to give

Audrey the feeling of a rapid decent, and he made sure his fingers slid into the back seam of her shorts at the same time.

"You're terrible. Did anybody ever tell you that?"

"Just about everybody I meet." Stephen's eyes grew expressive and he once again found that pleasurable seam.

"Now, it's my turn to whisper for help," said a roguish Audrey.

"Not! Can't whisper for help for at least an hour. That's the rule."

Audrey kicked the door wide open with the toe of her left white flat. "And who makes the rules?"

"The tallest one gets to make the rules. That's what my mommy always told me."

"And you always listen to your mommy, of course."

"Sure." Stephen held Audrey in his arms. He twirled once to the right, then once to the left. With mouths attached and without a warning or signal, he landed on the bed with Audrey in his arms.

"Oh, that was fun!" Audrey's smile was definitely back for a second time. "Can we do it again?"

"My back tells me no." They laughed, hugged, and rolled like thunder on top of the outdated comforter.

"I think it would be wise if I shut the door." Audrey got up and secured the door and curtain. She stopped to turn on the radio. Her oldies station tuned in.

"Do you remember what 'our song' was?" Audrey was once again testing Stephen.

"Of course, I do, Audie. How could I forget that? 1966 wasn't all that long ago."

"Over the years, I'd have an, 'I think of Stephen Grant week,' and I'd get out my annuals and I'd play 'Paul and Paula' over and over. Then, I'd put it all away and forget about you for a couple or three years. You've cycled in and out of my life that way," confessed Audrey.

Audrey continued, as she surveyed the clothes and various items that needed packing for the journey home. "I had this great idea about songs from the 50s and 60s. I really liked it, but I could never convince the right people that it could be profitable. I always get splinters of creativity, especially in the middle of the night."

Stephen didn't say a word, rather, tipped his head in curiosity, kicked his shoes to the floor, and propped himself on the bed to get comfortable.

"My idea was to update the songs that we, the majority of the population, grew up with back in the 60s. Take for instance 'Paul and Paula.' What happened to them? Did they live 'happily ever after,' or did they meet again years later, or did one of them die like in *Love Story*? I guess whatever happened is whatever the author says—right?"

"What do you think happened to Paul and Paula?" Audrey didn't wait for Stephen to respond, and then added, "I debated a lot about it before I wrote it down. I had to respect the integrity of the song. It was a happy, light song, and that had to remain." Audrey opened her suitcase and attempted to start straightening what needed to go inside.

"You have it on paper? You really wrote it down?" asked Stephen, when he had a chance to get a word in.

"Electronically speaking."

"And…?"

"I don't remember word-for-word, but it went something like this:

> *Hey, hey, Paula*
> *I'm so glad I married you.*
> *Hey, hey, Paul*
> *Nobody else could ever do.*
> *We'd waited so long*
> *For school to be through*
> *Paul, I'm so glad I married you.*
> *My love.*
> *My love.*

"They married and lived that 'happily ever after' fairy tale?" Stephen's eyes and voice appeared to question. "Fairy tales are only *that*, Audrey. They only happen in books and in people's minds. I gave up on fairy tales a long time ago. You always did live in that world."

Audrey was holding her navy blue and white lace nightgown in her hands as it was next in line for her suitcase. She abruptly turned in

Stephen's direction. "What *world* might that be? You're saying I don't see things in the light of the real world?" Audrey's voice became defensive.

"You write scenes, Audie, and then you want to play them out. When people don't follow your scripts, you leave yourself wide open and get shredded. You hurt yourself."

"Well, thank-you for your expert opinion and worldly observations about my life. If I get all lathered up, maybe it's because people only do about one-fourth of what they say they'll do. I don't operate that way. I give two-hundred percent. Always." Audrey threw her slightly wrinkled gown into her suitcase with a heavy right hand.

"I know that you give a lot, Audie, but you expect so much from people."

"I drive too hard, is that it?" Audrey placed both hands on her hips and took a stance that only the vintage mirror had seen just the day before.

"One might say that." Stephen now sat with his legs crossed on the bed. His temperament seemed to be more relaxed at that moment than Audrey's, and that in itself made her more annoyed.

"I make changes in people's lives, good changes, and positive changes. I have to drive hard in order to do that. People don't rise to a low expectation, Stephen. I commit myself to something, and that's just the way it is." Audrey had moved closer to the side of the bed.

"But you always want to be the captain of the ship, Audie. You can't always steer." Stephen was curt in his manners and firm with his voice.

"I've had to be in control. When I'm not in control, things don't get done. They just don't seem to happen unless I do them."

"They would if you'd let them." Stephen raised his eyebrows and cocked his head assuredly.

"Time is relevant! People like you don't seem to have a grasp of that." Audrey's eyes never lost contact with Stephen. "I've learned a lot over the years. It's obvious that *you* haven't."

"Well, tar and feather me! Damn it, Audrey, you're the one who's never grown up."

"*Me?*" shouted Audrey with total disgust.

"You've always lived in a rose garden. You've never seen the world for what it really is, for what it does to people."

"Well, thank God, there are people like me out there on this Earth. How can you think that good doesn't count?"

"Good isn't the issue here. Wanting to regulate everyone's good is."

"Wanting life to be the best it can be is wrong? Is that what you're saying, Stephen? Maybe, I was wrong then, never telling—" Audrey stopped abruptly in the middle of her sentence. She closed her eyes and tipped her face toward the ceiling.

"Never telling what, Audrey?"

Audrey looked at Stephen with a new calmness. She thought before speaking. "Never telling—never telling myself that life isn't always perfect. It doesn't always work out the way you thought it would when you were young and had dreams with wings. It isn't always…" Audrey paused and Stephen took over.

"Life can't always be built on dreams, Audie. That would be ideal, but it's not real." Stephen's response was genuine and loving. It was calm and Audrey knew it was true.

"Life is good for me, Stephen. I've had *wars* and hard years, but I've found peace with those things. Maybe I am a dreamer, but if I am, I don't want to go back to the alternative."

Stephen held out his hand to Audrey's side of the bed. "This isn't a dream, Audie. Our love never was." Audrey curled up beside Stephen as he snuggled her in his arms. "Maybe, the years have made you fantasize me into someone I never was. Only you can answer that. I don't know what your dream of me, or us, is in your mind, but I do know that you don't have to dream about my love for you. It's one of the only real things I know."

"Stephen, oh, Stephen." Audrey put her right hand on Stephen's cheek and spread her fingers around to the back of his head. Together, as one, they slid down on the bed. Audrey and Stephen moved in lyrical wonder. Their ardent touch accelerated with each moment, and they knew just how much each of those moments counted.

Stephen cupped Audrey's face in the palms of both hands as his body draped over hers. "You look radiant."

"I feel loved," said Audrey softly.

"You are," whispered Stephen. "You are."

Stephen and Audrey's bodies found each other once again, and their love, their eternal love, knew it had come home.

Chapter 23

Yesterday
All our troubles seemed so far away.
Now it looks as though they're here to stay.
Oh, I believe in Yesterday.

The voices of The Beatles were coming from the radio while Stephen and Audrey's voices quieted. Wrapped in the security of each other's arms, their naked bodies entwined one last time. Their image in the vintage mirror could not tell where Audrey began, and Stephen left off.

Her head danced on the pillows as the moisture of her body mingled with his. The enduring release of their love for each other had been satisfied again, and again, and again over the past thirty-six hours. As Audrey lay in Stephen's arms, she thought about how a sexual relationship was only one expression of love. Sex unites two bodies and releases their desire for one another. It binds them in a way no other touch can possibly do as it winds emotions in mysterious ways. Only time could unbraid these feelings in Audrey's soul as she would relive each scene over and over in her mind. She would place them in a special compartment of her brain entitled "memories of Stephen." This memory compartment, opened only at certain, safe times, could allow her to visualize the images and let them float alone—unencumbered by daily living.

There were other compartments in her brain that would struggle against the one called "memories of Stephen." These were known as reality and were more clearly marked by time, devotion, responsibility, love, and fulfillment. They too had titles: Jeff, Heidi, Scott, friends, career. Audrey knew that the struggle for dominance would be overwhelming some days. That is how the mind works. That is how guilt plays out its own game.

After the delicate pause following their act of love, Stephen's whisper interrupted her chain of guilt with, "It's knowing *how much* we love, that will stay with us forever." A song drifted through the airwaves and rain spattered against the windows. The sounds of life moved on and love held on tight for as long as it could for the two of them in Iowa Falls.

"Here's the newest forecast *radio ears,* it calls for rain. Did I say now? That's the same old thing I've been saying all spring and summer. At any rate, you'll be able to take the ducks for another walk. I guess by now, they're taking you." The DJ was trying to be funny but Stephen and Audrey could hear the rain splattering against the car, and the leaves on the tall oak in front of room 33 were swaying with unrest. Although there was no mid-afternoon sun to remind them, it was obvious that time had not diminished its pace.

"I need to shower and get ready. Oh, Stephen. I..."

"I what?" Stephen wanted to hear Audrey say, "I love you." She'd come close, but she never quite finished. Perhaps, she felt that it violated something between her and her husband. Perhaps, she didn't know just how she felt or perhaps—a lot—thought Stephen. For whatever reason, Audrey held back. Stephen didn't.

"I love you, Audrey."

Audrey kissed Stephen's chest and ran her right hand down the inside of his right thigh. When she was done, and before that burning again took control, she rolled to the edge of the bed. "I won't be long in the shower, and by the way, how many condoms do we have left from the two dozen you said you bought yesterday?"

"I grabbed the last ones off my dresser as we left the house. There were five."

"Five! You've got to be kidding me!" Audrey was quite emphatic and didn't know whether to snicker or sigh.

"No joke. Are you as good at math as you are in bed?"

"Stephen!"

"Well, since one of the last five is no longer—what number do you come up with?"

Audrey responded immediately, "I think twenty is pretty impossible for 45-year-olds."

"Good thing we're young at heart then."

"I guess we'll just have to make balloons out of the last four." Audrey smiled, and Stephen watched as she proceeded into the bathroom. Her small fanny jiggled only slightly, and the door closed behind it.

Stephen searched for his Jockey shorts, then he remembered he hadn't been wearing any and continued to dress. He noticed a fly swatter by the door and wondered if any winged intruders had been in room 33. Stephen opened the outside door and took a deep breath of moist Iowa air. The rain was coming down faster, and the drops seemed unusually large.

Audrey stepped out of the shower. She knew she had to leave Iowa Falls by no later than 6:00 in order to make it to Des Moines, check in the T-bird, and have time to get all of those airport things done before her plane left at 10:00. It was raining, and there had been flooding in Des Moines earlier in the day, so it wouldn't hurt to give herself another hour.

It wouldn't hurt, thought Audrey. It already hurt. It hurt like nothing Audrey had ever experienced before. She wrapped the stark white bath towel around herself and opened the bathroom door. She was still dripping wet and left footprints on the crushed aqua carpet as her senses were mesmerized by four, long, clear, white, cylindrical balloons attached to the outdated television. These were probably somehow stuck in the back panels that made them look like horns growing out of a hunk of charcoal sitting on the vintage desk, in room 33.

"Stephen Grant, you are an absolute idiot!" Audrey laughed hysterically and doubled over in the hilarity of the moment.

"I thought I'd create a going-away-party atmosphere. Do you like? I call it *condom art.*"

They both laughed, that is, until they cried.

Audrey bit her upper lip and rolled her neck from side to side to release the tension that was building up. "I think, I should leave by no later than 5:00 to 5:30. What do you think?"

"Your plane leaves at 10:00, right?"

Audrey nodded affirmatively.

"That should give you enough time. Des Moines has lots of water, so you'd better take I-35 all the way around instead of going down Fleur Drive. That always floods there by Water Works Park and Gray's Lake, even when there hasn't been this much rain."

"That's a good idea." They both knew the geography of Des Moines well as it sits in the middle of the state, has been the Capital of Iowa since it moved from Iowa City in 1857, and the airport has only puddle jumpers that connect to other small cities around Iowa. "What time is it?" Audrey once again addressed that proverbial question.

"'Bout 4:30." Stephen had glanced at his watch then back into Audrey's eyes.

Audrey took a deep breath, sauntered over to her suitcase, and paused while deciding what to wear on the circuit home. She pulled a beige set of silk and lace lingerie from the suitcase. It was one of Audrey's favorites. She always felt good and comfortable in that bra and bikini panties. That would be a good choice, she thought.

"Do you mind if I watch you get dressed?" asked Stephen with the manners of a Sheik.

"No. Actually, I want you to." Audrey added a nervous little giggle to the end of that statement.

The white towel that belonged to The Scenic City Motel dropped to Audrey's feet and Stephen's eyes scanned the symmetry of her naked form. He didn't miss a movement. He couldn't. Stephen drank of the moments and filed them in his memory for a keepsake. These were special moments, uncluttered by verbal messages. Moments of pure, undying love one man felt for one woman.

Audrey pulled her panties into place and leaned forward with her back toward Stephen as she adjusted the cups of her beige bra before fastening it. Stephen moved in close behind Audrey and wrapped his arms around her waist. He kissed her neck with gentle, moist tenderness and moved his hands over the softness extending between the silk and lace. Audrey exhaled as Stephen sustained her body in his arms and her heart in his hands.

"I'll be here, Audie," whispered Stephen. "I'll always be right here for you." He kissed his Audie one more time and backed over to the chair by the window.

Audrey continued getting into her denim skirt, and coral silk blouse. She chose a matching belt and shoes. She put her remaining clothes and cosmetics in her suitcase and turned toward Stephen with tears in her eyes. "Time goes quickly." Audrey tried smiling.

"It flies," added Stephen. "Don't they say, 'time flies'?"

"Yeah. I guess they do." Audrey tried smiling again, but the muscles of her mouth didn't comply.

"Hey. We'll see each other again—soon. I can feel it right here in my head." Stephen pointed to his knee.

The smile that was trying to come out of Audrey finally did. "You have two heads, Stephen. I don't think that's one of them." They both smiled.

"I promised I'd give Carol a call before leaving town. I'd better." Audrey picked up the phone and began dialing. "We've stayed just like sisters, you know. She knows my every secret—my past—right up until—last night." *My every secret, Carol knows. Her parents knew. Jeff and Heidi know—some. Stephen doesn't.* Audrey put the receiver back on its cradle and turned toward Stephen. Yes, she'd wait until she was back in Las Vegas to make that call. Distance and time could be friends, too.

"Stephen?"

"Wasn't she there?"

"I don't know. It didn't ring."

Stephen looked puzzled. "That's something it should do so they know you're there." Stephen was being sarcastic.

"I just wanted to tell you something, first. I mean, I've wanted to tell you this since we've been together...this time...since yesterday...since I saw you again." Audrey was anxious and had trouble getting an even flow to her speech. Not that she didn't know what she wanted to say; she did.

Stephen sat in silence, waiting, listening, anticipating.

"Well...it's about you...well, it isn't about just you...sort of just about you, though."

"Audie."

She just couldn't tell Stephen about Heidi this way. What way? When? How? She cleared her throat and turned back around facing Stephen, and she was once again composed as she clasped her hands in front of her face.

"It's just that I have a favorite word. I think that everybody does, don't you?" *Change the subject; that is a good thing.*

"A favorite word?" questioned Stephen as he cocked his head, wondering what Audrey was talking about now. "No, everybody doesn't have a favorite word."

"Well, I do. Do you want to know what it is?"

Stephen knew that he was going to hear Audrey's favorite

word, regardless of how he answered that question, so he just responded with a smile.

"*Harmony,* that's my favorite word." Audrey had been honest about that, but all of a sudden, she did not feel a lot of harmony in her life as she always strived for so she put the question right back to Stephen who still had a smile on his face. "So, what's your favorite word?" Her eyes grew large and bright with anticipation.

Stephen's response was swift, sound, solid, and solemn, "*Audie.*"

Chapter 24

Time was rounding its last corner and moisture was falling from Audrey's face as abundantly as it was from the sky. Stephen had carefully placed her suitcase in the trunk and started the T-bird so that the wipers could clear the windows. He hustled back to room 33. He tilted his rain-spattered head down and shook the drops away.

Audrey was standing outside the doorway, under the extended roof that covered the passing sidewalk. The door was open behind her. Stephen routed his gaze to the bed where they had completed their last act of passion with each other. The spread and sheets now rumpled lay lifeless, limp, and exhausted. The pillows, crushed, but straight and a small bedside light reflected in the mirror across the room.

Stephen looked at Audrey with insane grief and love. He took her delicate hands in his and held them close to his chest. He kissed her fingers, one at a time. Audrey could only watch as Stephen's lips touched her skin ten times in consecutive motion.

"I have always loved you, Stephen Grant. As long as there's a breath in me, I always will. Please, please, know that." Audrey's voice shook with emotion and sobs. She had said *the love word* to Stephen, to herself, to the room, to the rain, to the wind, to the world.

"Audie, your love feels so good and hurts so bad." Stephen slid Audrey's arms around his waist and placed his over her shoulders as he drew her next to him. "You are the first and the last love of my life. I could never love anyone or anything more than I love you. You have my heart, Audie, but then, you always have."

For about two minutes, not a sound came from the doorway of room 33. The air conditioner was off, the courtesy fly swatter was again resting on its hook, the DJ quieted, and two people in the vast sea of human life stood holding each other; their love, sung to the tune of their silent voices, filled the air.

"'Here's looking at you, kid.' Who said that, Audie?"

The slightest crack of a smile curled Audrey's lips. "Bogie. It was Bogie."

"What movie?"

"Casablanca."

"Where were they standing?"

"At the airport, he was letting her go."

Stephen shook his head. "No, Audie, you're wrong about that. Bogie wasn't letting her go. He was sending her to where she belonged. To where she would be happy, but he *never* let her go. She was with him—always."

"And always, I will be with you."

"I know, my Audie. I know."

As one shadow, they walked to the edge of the rain. The rain! It never rested from its mad rush that summer. Neither would Audrey's thoughts of Stephen.

"Audrey Harris Benway," Stephen cradled Audrey's head in the palms of his hands as he lifted her face toward his. "Promise me that you'll drive carefully and have a safe trip back. Call me when you can, but only when it feels right. And remember, *the harmony of life— is love.*"

"*I love you*, Stephen, and I love you loving me." Audrey's kiss was short. It had to be. She got into the car but couldn't tell where raindrops stopped and tears began. Between swipes of the blades, she could see Stephen. They forced a smile for each other as the wet, red, metal vehicle backed away. The tire tracks blended like a melting, soft-serve ice cream cone as the rains washed the muddy tread marks one into the other as swiftly as they left their imprints.

Chapter 25

Audrey had left with the words "I love you, Stephen" on her lips. He had waited to hear her say those words, and they felt so good. *Sometimes in life, maybe, silence isn't enough, maybe, words really do need to be spoken and heard in order to be completely felt and internalized by the soul.* Audrey had been so full of words and they came so easily to her. When she said those four words, 'I love you, Stephen,' he had no doubt, he felt no fear, and he, too, loved her, loving him.

Stephen stood in the falling rain as Audrey drove out of The Scenic City Motel driveway. He didn't have any feelings left to draw upon; they had all been used up, and he felt much like a single man caught dead in the eye of a hurricane; everything whirling around him, but no way out and nothing left to give. He couldn't blink the rain away from his eyes or feel the coolness as it was creeping into the late afternoon.

He took a few steps backward under the canopy. The rain was falling in front of him as he watched the T-bird until it completely rolled out of sight toward town on Highway 65.

Stephen entered room 33 once again. Audrey had checked out and he assured her that he'd shut the door. Maybe, she had left something behind. In a way, Stephen hoped she had. He surveyed the tops of the tables, desk, and bathroom cabinet, but found no visible traces of Audrey. He looked over at his *condom art* and smiled. He thought about taking them down or popping them, but decided to leave them for the housecleaner, as it would probably make her day. Stephen took hold of the doorknob but not before one last look toward the bed. For Stephen, it was not a long look or a sad look; it was a look of contentment. A warm flush ran through his body, and he felt Audrey's breath as he shut the door. In the rain, a black Cherokee waited for him.

****

Audrey knew that her drive to Des Moines would be a wet one. The rain seemed to be getting a bit harder as she drove down Highway 65. When she came to the corner of Washington Avenue, she remembered how she'd turned left to get to Stephen's almost 24 hours before. She wouldn't be turning left today and her mind stuttered in a repetitious, uneven flow of doubt, dissent, and desire.

Audrey glanced out the window to her left. A car came up beside her, and she knew that taking the right-hand turn was what she had to do. There were no choices to make now; those had come the day before. The car went straight and Audrey turned in the *right* direction.

Audrey drove by the Met, the Princess Café, Patty-Cake Bakery, Greenbelt Bank, and all of the familiar buildings that lined downtown Iowa Falls. She didn't see any of them. She didn't look at any of the buildings this time. Her attention focused on a single face rather than a multitude from the past. It was a face from now, not then. Images of Stephen's mustache and cleft and wrinkles and strands of gray hair bounced from the hood of the car as rapidly as did the raindrops. There was a smile and a touch inside the car with Audrey— Stephen was there beside her. He would travel with her in her heart, and she would be in his. They were passengers in life.

Audrey passed over the Washington Street Bridge with its double concrete arches underneath. The structure obscured her view of the river, but she knew just hours before, she and Stephen charged against its swollen current on *Emmy*. Stephen opened his soul and regurgitated his Vietnam experience to her. He cracked the shield in his heart and excavated the caves of his mind that this pain rendered. She was grateful to him and knew that it would be a beginning to his search for reality as he bridged his own war from the horrors of Vietnam to a life he could be part of, now.

The driver of an oncoming car blinked his headlights at Audrey as she reached the far side of the bridge. The sky was getting dark early, and Audrey heeded the advice from the driver by pulling her lights into action. The beams did not seem to go out too far as the rays of the lights were absorbed into the rain. The windshield wipers were not set up to full speed, yet, but from the looks of the rain and the forecast, Audrey might need to set them there soon.

Audrey passed the neighborhood school on the right side of the road, and a couple of blocks later, the kitty-corner house with Audrey's secrets locked into the walls underneath layers of paint. *Those secrets weren't going anywhere, they're comfortable where they are.*

Secrets. Secret words. Secret times of long ago. Secret worlds of today. Audrey shook her head as if setting it free from a tangled weave of sticky cobwebs. She had buried her secret from Stephen so many years earlier. It wasn't wrong to protect those she loved: Jeff, Heidi, Stephen, and herself. Are secrets lies or a shield? Are secrets…secrets if you share them with anybody? Audrey couldn't answer her own ambiguous questions, but she knew that she felt deceiving by not having shared more of herself with Stephen. *There will be time, another time. Maybe, in writing or over the phone, maybe I'll just wait until I see him again. Sometimes the past doesn't always have to be updated to the future. Maybe, some people do, but others don't.*

B-E-E-P! B-E-E-P! Audrey hit the horn as a car swerved toward her from the other side of the street. It was obvious that the driver was attempting to avoid a large puddle of rainwater, but that was ridiculous. "Excuse me!" Audrey shouted as she continued in the July rain that poured out of the dark Iowa sky.

She was at the edge of town. It was bound to be there. Audrey knew that the edge of everything comes at some time. She might not have wanted to face it, but she knew it all along. There was River Oaks, the Lutheran Church, and the baseball diamonds. No children were playing games on this rain-drenched day; their dreams of victory would have to wait.

A Highway 20 sign served as a visual marker, and the six miles between Iowa Falls and Alden were quickly covered. A small mall of about five stores had, years ago, attempted to draw shoppers from both communities; since the owners had not succeeded, it now looked more like a ghost town of Nevada than a modern effort to consolidate.

Audrey continued trying to think about things other than the past day and a half. She tuned in the radio. "We wish Winnie the Pooh could chase all of the clouds from these skies." The DJ was trying to lighten the atmosphere. "I don't think all of the characters in Pooh Corner would have much of a chance today, however. Forecast calls for continued rain. After this rain, we'll be in for more rain, and then, as if we didn't have enough, we'll probably get some more. Des Moines is getting the blunt of the current storm and several roads are closed. The airport is open. Some flights appear delayed, but they seem to be getting in and out. Allow yourself plenty of time and drive carefully wherever you're headed around the state. Better yet, stay at home and keep that dial tuned to…me! Here's an appropriate song from Richard and Karen Carpenter, they knew long ago about 'Rainy Days and Mondays.'"

Through Alden, past the Dows exit, Audrey was driving carefully, listening to music she loved, and thinking of how the events of the past day and a half would blend into her life. It wasn't a comfortable feeling. Audrey's thoughts turned to Jeff, Heidi, and Scott. Jeff would be thinking about what time he needed to leave home to pick her up at the other end of the flight. She'd give him a call from the airport and let him know if the flight was on time or late. He would be waiting with a kiss and a hug that somehow always felt the same each time, but oh, so comforting in that sameness that Audrey had come to expect over their years together. The hugs weren't bad or unappreciated or unloving, they just always seemed the same to Audrey. She wondered if her hugs to Jeff always felt the same to him. She hoped not.

Once Audrey arrived at McCarran Airport in Las Vegas, Audrey and Jeff would wait for the suitcase at the luggage pick-up. They would talk about their past few days—and teeth. She hoped that Jeff would be very talkative and have many client stories to tell, although, it had been the Fourth of July in Vegas too, so the dental office closed most of that time. She'd want to hear about Scott and what he'd been doing. How he'd dealt with the crash, booms, and bangs of fireworks. All of a sudden, Audrey felt guilty for missing the fireworks displays with Scott, as he did love watching them from afar, and all that Vegas had to offer with its generous displays at many holidays throughout the year. Yeah, she felt very guilty about that, too.

She wasn't sure if Scott would accompany Jeff to the airport at that time of night to pick her up. He went to be bed early and needed a full eight to ten hours of sleep each night in order to be ready for the demands of his job at the community workshop for disabled adults the next morning.

Audrey knew that around the perimeter of the luggage pick-up at McCarran, she and Jeff could watch the large viewing board advertising for various Casinos in Las Vegas. Siegfried and Roy from the Mirage were always on the screens with their white tigers, smiling faces, and European accents. Maybe this would help replace some of Audrey's usual conversation as well—Audrey hoped so. Jeff would carry the suitcase to the car that would be parked in the oversized lot, because he didn't like to use the parking garage at McCarran Airport. They would drive the three miles home, and although Audrey was usually talkative, she didn't know if she would be tonight. Perhaps, it would be better not to say much rather than take the chance of exposing something she didn't want to. She could talk about Carol, Sandy, and other Iowa Falls cronies without mentioning the name of Stephen. She could certainly find a lot to say about the rain and a little red Thunderbird. Yes, she knew exactly what Jeff and she would do and talk about and that was so comforting. After all, that's what gave Audrey her calm and harmony in life.

Scott would most likely be in bed, but he always got up to give Audrey a groggy "hello" and "good night" if she came in late. Audrey smiled at that thought. Scott was her *gift* in life, and his kisses and hugs never seemed the same. He'd kiss, hug, and curl back up in his bed to be tucked in along with his *Star Wars* theme comforter. Scott would fall asleep with the assurance that his mother was back in her proper place. Back to support him and protect him from people who didn't always understand and had little patience for the "Scott's of the world." He was vulnerable. Audrey loved him for that trait and would give her life to defend him. That's what mothers do. It's called—love.

Since it would be late, Audrey and Jeff would get ready for bed in the same manner they'd gotten ready for bed the past twenty-six years. Jeff would say something like, "Glad you're home, honey," and then it would be one extreme or the other. He would give her a quick kiss, roll over on his stomach, and be asleep in five seconds, or he would want to make love. Audrey hoped that tonight, it would be the first. She could say she's too tired if he wants to make love. It's not that she wouldn't want Jeff's affection, but not tonight, just not tonight.

Chapter 26

A car was coming up behind Audrey at a rapid pace. She could see the white Chevy in the rearview mirror and wondered why on Earth they would be going so fast with all of the rain. She kept a steady foot as the car passed her, spraying even more water on the windshield. She adjusted the wiper blades to a faster speed.

Stephen was surely home by now. Audrey tried to picture him in his house as she shifted her mind once again from Vegas to Iowa. She wondered if he'd found the buckeye she'd left on his table. That was a special buckeye. How it had lasted all of those years was a surprise to her. Buckeyes must have a real hard shell, because living in the corners of a woman's purse could not have been easy all of those years. She could visualize the smile on Stephen's face just thinking that he might be holding it in his hand at that very moment. Stephen had a whole tree filled with buckeyes but that particular one was unique for sure. Audrey was glad that she'd stopped to get a few more from his yard on her way out. Maybe, those would become unique as well.

The cornfields were waving to Audrey as she sped beside their fences, worn down by the years. A post was missing every so often and left the wire dangling, inviting intruders into its abundant, golden treasure. "Knee high by the Fourth of July," that's how the corn was to grow if it would be ready for the late summer and the Iowa mouths hungry to partake of every kernel. The corn's ears hadn't listened well this year, surmised Audrey. The rains had come, and what promised to be a good harvest in the spring could not possibly be manifested by the bushel this fall. Even if the rain quit at that very second, many of the farmers would still be suffering and there were no lighter skies in the forecast.

Audrey's mind continued to shift between home, Stephen, and rain. Between right and wrong, wet and dry, the questions kept calling for answers Perhaps they were all too fresh and Audrey's immediate need seemed to be to concentrate on the deluge of rain that fell from the Iowa sky.

"How much longer before we get there?" Audrey was reminiscing aloud and thinking about how many times she had been on this road going to Des Moines with her family. As a little girl, she would always ask that question whenever her family got in the car to go anywhere.

"Just over the hill and around the corner," Audrey tested herself. "Now, who said that? My daddy did. That's who." Audrey smile broadened just thinking about her father who had passed away a few years earlier. He was really the favorite man in Audrey's life, and she always knew it. He had named Audrey after his hero, Audie Murphy, the most decorated American Army soldier of World War II, laid-to-rest in Arlington National Cemetery, in Washington D.C. Murphy had become a movie star, and it was a father–daughter ritual every Friday night to go to the Met Theater for the weekly cowboy movie. Many of the movies of the 1950s starred Audie Murphy, the baby faced hero from Kingston, Texas. Only Audrey's father and Stephen ever called her Audie, and they both always said it with a sense of pride in their voices.

Audrey could sense the uncanny presence of her father in the car with her today. It was almost as if he were riding shotgun alongside a stagecoach on celluloid.

As Audrey and her red T-bird approached Williams, she could see a set of lights coming up the other side of the hill. In fact, it looked like two sets of lights, probably one behind the other. A car was also following rather closely behind her once again. None of these were unusual things as their glow appeared illuminated between the rain and the short metal guardrails on both sides of the highway that separated it from the thirty-foot drop. Not unusual—except that they belonged to a pickup that Audrey could see happened to be on *her side* of the highway. *On her side of the highway!* Were they all on *her* side of the highway? *What was going on?* Was it an illusion from the rain? Audrey knew that accidents happen quickly, and there's no time to think or plan or adjust. She wiped her eyes with the back of her right hand while keeping her left hand on the steering wheel. It had to be a fast swipe across her eyes, because she needed both hands that were now wet with perspiration. The road was wet and slippery, and the rain was blinding on the hill. The car behind wouldn't back off. *Why not?* "Please, please, God…Where are you? What do I do? Help me, now."

B-E-E-P! B-E-E-P! Audrey laid on her horn with a prayer on

her lips, tears streaming from her eyes, and her daddy's image sitting beside her. There was no shoulder, only the small metal rail on either side of the road. As sweat poured from Audrey's body, her face flushed with fear. Her hands clamped tight to the steering wheel as she attempted to maneuver it one direction then the other. There was nowhere to go! Audrey's right shoe slammed firmly against the brake pedal: pumping—holding—pumping—holding! The road was wet, the brakes were wet, the lights were blinding, everyone's tires squealed, *sliding, sliding, sliding!*

"*Daddy! Daddy!*" shouted Audrey at the top of her voice. "*Hold me*! *Catch me*! *Daaaaa Deeeee!*" Audrey's voice faded as the word "Daddy" hugged her lips. Then—she was silenced.

Metal mangled on this July evening in the hot, wet Iowa air. What spilled on the road and down the thirty-foot embankment matched the color of Audrey's red Thunderbird.

The spirit of Audrey's daddy was there, but to catch her would have taken a miracle.

Chapter 27

Stephen discovered the buckeye that Audrey left on the dining room table. "She doesn't miss anything," he said aloud.

He swished it around in his left hand, tossed it in the air a couple of times, and wondered how it could have survived all these years in the bottom of a woman's purse.

Stephen grabbed a can of Coors from the fridge and popped the tab. He stood watching the rain out of his kitchen windows as he took the first gulp. The radio, still tuned to the oldies station as Stephen occasionally glanced at the unset table.

His thoughts were of Audie, and how much he already missed her. He wanted her always to be a part of his life; no matter how far between those parts would be. He could never let her out of his life again.

Stephen wondered if Audrey was happy in her world. She hadn't talked a lot about her husband or her children, Stephen hadn't asked. All of a sudden he thought, *she talked a lot but I guess, we talked about me and us, not her.*

Stephen knew some things about Audie. He knew that her hair was curly and lighter than it had been in the past. He knew that she was diabetic, liked kiwi, fat free food, matching shoes, fancy lingerie, music, and giving quizzes. She could name muscles and facts about Iowa Falls, and she remembered everything.

She could recite poetry that he hadn't heard in nearly thirty years. He knew that Audrey was sensual, romantic, and alive, and he knew that she loved his touch. Stephen knew that Audrey cared deeply about old friends, people, and places, so why didn't he know how happy she is or isn't? Why hadn't he asked? Why couldn't he tell? *Damn, damn. When she calls, I'll ask her when she calls.* Stephen took another gulp of his beer.

Stephen knew all of those things about Audrey, and he knew one thing more; he knew how she made him feel about himself. Stephen felt loved for the first time in many, many years, and it was something he discovered he had within himself to give back.

He wasn't afraid of giving to Audrey. He wasn't threatened. He wasn't pretending to be something more than who he was. Stephen knew that he wasn't an island unto himself anymore and he came alive for about thirty-six hours as if playing a role in *Brigadoon*. He cared.

Stephen Grant cared.

Chapter 28

"We interrupt our broadcast to bring you a late news bulletin," the oldies radio station announcer from Iowa Falls proclaimed. "We have just received information concerning what we think is a fatal car accident on Highway 20 near Williams. We do not know the victim's identities. We'll have more information as it becomes available."

Stephen's beer suddenly soured in his mouth. It had been just the right amount of time for Audrey to reach Williams. "Nah, she'd be further than that," shrugged Stephen. "Audie's safe and on her way to Des Moines; probably somewhere on I-35. Let me see, it's been about thirty minutes." Stephen stared at the kitchen clock.

Thirty minutes in his life since he last touched Audrey. Where would she be in thirty minutes? The blood rushed from Stephen's head. "My God—where?" Stephen squeezed the can of Coors he was holding with the same amount of passion that had consumed him while making love to Audrey. Its contents, erupted by his might, foamed in a puddle of apprehension, ran from the kitchen island, down its sides, and landed on the floor.

Stephen flung the door of his black Cherokee wide open and mounted its leather seat with the force of a steed. His hands were sticky with foam from the Coors he'd cracked open, and the beer mingled with the rain and sweat. He hadn't taken the time to shut the door leading to his prized gym equipment in his garage. He hadn't grabbed his jacket to repel the rain falling from the Iowa skies. Stephen couldn't think of anything but his Audie. The lines on his forehead, around the sides of his eyes, and the downward curvature of his mouth were a study of trepidation, carved by the hands of love.

The black Cherokee sped through the rain soaked streets of downtown Iowa Falls—past the Met Theater, the Princess Café, past all of the old houses, across Washington Street Bridge and the baseball diamonds and Armory on the left side of the road left in a blur. Stephen's heart, harbored in his throat, and his pulse thundered in the temporal lobes of his brain. Audie! Audie! It just couldn't be his Audie!

As the black Cherokee topped the Williams' hill, sirens, lights, and smoke encompassed the scene. Stephen now filled with the same sense of uncertainty he had known in Vietnam as his oversize tires ended their skid and he hurled his legs out the door. The Cherokee's fog lights forged a path in the tall side-grass to what remained of the short metal fence, before the thirty-foot drop. Rain continued to fall, but Stephen's eyes, mind, heart, and soul could only focus on what he would see at the bottom of that Iowa gully. It couldn't be a blood red Thunderbird, not today, not his Audie!

An Iowa State Trooper, Doug, was one of the first responders to the scene of the accident. He shouted above the sirens and driving rain, "Stephen, what are you doing here?"

"Get out of my way, Doug!" Stephen flung his arms wide in both directions with one mighty stroke.

"You can't go down there!"

"BET MY ASS! Aaaauuuuuudddddeeeeee!"

The sound of her name permeated the air. Stephen, crumbled to his knees.

Chapter 29

"'…Surely, goodness and mercy will follow me all the days of my life, and I shall dwell in the house of the Lord forever.' Audrey Anita Harris Benway was one lovely woman. A driver, who had too much to drink, and a season of too much rain, took her from her family and friends. I wish this kind of killing could end with Audrey, because she would like that. She is the one who would have sacrificed for that reality. We ask ourselves, did Audrey do wrong, and we find only one answer, no. Audrey loved and laughed and lived with a passion so real and intense that she left most of us standing and wondering where we'd been."

The minister was sincere, the Congregational Church filled, and the rain, the relentless rain, accentuated the mood. Audrey's family decided to bury her next to her parents and in the family plot in Iowa Falls, close to the roots she so loved, and they, themselves, would make yearly visits.

The minister from Iowa Falls continued, "Over the years, Audrey never visited Iowa Falls but what she didn't stop by to say 'hi' to me. She was my good friend and yours. I baptized Audrey, and today, I am here to honor her life. She was a daughter, a wife, a mother. Audrey healed people both physically and emotionally. Her smile lit the air we breathe and her warmth, well, what can I say about Audrey's warmth that you, her friends and family didn't feel?" The pastor went on about Audrey, her commitments, her life over the past quarter of a century. All of the things Stephen had missed.

Stephen had known Audrey on the borders of her life. He was the one who had first made love to her, and he was the man who last held her in his arms. Sandwiched in-between had been a lifetime of living, day-to-day existence with its pleasure and pain, its monotony and exuberance. Stephen wished he had known more about Audrey, but what he had known could be wrapped around his body like the first pair of wings on a firefly; there for balance in flight and protection during rest.

Stephen studied Audrey's children in their deepest hours of despair. Heidi was tall, much taller than Audrey was, and beautiful. She looked full of the same spirit that propelled her mother, her navy blue dress fit her figure well, and she wore matching shoes. Her long dark curls Stephen was certain were not in disarray under most circumstances. Heidi's fingers were slender as she brushed the hair from the side of her face, and at that moment, Stephen wondered what size shoes she wore, and if she liked kiwi because it was pretty. As Heidi's face turned toward Stephen's, he saw the dominant cleft in her chin. *Audrey had mentioned that—hadn't she?*

Scott! Stephen wasn't sure just how old he was. Audrey had told him that Scott worked in a community workshop, but it was obvious she had neglected to mention his other features. He was short, with a round face, little ears, and distinctive eyes. Scott had Down syndrome. Stephen hadn't known that about Audrey's life. Did she possibly think it could have influenced his love for her? All that she must have gone through in the torment of her acceptance and in the trial of life as it went on day-to-day. That had been her hell, but Stephen could tell it had been her heaven as well. Scott was an obvious tribute to Audrey's will and knowledge. Maybe he didn't understand everything that was going on but he was a monument of strength and a comrade to his father. Stephen could tell that, over the past years, Scott and Audrey had been good teachers for each other. Audrey had every reason to smile down upon her family. *To be loved by her, I was in a special class to be loved by her.*

There sat Jeff, the one man in the entire world whom Stephen had once hated. He no longer felt hatred and resentment toward him, but pity and envy in a simultaneous circle: pity for what he had lost and envy for the years he had with Audrey.

"My mother was my best friend." Heidi was speaking from the front of the church in a voice reminiscent of one that Stephen had heard before. "Oh, how I will miss her." Heidi paused to wipe the tears from her eyes. "'Did you ever know that you're my hero? You're everything I wish I could be. You are the wind beneath my wings,' mother. Who sings that? My mother would always ask, 'Who sings that?'"

Heidi laid a small piece of paper on the pulpit in front of her. "Well, I have a very short one for her. Who said this, mother?

And the Lord said, 'Do not weep for she is at peace.

She will rest with Me until you come.
Then we shall all sing and dance together.'

"The answer is me, Mom, that one's by me." Heidi's cries were soft and mellow as her father escorted her back to her seat. Stephen Grant again noticed the cleft in her chin—and he, too, cried.

The cemetery was soggy, but the rain was kind enough to pause for a couple of hours. An elaborate spray of yellow roses draped over Audrey's coffin as friends gathered for a last good-bye. The minister was brief in his message and once again gave a praise of thanksgiving for a life that had touched and changed so many around her.

"Audrey, every one of us will miss you, each in their own special way, and when their heads are bowed in prayer, may they remember the good you did in the name of the Lord." It was time for "The Lord's Prayer," one of Audrey's favorites, to be recited in unison as the minister stepped back.

Carol stepped forward when the minister had finished and began, "Audrey and I were best friends since the first grade. We played, we sang, we dreamed, and we shared the secrets of each other's worlds. We grew up together and evolved from having to have our needs met, to being the ones who fulfilled needs in others. Audrey was so good at that." Carol wiped the tears that were streaming down her cheeks.

"A couple of years ago, Audrey told me that at her daughter's wedding, someday, she hoped that I would sing "Through the Eyes of Love." This occasion is far from the joy that will be on that day. However, that song meant a lot to my best friend. I can't possibly sing more than…just a bit, but this is my last gift to a woman I truly loved.

"Knowing you're beside me, I'm all right.
Please don't let this feeling end
It might not come again, and I want to remember.
Reaching out to touch you
I can feel so much.
Since I found you,
Looking through the eyes of love."

Carol's voice faded, and the moisture in the air absorbed the strains of her song. Through it all, Stephen was silent as his soul searched for a measure of understanding, and his heart, for a moment of peace. He wished he had someone to cling to, to hold on to, and to care about at this very moment. He wished he had someone who cared for him like Audrey's Scott and Heidi cared for their father as they clung to each other like roots flowing from the same vine.

Chapter 30

Cole and Carol planned a gathering after the funeral at their home for Audrey's family and friends. Stephen felt obliged to attend. His mind was there but his heart settled deep into the Iowa soil.

"Glad you came, Stephen, I was in hopes you would." Carol greeted Stephen at the door with a hug. "We've had some sad days." Her eyes filled with tears.

Stephen nodded and sniffled. "This was nice of you, Carol. You and Audrey were so close. I know that. Audie liked this sort of thing. I know she would approve." Another short hug, released quickly, and Stephen moved into the kitchen with its bay window that opened to a view of pine, oak, and rosebud trees that had already blossomed for the year.

A young woman in a navy blue dress with matching shoes came over to the window seat and settled into a more relaxed pose. Stephen observed her mannerisms and their likeness to Audrey's, but he couldn't take his eyes off her face. Many of her gentle features matched Audrey's: the blueness of her eyes, the coarseness of her hair, the clearness of her skin. Many were Audrey's—many were not.

"That was beautiful, what you said about Aud—your mother," said Stephen.

"Thank you. I don't know what I'll do without her. She was my best friend. Did you know her very well?" Heidi had responded graciously to Stephen's comment, as he knew she would.

Stephen's eyes clouded as he lowered them to the kitchen tile. He cleared his throat. "I think I knew her well. She was…she was a good friend. Always."

Stephen did not want to stare, but his eyes could see nothing but Heidi. He recognized the high cheekbones from somewhere. He saw the fullness of her lips. He identified the cleft in her chin. Stephen caught a glimpse of his own reflection in the bay window, and suddenly—unlike the temperament of the day, life became clearer.

"Are you all right, honey?" asked Jeff as he placed his right hand on Heidi's shoulder. Audrey's husband had approached.

Jeff wasn't quite the image Stephen had depicted him to be. He was short, a bit pudgy, shirt buttoned high with cuff links on a hot day, and a conservative tie. His shoes shined in spite of the weather and his hair, thinly pulled to one side.

"I don't think I'll ever be all right again, Dad, but I'm okay, right now."

Jeff squeezed Heidi's shoulder and immediately extended his hand to Stephen. "I'm Jeff Benway. I know a lot of Audrey's friends from Iowa Falls, but I don't think we've met."

"Stephen Grant," he said as he returned the handshake.

"Do you live here in Iowa Falls?" inquired Jeff.

"Down by the river."

"Can we go on the river this time, Dad?" Scott, who was standing next to Jeff, asked.

"Not on this visit, Scott." Jeff's response was patient. "Maybe, next time we're in Iowa Falls. We'll be back, you know."

"My mom will always be in Iowa Falls now. Did you know that?" Scott, with a bit of a smile on his face, was addressing Stephen. Scott knew a new fact and he wanted to share it.

Jeff answered, "That's right, Scott. Mom loved it here, and she'll always be here now. She's resting by Grandpa and Grandma in the cemetery." Jeff was matter-of-fact in his response to Scott as Carol approached the group.

"Heidi told me what you're going to place in your garden in Vegas for Scott especially," said Carol as she faced Jeff. "That will be special and healing."

"We hope so, Carol. We're all going to need that, you know. We're going to call it *Mom's Harmony Garden*. Harmony was Audrey's favorite word. I think she'd like that, and we'll put a bench there for Scott so he can sit and talk to her any time. I don't know how I'll manage without her. I really don't know. Maybe this will help all of us just a little bit." Jeff's voice quivered as it tapered off.

Stephen was a part of this conversation only as it tore through his brain and drained out into the bulging membranes of his eyes. The *harmony* of Audrey's life would lie at rest, and he knew, that she knew, she was loved by him as well as by so many others in her life.

Everyone in the circle took a step back and collected their thoughts as Cole approached the small group by the window. "Jeff, can we have a private moment—it's hard to find one."

"Sure," and the two stepped aside.

"How is Heidi doing on the dialysis?"

"Oh, Cole, thanks so much for setting the session up over at the medical clinic while we're here in Iowa Falls. It's more important than ever that she keep the routine up." Jeff's eyes teared. "It's been hard, and I look for much harder ahead. You know, Aud just kept all of us going in the right directions and without her—"

"I know, I know. Carol will keep in close touch." Cole put his hand on Jeff's shoulder.

"Dad. Dad, the man with the mustache over there," Scott was pointing to Stephen and talking in his *outside voice.* "He has a pon-ta-loon on the river. I want to go on it, *now."*

Jeff looked confused, so Cole stepped in to offer a welcomed, helping hand. "Scott, that is your new friend, Stephen, and yes, he has a pon-toon on the river. It's like a boat."

"Yes, and I want to go on it, *now.*"

Heidi and Stephen could hear the ruckus from just a few feet away and took steps to remedy it.

"Scott," said Heidi in a calming voice, "please use your *inside voice* like mother taught you. We are in Carol and Cole's house, and we always use an *inside voice* when we are *inside.*"

"I'm sorry, Heidi. Yes, mother taught me that. I want to go on the pon-ta-loon, *now!"* whispered Scott.

"Scott," Stephen spoke up, "we can't go on my pontoon now. It's raining, and we have other important things to do today. When you come back to Iowa Falls sometime, I promise to take you for a ride on my pontoon. Give me five and we'll know that's a promise between us." A High-Five sealed a promise between Scott and Stephen that would someday be kept.

Jeff shook Stephen's hand with a firm grip of approval. "You saved the day, sir, and I thank you. I think we were just about to visit a minute ago. Did you know Audrey long?"

"I graduated with Audrey," replied Stephen.

"I think she'd spoken of you before. Audrey talked a lot about her friends. Audrey talked a lot, about…a lot." Heidi, Jeff, and Stephen all seemed to nod at once, and a smile of fondness locked them in a common bond of verbal memories. They all needed a smile about then.

"The birds are happy today, Dad." Scott was watching a pair of blue jays perched in a tree not far from the bay window.

Heidi injected, "They're not *real* happy, Scott. No one is *real* happy today."

"Well, look, Heidi. They're blue jays. Mom read me a story about how blue jays talk. I know they're happy."

"They probably are, Scott," assured Jeff. "Scott knows a lot about animals."

"Yeah, I do. My mom always taught me about animals. Do you like ferrets?" He was asking Stephen. Scott ran much of his speech together in a cluttering manner that made it difficult for many people to understand. Stephen didn't seem to have as much trouble as most.

"Ferrets are one of my favorites, Scott. I had a pet ferret when I was young."

"What is his name?" inquired Scott.

"Maynard *was* his name," replied Stephen as he surprised himself at retrieving that piece of childhood trivia.

"Is Maynard here today?" Does he eat bugs?"

"I don't have Maynard anymore, and yeah, he did eat bugs."

Heidi and Jeff both smiled at Stephen. Not everyone had patience with Scott's questions, and on this particular day, under these circumstances, it was nice to find a stranger who would converse with him.

"Oh, no!" Scott was pointing out the window, holding his stomach and laughing hysterically. "Look at the funny cat. His tail is—"

"Remember last time we were in Iowa Falls, Scott, mom told you about the squirrels? That's an Iowa squirrel and he eats acorns." Heidi explained much like Audrey might have.

"Can I have him, Dad? I want to take him home."

"He's wild, Scott. No." Jeff was brief. Scott showed a bit of a pout but Heidi was right there on the uptake.

"Scott, would you please get me a 7-Up?" requested Heidi of her brother. Heidi was tolerant of Scott and she knew how to redirect his energy and calm his behaviors that could erupt easily.

"Sure, Heidi." Scott directed his reply to Heidi and then turned to Stephen. "You should name your ferret Heidi. Do you think I can have a squirrel with a big tail?"

Heidi rolled her eyes. "Scott! That will be one 7-Up, with ice, please."

Scott grinned because he loved teasing his older sister and upon accomplishing that task, he turned and obeyed her command.

Stephen had thoughts of his own at that moment. *He remembered Audrey saying how her son, Scott, would love the tails on the squirrels as they ascended the path after the pontoon ride. He could tell the complexity and enormous task it had been to raise a child with Down's syndrome. To teach her daughter and her son so well was beyond anything Stephen could wrap his mind around on this rainy day.*

Carol assisted Scott with a 7-Up for Heidi and a Dr. Pepper for himself. Scott returned to the bay window with the Dr. Pepper.

"Did you forget anything, Scott?" asked Heidi.

"I've got it, Heidi," said Carol as she approached. She leaned between Stephen and Jeff in order to hand the glass to Heidi.

"Thank you, Carol, you too, Scott."

"What would you fellas like?" Carol was asking Stephen and Jeff.

"Coffee'd be great, Carol. Thank you," replied Jeff.

Carol looked at Stephen's chin, but she felt his penetrating eyes directed at her. Without lifting her head, she rolled her eyes up to meet Stephen's. His eyes were full of more than what he wanted to drink. They seemed to be overflowing with questions that he implored to have answered.

"I'll take coffee, too, Carol. Let me help you with it." Stephen put his hand on Carol's back and walked her to the other end of the kitchen toward the coffee pot.

"Carol." Stephen didn't want to draw any attention to their conversation. He got a cup, and as he poured it full of java, he turned his head in her direction. "We need to talk, don't we?"

Carol didn't reply.

"Can you meet me tomorrow? Breakfast, lunch, anytime you say." Stephen was emphatic.

"The Princess, at ten o'clock all right?" asked Carol.

188

"I'll be there. Carol—?" Stephen cut his question short. Her look was all he needed.

Carol returned to Jeff with a cup of coffee and a heavy mind. Two men, in the whole world, two men had loved Audrey. They had both given her a child and she knew that Audrey loved them back. Audrey had to make a choice, however, and for whatever reasons, she did so. She made a life with Jeff, a good life, a protected life, a prosperous life, and a caring life.

As Carol handed the cup to Jeff, she thought of how he must now face life, void of twenty-seven years filled with Audrey. The days would have to be—rewired. Like time, wound in a circle, whose hands knew no direction. Jeff always wanted to appear to be the one in control, but Carol knew it was Audrey who was the cement in their lives. Audrey was the one who had learned to make decisions, and she committed herself to whatever those decisions were. Audrey had raised Heidi and a handicapped son. Audrey always said, "It was other people who were handicapped, not Scott. He didn't care about what he didn't understand. It was the others—the normal ones—who were afraid of anything *they* didn't understand." Audrey worked while Jeff finished dentistry school, and then pursued her own degree and career in physical therapy. Audrey never lost faith in anything she tried. *Where will Jeff be? Did he know all that Audrey was in their lives? He'll surely know, now.*

For Stephen, who held in his mind, secrets that would forever remain as such. He would not share them with anyone. They were too special to share; too unbelievable to be real, and too painful to be totally remembered. Now, he had another reality to face. A reality in the form of a daughter he'd never known existed. Carol wanted Stephen to know. She had one night to sleep on it, to find out what he wanted to know and to determine what she should tell him. She was Audrey's confidant and the truest of friends. One night would determine the strength of that friendship as opposed to the need of its resolution.

What would life be like for her without Audrey in it anymore? Almost forty years of Audrey's voice as it came tumbling over the phone in words like, "Hi, Sis, are you having a good day? It's sunny here today; how is it there? What do you think I should do with Scott when he…" All of these and more would no longer be heard. Carol wouldn't receive those funny cards in the mail for no reason and flowers on her birthday would never again carry the message, "Sisters Forever." She would not meet Audrey in Iowa Falls or Las Vegas or Atlanta or anywhere. Theirs was a friendship that would eventually find calm in the acceptance of death; a journey that would take a long time.

For Heidi and Scott, Carol's heart could find no peace or answers on this day, not on this rainy day. Perhaps someday, when the sun was shining and the clouds no longer formed grotesque shadows over the Iowa fields and on top of the houses, maybe, some peace would come for Audrey's children. *Harmony, is something that everyone strives for in their own life, but few find, because life's boundaries are fragile and can change without an instant of warning. Harmony is love, and that love must be renewed every day—while we are living.*

****

Stephen and his silence attempted to blend into the friends who had come together on this day in July. He enjoyed seeing Doug, Sandy, Dan, and a crew of Iowa Falls Cadets who had gathered in shadows of sadness and loss, joy and pain. He listened, and in that listening, he heard echoes of hearts and souls that reached out, each searching for some meaning to this existence, some inner sense of being, answered by life itself. The harsh view of a yellow sky came to Stephen's mind. The smell of death shrouded his every sense, and Audrey's words, "I'm glad Westy had a friend like you to give his last smile to; you'll carry it with you forever," ricocheted within his mind. *Who said that?* Stephen asked himself in continued silence. *Now, who said that?*

"Good to see you, Stephen." Doug, the Iowa Trooper was speaking.

"You too, Doug. The last time was a bit—"

"It's okay, Stephen. The scene of an accident is always complicated, and when you know the victim, it wrings your heart out. I always think I've seen the worst, and then there's something else that comes along. I didn't know you were so close to Audrey."

Stephen's head shook vertically as teeth marks formed on his lower lip. "Yeah, we were close."

Doug sensed Stephen's mood and knew from the scene of the accident what they meant to each other.

"Audie was very special to me." A lone tear slid down Stephen's face.

"Let's meet for a beer one of these nights at Brewski's Bar. I'll give you a call."

"That'd be great, Doug, let's do." Stephen nodded, knowing that Doug had always been his friend, and he was there on that rain soaked hill in Williams. As Stephen had sunk to his knees that day, knowing his Audie was gone, Doug was the one who held Stephen in his arms, just like Stephen had cradled Westy on the bank of that river in Vietnam. Caring—one friend to another—Doug cared about Stephen.

The rain was once again drenching Iowa, reminding her inhabitants that control was in someone's hands other than their own. The day had been long and the strain was evident on the many faces that had come to honor Audrey's life.

Heidi stood watching as heavy raindrops pounded on the wooden canopy covering the back patio. The drops knocked to get in, to find shelter, from one another, but the rain was met by structures that repelled its arrival and told it to stay away.

"You resemble your mother," said a voice from behind her.

Heidi recalled it was Stephen-somebody speaking to her as he exited the French doorway leading to the back patio. "Some people think so, but I don't, not really. I'm old enough though to know that's a real compliment. My mom always cared about how she looked." Heidi paused as she sat down on the porch swing that moved easily on its suspended cables. "Carol said that Iowa's becoming a swamp these days. Does all of this rain affect you?"

Heidi—Stephen liked the name Audrey had chosen for their daughter. It fit her well. She seemed confident, poised, and intelligent. *Audrey's life had come full circle.* Stephen leaned against a white post, placing his coffee on the railing that surrounded the patio. Heidi's concern about people she didn't even know was genuine. Her attitude was a dog-ear in pages written upon by her mother. Before Stephen stood a replica, an assurance that life had only turned a corner, leaving in its tide, the sediment of good.

"It doesn't affect my day-to-day job, but yeah, what happens here in the Midwest affects us all, eventually."

"They predict the worst will be in Southern Iowa and Missouri. The Mighty Mo just can't hold it all," said Heidi as she watched Stephen retrieve his coffee mug from the railing and take a gulp. "I hope the winter's a mild one for you."

Winter…I have to get through the rest of today. July and the summer. Then and only then, can I think of Winter.

Chapter 31

As Carol arrived at the Princess Café, she glanced at her watch. It said 9:50 as she entered through the door and passed the marble soda fountain with its bar stools. Stephen's face towered over the top of one of the high backed booths on the right side of the Café. He raised his eyebrows as if Carol could have possibly missed him. A couple other patrons of the Princess sat down the other aisle.

"Hi, Carol. What's Doc been up to? I haven't seen him for a while. Guess I should consider myself lucky." One of the customers recognized Carol as he chuckled at his own joke.

"Good morning, Nelson. Docs around but keeping pretty busy. Shall I make an appointment for you with him?" Carol had returned the barb in Nelson's direction as she walked back to Stephen's booth.

"Not until I need him. Just tell him 'hi' for me."

"Will do, Nelson, enjoy your breakfast."

"Thank you for meeting me, Carol, I went ahead and ordered coffee for us. Would you rather have something else, like breakfast?" Stephen stood as Carol sat down in the seat across from him.

"Coffee's fine, Stephen. Carol helped herself to the Sweet-N-Low and began stirring slowly. As the liquid swirled in Carol's cup, she caught a glimpse of Stephen's reflection in the etched mirror that hung on the wall beside the booth. Stephen looked tired, drained, and pale. The strain and grief he had been suffering over the past few days had taken its toll. He hadn't bothered to shave that morning. Carol didn't think he had shaving on his mind.

"Audrey's family left early this morning. Their flight is leaving about now." Carol knew that it might relieve Stephen's mind up front if he knew they had distanced themselves from him.

Stephen shook his head affirmatively. "How old are Audrey's kids?"

"Scott's 19, now, and a nice young man. What did you think of him?"

"I agree. He is nice. It couldn't have been easy for Audrey."

"It wasn't, and it certainly won't be easy for Scott, now—he depended a lot on his mother. They were good teachers for each other."

Stephen and Carol both took a sip of their coffee, avoiding the up-coming question.

Stephen could no longer wait. He couldn't edge into it anymore. He had to know. "Is Heidi mine? Is she, Carol?"

"Heidi is twenty-six years old, Stephen. She's not a little girl." There was a long pause, an uncomfortable long pause. "Heidi has always been Audrey's."

"And? Is she, Carol? I *have* to know."

Carol took a large gulp of her lukewarm coffee. She never thought that she'd find herself in this position—revealing her truest friend's deepest secret. Whether she'd agreed with Audrey about never telling Stephen really didn't matter. What did matter was her loyalty to Audrey.

"Stephen. Would it make any difference to anyone? Now?"

"It would make a difference to *me*. The looks are unmistakable. If I'd never seen her, I'd never have known."

"More coffee?"

Carol responded to the server's question with, "Please, for both of us."

Stephen had turned his head toward the mirror, away from the server. His forehead wrinkled with anxiety, and the reflection of his eyes sunk into the shine on the black tabletop. The server poured the coffee and was on her way.

"Why didn't she tell me?" Stephen was looking directly into Carol's eyes. "Audie never told me, Carol? Maybe, I was supposed to know, somehow. God, how was I supposed to know?" Stephen didn't expect Carol to deceive Audrey's long-standing confidence, but she didn't have to, *he knew.*

"Things were much different in the sixties, Stephen, than they are today. You know that. There were only two choices back then: illegal abortion or girls went to "homes" in cities and then put the baby up for adoption. Audrey wouldn't even consider an abortion even though her parents suggested it. When Audrey found out she was pregnant, it was a terrible scene with her parents. I was by her side, because she asked me to be. You can imagine how they reacted. It was late August and you thought Audrey was going to the University of Iowa. She didn't. Instead, her parents made arrangements for her to live in a home for unwed mothers in Omaha until the baby came. The plan was for adoption."

Stephen cried with silent tears as he squeezed Carol's hands from across the table.

Carol continued. "About six weeks into her stay in Omaha a very wonderful young, brilliant dental student walked into her life. He was a student at Creighton University School of Dentistry. He simply adored Audrey from the moment he laid eyes on her."

"I can understand that," Stephen forced the sentence on a short, single breath of chocked up air.

"Jeff was older, more mature, had a clear direction in life. Audrey was honest with him, and when he met her parents, they knew he would take good care of their daughter and her child. I drove to Omaha and was Audrey's maid of honor. Jeff has always treated your child like his. I can assure you of that, Stephen. Heidi is…Heidi is everything you'd expect, and you'd be proud of her, Stephen. She graduated from college and works at a bank in Las Vegas. She lives in her own apartment, but helps Jeff a great deal with Scott. She's done well. She's engaged to a great guy who works as an executive for one of the big casinos in Vegas. Audrey and Jeff did a fantastic job raising her; they are great parents."

"But, how didn't I know? I loved Audie. I always loved Audie. I don't understand."

"Audrey tried to tell you one time—when she first found out she was pregnant. She claimed that she just couldn't tell you. I didn't always understand it either, Stephen. Somehow she felt responsible for getting pregnant. It was her way." Carol wasn't about to put any blame on Stephen this many years after the fact. She didn't know if he was to blame, if Audrey was to blame, if the times were to blame.

"Every time we had a class reunion, Audrey always thought you'd be there. You never were. When she found out that you lived here in town again, a few nights ago, I didn't want her to see you. I advised her not to stop by your house. I *knew* she would."

Stephen looked at Carol with caution in his eyes at that statement. Then, Carol continued in her explanation. "Stephen, there are some people in your life who you just never can get over. They can hurt and love you at the same time, mostly, because they were there at the tender, emotional, and formidable adolescent age when you began your life's journey. For *you,* it was Audrey. For Audrey, it was *you.* You had the most precious time with her back then as she first began her journey and, again, as her journey ended. If Audrey decided not to tell you about the baby, I know she had a reason. Audrey was smart, and she was strong. Maybe she tried to tell you, Stephen—maybe she tried."

Stephen loosened the grip on Carol's hands and thoughts of how Audrey had tried to tell him about their child dipped into his brain's short-term memory compartment of July fourth and fifth. "Of course, she did, Carol. She tried a couple of times, but I guess just not the right times for her. That would have given Audrey her *harmony*—the thing she searched for all of her life."

"Maybe, Stephen. But maybe by not telling you, her harmony was fulfilled."

All Carol and Stephen could do for about three minutes was sit in silence and allow the cobwebs of life to be dusted from their anguished labyrinths that had been blown in by the winds of time. Carol reached for a hanky she had tucked in the pocket of her shorts. She shook it open and wiped her eyes.

The server returned, but paused only for a second, and without a word, proceeded down the aisle.

"Heidi knows that Jeff isn't her biological father?" Stephen wanted continued clarification.

"Yes. Audrey told her several years ago. It was a time when she knew Heidi could understand. We talked about it for weeks over the phone before she finally told her. It was a major decision for Audrey, but it seemed appropriate under certain circumstances that were happening in Heidi's life at the time."

"Like what?" Stephen continued.

Carol had gone far beyond where she'd planned in revealing Audrey's life to Stephen. She felt uncomfortable and betraying.

"Stephen, Audrey always handled everything well when it came to her children. She was a wonderful mother."

"I can tell that. I never got to see her, hold our baby," Stephen dropped his eyes.

Carol wiped her eyes with her handkerchief. "If I knew

anything about Audrey, it is that she loved four men in her life; her father, her husband, her son, and *you*."

Stephen had not hurt when he hadn't known the truth. If *the truth can set you free*, then why did he feel like a prisoner of the past?

Stephen walked Carol to her car. "Thank you, Carol, thank you for your honesty. I wish I could say that I feel better, but I don't know if I can."

"It's all new for you, Stephen. New is hard, sometimes."

Stephen leaned on the side of the car. "This whole week has been something out of a…out of a novel." Stephen brushed his forehead with the back of his hand.

"It's a week that will go on for a long time."

"That's right, Carol, a long, long time, that's for sure." Stephen opened the door for Carol, and she slid in behind the steering wheel.

"Take care of yourself, Stephen. Treat yourself well."

"I've learned a lot this past week, Carol. A lot about Audrey— lot about myself, too."

Carol added, "Life isn't always fair, Stephen. We're given choices, and we make them based on logic and feelings at any one given time in our lives. Always love Audrey for who she was, and forgive her if she didn't match all of your expectations. Any time you want to talk again, I'm here for you."

Once again, the clouds were tumbling overhead in downtown Iowa Falls as the hungry, noon crowd was moving into the Princess. Stephen had not eaten yet today nor did he have any plans to do so.

Chapter 32

The winter of '93 was anything but mild. Its brutal cold and early snows forced hard times for Iowa's people and her land. March arrived with grateful anticipation and with little precipitation. It was the driest March on record in 122 years, and farmers in Hardin County anticipated preparing their fields for seeds of oat that would be planted in late April or May.

The bad farm news and forecasts continued as Stephen often reluctantly read the *Hardin County Times-Citizen*. Sometimes, the newspapers would stack up on his coffee table before he'd sit down with a cup of coffee and attempt to digest the latest in area news. The paper claimed that Iowa's oat production in 1993 fell to the lowest level since records were kept, dating back to 1866. "The topsoil moisture might be a little dry, but there is no shortage of subsoil moisture due to the floods of the summer of '93. Oats were ready to grow if their roots could spread out for nutrients in the compacted soil."

The umbra of winter, for Stephen, was long and cold, and the hours had come and gone, not with exuberance but with monotony. They had seen little of the smiles Audrey left as shadows upon his pillows and walls, and the guitar was again collecting dust as it stood *watching* from its corner of the world.

Stephen's dining room table remained unset. He did not expect any company and his need to feel polished had been met, or its importance had been resolved. A lone buckeye rested gently in the glass hutch, alongside the crystal goblets.

Stephen had added a new magazine to his collection of reading material. He subscribed to *Vietnam*. He just looked at the pictures in the first couple of issues, but now, he'd begun reading. Continuing to sort the pieces of his jigsaw puzzle had become an obsession during those dark days of winter. Stephen's feelings hadn't changed, but his perception and understanding of the Vietnam War itself gave him a new perspective on those years, and a reason for his having been a part of it all. Vietnam was becoming *real,* and in a *real* world, he could deal with ghosts.

Stephen told his daughter, Emily, many times over how much

he loved her, and the enormous pride he felt for her. When she visited over Christmas, she and Stephen picnicked on her namesake, *Emmy,* as she slumbered in her winter quarters. Crisp Kentucky Fried Chicken crackled in their mouths as the voice of Dan Fogelberg and the keys of Richard Yusko floated on the dry, winter, Iowa air. They once again designed a snow-bunny of white. Only one—only one, who stood as a sentinel on the side of Stephen's house, ears reaching to the sky, whose name was HOLLAND.

Heidi. Stephen often thought of Heidi. How could he NOT have known? How could Audrey not have told him that he was a father all those years ago? He had to stop asking questions that had no voice to respond. Heidi was a grown woman. She was all Stephen could have ever hoped for in a daughter, but the glory and pride belonged to Audrey and Jeff, not to him. Maybe, one day Stephen and Heidi would meet again. He knew that the maybes of life were many and unpredictable.

Stephen's rural gas truck rolled down the country roads of Hardin County, Iowa, and filled both commercial and farm tanks of its modern necessity. He managed to cross over gravel and dirt roads where the summer floods had damaged bridges, and he blazed paths where only promises should have gone during that winter of '93. The farmer's bills could not always be paid with the words, "Federal Reserve Note" written across the top, as their expenses could not be met in tens and twenties. Stephen filled his freezer with Iowa's best pork and beef as payment. Jars of homemade jellies and preserves lined his cupboards and he accepted handwritten "Notes of Promise" signed by this nation's most trustworthy and honest people. It was new. It was risky. It felt good. At last, it felt so good.

Just when the Iowa farm woes were out of the news, in they popped again in early May 1994. The *Des Moines Register* printed, "The Iowa Secretary of Agriculture announced that due to the floods of '93, Iowa had been knocked from its long-held leadership positions in major agricultural production categories." With God on their side, Iowa might be able to recover financially in a year or two. "The state had dropped to fifth place in net farm income and most of the livestock showed the smallest inventory since the 1920s."

May of 1994 was welcomed at Stephen's house, where the

river drifted along behind with lilies, peonies, and lily of the valley as they began to wave along its perimeter. He enjoyed the late blooming lilacs as he waxed his Harley on this particular evening, and the few fireflies that were out in May were beginning to dance to the tune of their souls.

Stephen cut a fresh bouquet of lilacs as Audie so loved and put them in a small jar. He carefully placed the jar inside the left bag on the back of his Harley and swung his right leg over the seat. The roar of the engine, tuned to perfection, as his hair blew from beneath his helmet.

As Stephen approached the cemetery, he slowed his Harley to a roll and was cautious as if not wanting to intrude upon those who were sleeping. He turned off the light and the engine when he came to Audrey's grave, just as he had done so many times before. He drew the lilacs from the back bag and placed them by her head.

"For you, milady," he whispered like a prayer.

Stephen sat for a long while and knew all he would miss. He would not see Audrey's face, feel her skin against his, watch her comb her hair, drink her coffee, smile, or cry. He would not watch her dress, undress, caress his guitar, put on her lipstick, or hold his hand. He had never seen her hold their daughter, nor would he ever hear her tell the stories of *her war*. There was no way of knowing how much their lives would have intersected, but Stephen knew that Audrey had always been a part of him, and she would echo in his life forevermore.

As Stephen was ready to leave the cemetery, a firefly landed on a lilac to signal his desire.

"My Audie, you were wrong about only two things: in Casablanca, Bogie *never* let her go, and it is *I—I who dance with fireflies—and you.*"

About the Author

Kathie's love of writing began when she was in the second grade in Iowa Falls, IA. Today, she is the author of two new books on autism, *Tears of Laughter ~ Tears of Pain* and *I Never Told My Son He Couldn't Dance,* and a children's book, *Bayo, The Boo Cow.* Kathie has authored numerous articles for many national magazines and her short stories and poems are renown in the world of autism and appear in various anthologies. Kathie writes on-line continuing education units and presents live webinars. Kathie Harrington, M.A., CCC-SLP (speech/language pathologist) graduated with her Master's Degree from Truman State, Kirksville, MO. She is the owner and president of a private practice, Good Speech, Inc., Las Vegas NV. Kathie is a weekly blogger at *ADVANCE,* for Speech/language Pathologists, KathiesWorld.com, and On the Road with Humpty Dumpty.com. She is an international presenter on the topic of autism and language development. *To Dance with Fireflies* is Kathie's first novel but the sequel, *Only a Hero,* is well underway and her husband, Tim, is confident it won't take her long to complete. Tim knows Kathie well after forty-five years of marriage. Tim and Kathie have two grown children whom they transplanted from the fields of the Midwest to the bright lights of Las Vegas some twenty-six years ago. Kathie can be contacted through her website at:
www.kathiesworld.com or at kathieh2@cox.net.

CPSIA information can be obtained at www.ICGtesting.com
Printed in the USA
LVOW011915130313

324130LV00017B/957/P